THE DYING ROOM

Copyright © 2015 Debra Webb, Pink House Press

Edited by Marijane Diodati

Cover Design by Vicki Hinze

PINK HOUSE PRESS
WebbWorks, Huntsville, Alabama

First Edition March 2015

ISBN: 0692323120
ISBN-13: 9780692323120

THE DYING ROOM

A FACES OF EVIL NOVEL

DEBRA WEBB

PINK
HOUSE
PRESS

CHAPTER ONE

"It won't be long now." Wilson Hilliard was dying a slow, agonizing death. If God had any mercy, he would have ended his wretched existence long before now. But then, he and God had never been on very good terms. Between the stroke that had paralyzed him six years ago and the cancer eating away at his insides, he was most certainly paying for his every sin and he wasn't even dead yet.

His friend tucked the covers around him. "Now, now, Mr. Hilliard, none of us knows when our hour will come."

Wilson managed the strength to laugh. "True. True." He patted the man's hand. "You've been a loyal friend, Bernard. I wish I could compensate you properly."

Bernard smiled down at him. "It's a privilege, sir. You rest now. You've had enough excitement for today."

"Show me the photo once more and tell me again what he said." Wilson felt almost giddy even though he'd heard the story twice already.

Bernard's smile stretched into a grin as he leaned close to whisper. "First, he pleaded and cried like a small child." He held his cell phone where the photo he had taken could be seen. "Then, when he understood his pleas were falling on deaf ears, he said: *God have mercy on my soul.*"

Despite the agony tearing at his body that the pain medications couldn't touch, Wilson laughed until he lost his breath. When he could breathe again he sputtered, "The very idea. God has no mercy for men like us. Apparently, our old associate wasn't listening all those Sundays he sat in church with his lovely wife and perfect son."

"I think not," Bernard agreed.

"They deserted me." Anger stung Wilson's eyes. He was old, his mind feeble or he would never allow even a moment of weakness. "I gave them every-thing, and when I needed them most they turned their backs on me."

Bernard nodded, his face somber.

"It's very much as your Mr. Durham said," Wilson concluded, as much to himself as to his friend. "I've been left to this…" He looked around the room, his sight failing him, too. He could scarcely see the drab wallpaper, torn and peeling, or the faded, tattered curtains. "*Dying* room."

"We're making the best of the situation, sir."

Bernie's optimism lifted his spirits like a ray of sunshine after an endless winter rain. His promises made these final days bearable. "I want them to know what it is to feel this agony…this *emptiness*. I want each one of them to recognize their fate as they draw a final breath in their own dying rooms."

"I will see to it, sir."

"You have the list?" Wilson wished he could be there in person to watch.

Bernard patted the breast pocket of his light wool jacket. "I do."

Wilson nodded. "Good. I'll hang on then for as long as I can. I refuse to go to hell until I know they're all there waiting for me."

"All is in order, sir," Bernard assured him. "The work will be quick. I will not fail."

Wilson closed his eyes with complete confidence that all was as it should be. For the first time, he looked forward to dying.

CHAPTER TWO

Sylvia Baron picked up the small silver baby spoon. She traced the name engraved there. *Burnett.* Her best friend's baby was due in only three weeks. Sylvia felt a smile tug at her lips. She couldn't remember the last time she'd claimed anyone as a best friend. Maybe in her undergraduate days. *Before.*

Before her life had changed.

"Do people really use those?"

Sylvia blinked away the memories and looked up as Jess Harris Burnett, Birmingham's deputy chief of Major Crimes, joined her at the gift table. "I can't say for sure," Sylvia teased, "but there are those who accuse me of being born with one in my mouth." Sylvia held the silver spoon next to her face. "What do you think?"

Jess laughed. "I'm afraid this child," she rubbed her round belly, "may be accused of the same if Katherine has anything to do with it." She surveyed

4

the gorgeous flowers, colorful balloons, and silk streamers adorning her mother-in-law's family room. "The decorations alone for this party must have cost a small fortune."

Sylvia returned the spoon to its satin lined box. "This is her first grandchild. They say parents and grandparents always go a little overboard with the first one."

Her eyebrows merging together in concern, Jess touched Sylvia's arm. "You look distracted. Is something going on with Nina?"

Sylvia shook her head. "Nina's doing great." Since moving to the clinic in New York last October and participating in that incredible new drug trial, her sister had made a complete turnaround. It was amazing and Sylvia could not be happier. "If she continues on her present course, she'll be released to the care of her psychiatrist here next month. She'll be living at home again for the first time in more than ten years."

"I'm so happy for your family."

Sylvia nodded. "Thank you. Mother and Daddy are ecstatic." Nina's recovery was nothing short of a miracle.

"You two look as if you could use some more punch." Gina Coleman, the person who probably knew Sylvia better than anyone, joined them. In each hand, Gina carried an elegant crystal cup filled with Katherine's secret punch recipe.

Sylvia lifted a skeptical eyebrow. "It's after five o'clock. You're an award-winning investigative television journalist, and you couldn't find anything stronger than punch."

Gina grinned and extended a cup toward her. "Don't I always take care of you?"

Sylvia accepted the cup and tasted the refreshment. "Hmm." She sent her friend a pointed look. "If Katherine finds out you—"

"She won't." Gina passed the remaining cup to Jess. "The virgin recipe for the mother-to-be."

"Thank you." Jess cradled the cup in both hands.

Gina moved in closer. "So, what's up?"

Jess shrugged. "Sylvia hasn't spilled yet."

Sylvia made a face. "Nothing is *up*. I was lost in thought, that's all." She glanced at the klatches of women gathered around the room. A dozen little huddles, all discussing the hottest gossip or newest recipe or maybe the latest white sale at Belk's. The wives of doctors and lawyers and daughters of old money families, women Sylvia had known her entire life. Few had the first idea how cold and brutal real life could be.

Enough with the pity party, Sylvia.

"There she goes again," Jess said, drawing Sylvia's errant attention back to their intimate huddle. "Are you sure you're okay?"

Sylvia downed her spiked punch. "I think I've had a little too much baby today."

Gina patted Jess's belly. "She doesn't mean it, little one. We're going to spoil you rotten."

Sylvia scowled. "If you have to know, today is kind of a sad day for me. I lost someone special on this day back...when I was in Paris."

"I remember when you were away." Gina nodded slowly as if she were searching her memory. "You took a semester off before starting med school. I was so pissed that my parents wouldn't let me go with you."

"You fell in love in Paris?" Jess set her punch aside and planted her hands on her hips, emphasizing the swell of her belly. "Do tell."

She should have kept her mouth shut. Sylvia heaved a big breath. "Not a boyfriend. Just a special...*friend*."

Gina squeezed Sylvia's shoulders in a quick hug. "I'm sorry. You never said anything."

And she never would.

"What am I missing?" Lori Wells joined the huddle. She looked from Jess to Sylvia and then to Gina. "Who died?"

Despite herself, Sylvia laughed. Jess and Gina joined the outburst.

Lori looked confused. "You three cannot be drinking the same punch I am."

"I can change that for you, Detective," Gina said. "I know where Katherine keeps her elixir."

"Actually." Lori smiled widely. "I can't have alcohol."

Jess gasped. "Are you serious?"

Lori nodded. "I took a pregnancy test this morning." She literally shook with excitement. "It was positive! Chet is over the moon!"

"Wow." Sylvia tried to sound excited but the word came out a little flatter than she'd intended. "That's great." She turned to Gina. "If you get pregnant, I'm looking for new friends."

The ladies laughed again. Sylvia was very happy for Jess and Lori. She really was. It was just tough, particularly today. Damn Katherine Burnett for picking this day to have Jess's shower.

"No matter how certain you are that you don't want children, when you fall in love with the right man," Jess glanced at Gina, "or woman, you may change your mind. When I started my career, I didn't see myself having a child *ever*. And look at me, I'm huge!"

"You look wonderful." Gina hugged her.

Gina was right, Sylvia admitted. Jess glowed. Her long blond hair lay in soft curls around her shoulders. The elegant blue dress molded to her baby bump in a bold, modern fashion. The low-heeled pumps left something to be desired, but Sylvia understood the choice. She watched as Gina and Lori reassured Jess. The two looked equally gorgeous in their figure flattering sheath style dresses. Both had those dark, exotic looks gained only through good genes. Sylvia considered herself the plain Jane of the group. Though she'd added red highlights to her brown hair, it was still just brown. Her brown eyes were ordinary. She'd spent most of her life trying to make up for her average appearance with attitude and intellect.

She scanned the room again, noting all the women her age. All were married or had been at least once and were rearing offspring. Sylvia was forty-four years old and divorced. The failed marriage hadn't resulted in any children. She had used the excuse that she was too busy for children. The truth was she had pushed aside anything that might have gotten in her way of building a respected career—her daddy's greatest wish for his daughters. Senator Robert Baron had preached strength, ambition, and independence from the time Nina and Sylvia were born. Her marital status, however, wasn't her daddy's fault. The senator had never made any extraordinary demands on his daughters. Somehow Sylvia had taken on that burden herself. Perhaps, it had happened after Nina was diagnosed with such a horrific and challenging illness. Maybe Sylvia had decided she needed to make their daddy proud enough for both of them.

She dismissed the absurd line of thinking. There was no one else to blame for the choices she had made. There was no taking back one choice in particular and no changing the result. What was done was done. Now, she lived with the consequences. Pretending it never happened had been so much easier until recently.

"Excuse me, ladies."

Sylvia and her friends turned to the young woman who was a member of the staff catering the elaborate baby shower.

"Mrs. Burnett said I should tell you that your cell phones are ringing nonstop in the guest room."

Punch cups were set aside and thank-you's tossed over shoulders as the four hurried from the room, down the hall, and to the last door on the right. As Katherine had said, at least four cell phones were making noise, each with its own unique ring tone.

Sylvia's call went to voicemail before she could catch it.

"Yes, Sergeant," Jess was saying to her caller. She listened a moment, her face shifting to a troubling expression, "I'll be right there." She ended the call and looked from Lori to Sylvia. "We have a murder."

As much as Sylvia hated to hear of anyone's death—especially by homicide—she was grateful for the excuse to leave the festivities. As Jefferson County's associate coroner, she had learned a long time ago that relating to the dead was far less complicated than interacting with the living.

Not once in her career had Sylvia let down the dead, which was more than she could say for the living.

CHAPTER THREE

The well-kept English Tudor sat in one of Birmingham's most prominent historic neighborhoods. Deputy Chief Jess Harris Burnett scanned the quiet street as she emerged from Detective Lori Wells' Mustang. The landscape lighting illuminated the line of yellow tape that marked the property as a crime scene.

"The victim is retired Jefferson County Circuit Court Judge Harmon Rutledge, age seventy-two," Lori said as she put her cell phone away and joined Jess on the sidewalk. "Chet says it looks as if someone imprisoned him in his library and spent a day or so torturing him."

"He lives alone?" Jess showed her ID to the officer guarding the perimeter.

Lori did the same. "He's lived alone since his wife died two years ago. The housekeeper came by this evening to make a grocery list since she does the shopping on Mondays. She discovered the body and made the call to 9-1-1."

The front door opened and Sergeant Chet Harper stepped back for them to enter. "Sorry to interrupt the baby shower, Chief."

"I was ready for a break." Jess hesitated in the entry hall to pull on gloves and shoe covers. "Congratulations, by the way."

Harper grinned and ducked his head. Jess tried to hide her smile. For such a tough guy, the man was a big softie when it came to his relationship with Lori. They were getting married in June. Jess was the matron of honor, and she couldn't be happier for the two of them. With Harper's dark, handsome looks, their child was bound to be gorgeous.

"Thanks, Chief."

"Bring us up to speed, Sergeant."

Harper led the way through the massive house. "Cook is talking to the neighbors. Hayes is in the kitchen interviewing the housekeeper."

The entry hall cut straight through to the back of the house where a set of French doors led out onto a terrace. At the French doors, the hall went left and right. The kitchen was visible down the hall to the right.

"The victim's library is this way." Harper gave a nod to the left. As they moved in that direction, he gestured to the first door they encountered. "There's a basement down those stairs. Looks like it's used more for storage than anything else. No indication anyone's been down there recently."

Jess was grateful trudging down the stairs to the basement wasn't necessary. The more her belly expanded the less sure-footed she became. Primarily because she could no longer see her feet! *Only three more weeks.* Her nerves jangled with excitement each time she stopped long enough to consider that in less than a month she and Dan would be holding their baby. The notion of seeing Dan with their child in his arms made her heart beat faster. They had chosen not to learn the baby's gender before it was born. Jess had already decided the baby was a girl. Dan, on the other hand, was equally certain they were having a boy.

Thinking of Dan, she should probably text and let him know she would be late for dinner—not that he would be surprised. As Birmingham's chief of police, Dan Burnett was well aware that a cop's job rarely fit a nine-to-five schedule. Jess's somehow seemed to never fall into any sort of normal timeline.

The elegant library smelled of feces and urine. Sylvia and a couple of forensic techs from the BPD's Crime Scene Unit were already at work. A good-sized room, the shelves that lined the walls were filled with legal volumes. Rich paneled walls with intricately carved details showed anyone who visited that this was no ordinary room. Great attention had been paid to every aspect of the design and décor of the opulent room. From the coffered ceiling and mahogany furniture to the gleaming wood floors, the space made Jess think of a historic courtroom she had seen in Boston.

The victim was a white male. He wasn't a large man, but he appeared fit. His hair was a distinguished color, more white than gray. He wore a white t-shirt and khaki slacks that were stained by his body having relieved itself.

Sylvia looked up from her work. "Daddy is not going to be happy about this."

"Was the victim a friend of your father's?" Jess moved to the center of the room where the victim was secured to a chair. Nylon ropes bound his wrists to the arms of the chair and his ankles to the chair legs. Another wider band of nylon was used like a safety belt around his waist and held him in a seated position.

"They hadn't been friends in a long time." Sylvia removed her thermometer from the incision she'd made just beneath the ribcage on the victim's right side. "The two hadn't spoken in years, but I think Daddy always hoped they would one day clear the air." She read the thermometer. "Taking into consideration his body temp and the state of rigor, I'd estimate time of death at around noon today."

Jess considered the wall directly in front of the victim. Other than the floor-to-ceiling window that towered behind his desk, most of the walls were filled by bookshelves. This space, however, had been reserved for a grand portrait of the judge. The portrait had been removed and set on the floor a few feet away. Great care had been taken in filling the newly emptied space with photos and newspaper clippings. The brass light that would have spilled a warm glow over the painting now highlighted the photos and newspaper clippings, many of which were less than flattering to the judge.

"It looks as if someone carried out a little payback."

"Well." Sylvia peeled off her soiled gloves and reached for a fresh pair. "The judge certainly had a reputation for controversial rulings."

"There's significant bruising." Jess covered her nose with the back of her gloved hand and leaned forward for a closer look at the victim. "Are those Taser marks on his neck?"

Sylvia had lifted his t-shirt to access his torso. She gestured to his abdomen. "The bruising is maybe a day old. These," she indicated the marks on the right side of his neck, "are definitely Taser burns."

"To disable him maybe." Jess crouched down next to Sylvia to inspect his neck, wrists, and hands. "I don't see any indication that he fought his attacker before he was restrained, or that he attempted to free himself from his bindings."

Sylvia pointed to his upper arm and the needle mark visible just above his elbow. "I'm guessing the killer kept him drugged, at least to some degree."

"Any children or close friends?"

"A son who lives in Nevada." Sylvia stood. "As for friends, the judge didn't have any real friends that I can think of. He had associates."

Pushing to her feet, Jess suppressed a groan. That move was becoming more difficult all the time.

"The sooner you can give me cause of death, the better."

"Once we get him to the morgue," Sylvia assured her, "the judge will go straight to the head of the line."

Jess thanked Sylvia before joining Lori at the collage of unflattering newspaper articles. "I'm guessing this wasn't meant to be a tribute to all the judge's accomplishments."

"I don't think so." Lori tapped an article with its accompanying photo and then another and another after that. "All of these are cases the judge presided over, which created considerable controversy. I remember reading about him. Most people considered him a hard-ass with no compassion."

"So this may have been a family member of a defendant who feels the judge ruled the wrong way." It certainly wouldn't be the first case of revenge Jess had investigated.

"Or someone who wanted it to look that way," Lori offered.

Jess surveyed the articles once more. "These clippings aren't new." She pointed to the yellowed edge of one. "Someone has been collecting and keeping these for years."

"So our killer's animosity has been building over an extended period of time."

"Until he decided it was time to act," Jess agreed. "Let's begin with these cases. See if the killer was trying to tell us something."

While Lori photographed the scene for their case board, Jess moved around the rest of the room.

None of the books appeared disturbed. The desk was uncluttered, the drawers organized and neat. No computer, not even an iPad. After a bit more poking around, she went in search of Harper. She found him in the corridor headed her way. "You find anything?"

He shook his head. "The rest of the house is undisturbed. Not one thing appears out of place. Our perp was careful."

"Did the housekeeper notice anything missing?" Jess suspected the answer would be no. She was reasonably sure this was not about financial gain.

"Hayes finished taking her statement." Harper hitched his head toward the other end of the corridor. "He walked through the house with her, but she didn't spot anything missing or disturbed."

"Good. Did you find any indications of forced entry? A window maybe?" If the judge had welcomed his killer into his home, then the suspect pool could be narrowed somewhat. Then again, this was the south, most people invited folks into their homes whether they knew them or not.

"I checked all the windows and the doors," Harper said as they moved toward the opposite end of the corridor. "I didn't find any indication of forced entry. The judge's car is in the garage. There's jewelry in the master bedroom. A hundred bucks and several credit cards in his wallet on the bedside table. The keys to his Cadillac are on the hall table. His gun cabinet is unlocked and stocked with weapons and ammo."

"Apparently, our killer wasn't interested in easy cash," Jess noted. Harper's findings confirmed her conclusions that robbery was not the killer's primary motive.

"If he was he sure left plenty behind," Harper agreed.

"I'd like to speak with the housekeeper now."

As if he'd read her mind, Lieutenant Clint Hayes exited the kitchen and headed their way. "We're ready for you, Chief."

Harper hitched a thumb toward the front of the house. "I'll catch up with Cook and see how the neighbor interviews are going."

'Thank you, Sergeant." Jess shifted her attention to Hayes. As always he was dressed as if he were headed to a GQ cover shoot. Harper and Cook still teased him from time to time about having stock in Armani and Ralph Lauren. "What do we have, Lieutenant?"

"Valerie Neely, sixty-seven." Hayes led the way to the kitchen. "She's worked for the judge for twenty years."

"Hopefully, she knows some of his enemies." When a man ended up dead and it wasn't about money or a woman, he most certainly had at least one enemy.

Valerie Neely was a short, stocky woman. She dressed for function and wore her gray streaked hair in a serviceable bun. Five minutes into the interview, Jess decided she'd missed her calling as a drill sergeant.

"So you made dinner for the judge on Friday?"

Valerie nodded. "Fish with rice and broccoli."

Jess tapped her notepad with her pencil. "Why don't you make your shopping list on Fridays, Valerie? You work long hours all week, why take part of your Sunday evening to come by."

She shrugged stooped shoulders. "The judge likes me to check on Sundays. I like my job so I do things the way he wants. I knew something was wrong as soon as I opened the door. It was unlocked and the security system was off."

Jess could understand her reasoning about the job, though keeping her boss happy had never been Jess's strong suit. The housekeeper's statement helped determine the timeline they were working with here. As late as seven on Friday evening the judge had been fine. Whatever happened, it took place during the thirty-six or so hours that followed. Accurate timelines were essential to solving any case.

"Valerie, you've been immensely helpful. I have just a few more questions."

The older woman's patient gaze remained on Jess. "Fire away. I'd like to get a few things done around here. The judge..." Valerie cleared her throat. "His son shouldn't come home to find his library...like that."

"I'm afraid the whole house is part of our crime scene, Valerie. You won't be able to touch anything or even come back inside after this interview until we release the scene. That could be a while."

Valerie heaved a burdened breath. "Well, get on with it then. I'd like to be home before bedtime."

Jess looked over her notes. The housekeeper had already stated the judge had no enemies that she knew of. No friends either. She didn't get into his business, she insisted. He rarely had company or phone calls when she was on duty. He saw his son and grandchildren once a year around Christmas. He visited the cemetery each Sunday morning and left a single long-stemmed rose on his wife's grave. Otherwise, he read and piddled in his garden. He'd already planted potatoes and prepared beds for the other vegetables he enjoyed. The gardens, Valerie explained, had been his wife's passion. The judge insisted on caring for the gardens just as his wife had.

"Do you review the judge's mail?"

Valerie shook her head. "I take it from the mailbox and lay it on his desk. He goes—went through it himself."

"But you had it in your hands from the street to his desk," Jess countered. "Surely you looked at the return addresses occasionally."

A noncommittal shrug lifted the stern woman's shoulders. "Utility bills, cable, insurance, stuff like that."

"Nothing that looked suspicious to you?"

She executed another firm shake of her head. "No, ma'am. Just the usual stuff everyone gets and the occasional junk mail."

"No visitors who seemed unhappy with the judge? Was there ever a time when he was threatened by someone relative to a case? Did he ever receive any hate mail?"

"None that I was aware of. He kept his business to himself."

"Did the judge have a cell phone or computer of any sort?"

"Absolutely not. He hated them. Before he retired, he used to complain that even his staff was lost without all their computers."

There were times when Jess hated them, too. "How was the relationship between the judge and his son?"

"The judge always said the best thing that happened to his relationship with his son was when the boy moved out west. They haven't argued since."

"So the judge and his son weren't on good terms?"

Valerie chuckled. "Obviously you didn't know the judge. No one was on good terms with him. You want to know who his enemies were? Pull out the phone book for the greater Birmingham area and pick a name."

So much for narrowing down the suspect pool.

CHAPTER FOUR

Sylvia removed her gloves. "The blows that caused the bruises on his abdomen didn't do any real damage." She indicated the torso of the victim with its freshly sutured Y-shaped incision, and then the damaged tissue on his wrists and ankles. "The ligature marks, as you know, resulted from being restrained. He was remarkably physically fit for his age. I can only hope my heart will be in such good condition when I'm in my seventies."

"What about the Taser marks?"

"I don't think the Taser is what stopped his heart, but I can't completely rule it out at this point. We'll know more when the tox screen results are back."

"So he didn't have a heart attack."

"He did not."

Jess considered the victim. "How long before you have the tox screen results?"

"The lab is putting a rush on all results related to his autopsy." As much as she wanted to help move the investigation along, there was little else Sylvia could conclude until she had those in hand. "We may have some results by tomorrow, and I should have most within seventy-two hours."

Jess removed her gloves and tossed them in the same hazardous materials bin Sylvia had used. "Let me know the minute you have something."

Sylvia followed Jess into the corridor. Lori spoke quietly with a caller a few feet away. "You look a little tired today, Jess. Did you get any sleep last night?" The woman was only days from having a baby, she should be taking it a little easier.

"A couple of hours. It's hard to sleep when I first start a new case." Jess wrestled the straps of that big black bag she carried a little higher on her shoulder.

Sylvia had gone to a lot of trouble to find an exact match to the bag Jess had lost in the fire at Dan's old house. Jess had been carrying that enormous black leather bag when she first waltzed into Sylvia's life last year. Jess swore she carried her life in there, and Sylvia had come to see that her friend wasn't kidding.

"We've been sorting through the cases posted on the judge's library wall," Jess went on. "Forensic techs are going through fingerprints. So far the only ones we've identified are those belonging to the judge and his housekeeper."

"Chief." Lori tucked her phone into her bag. "Lieutenant Hayes tracked down the brother of the guy who was executed last year. He's agreed to an interview."

"One down and a whole lot more to go." Jess looked toward the autopsy room door. "Judge Rutledge sentenced more defendants to death than any other judge in Alabama's history. He had a reputation for overriding a jury's recommendation of a life sentence when death was what he wanted for the defendant."

Sylvia recalled well the headlines and her father's comments when, after turning seventy, Rutledge was finally forced to retire. "The media referred to him as the grim reaper."

"Do you remember when a bomb was delivered to his home?" Lori asked.

"I do. It was the summer after my junior year in college." Sylvia nodded. "The judge and his wife were away that morning. The housekeeper he had at the time was killed. I think the bomb exploded unexpectedly as she brought it into the house."

"We're trying to locate a sister," Jess said, her expression indicating that she, too, recalled the awful event, "the only remaining family of the man convicted in that case. He was executed two years ago."

"You think the killer might be female?" Considering the obvious signs the judge had been drugged with something, Sylvia supposed the idea wasn't outside the realm of possibility.

"She may have hired someone to do the deed." Jess shrugged. "We haven't found any financial issues or bad habits on the judge's part. Beyond his propensity to enforce the capital punishment statute, I'm not seeing any sort of motive for murder."

"Maybe several of the families banded together to punish him, "Lori suggested, "for doling out death sentences to the loved ones they believed to be innocent."

"With a strong enough motive anything's possible," Jess granted. "With Rutledge's history, we could be looking at hundreds with sufficient motive."

"Were you able to reach his son?" Sylvia couldn't remember the last time she'd seen Harvey Rutledge. Not since high school.

"I spoke to him late last night. He sent me a text this morning saying he had a flight into Birmingham around six this evening." Jess checked the time on the wall clock above the autopsy room door. "He's probably landing about now. I don't know how much help he'll be. He hasn't seen or spoken to his father since Christmas." She frowned. "How could Rutledge pretend his own child didn't exist 364 days out of the year?"

Sylvia shook her head, the words she wanted to say clumping into a hot ball of hurt in her belly. "I'm sure the son can shed some light on their relationship."

"Maybe so." Jess flashed her a smile. "Thanks for the update. Call me as soon as you can with those tox screen results."

Lori gave Sylvia a wave as the two rushed away. Sylvia returned to the autopsy room, donned a fresh pair of gloves, and prepared the body for storage. There were morgue assistants she could have called to do this part, but the familiar movements kept her mind off other things.

After more than twenty-two years, she couldn't understand why the past had to come back to haunt her now. In all likelihood, it was the endless talk and fuss around Jess's pregnancy. Now, yet another of her friends was expecting. Lori's baby was scheduled to be a Thanksgiving delivery, which meant more baby showers and celebrations in the coming months.

Sylvia groaned. The trouble had started at Jess and Dan's wedding just before Christmas last year. She'd never been one to act on impulse. At least not when it came to sex. That night it was as if her hormones simply wanted to punish her for what might have been. Her parents had long ago stopped asking when she was getting married again so they could have a grandchild. Whatever this unsettling and confusing longing was, it appeared to be an internal struggle. Had some errant brain cell decided she deserved to relive the one regret in her life over and over?

The memory of how and where she'd spent the night after Jess and Dan's wedding abruptly flashed through her mind. Sylvia groaned again. "I still can't believe I did that." She stared at the judge, stalling in the closure of the body bag. "I really am quite screwed up, Your Honor. I'm reasonably sure there's no repairing me."

As she prepared to close the bag, the slightest hint of blue amid his hair gave Sylvia pause. She parted the thick white hair and searched. Often times, the elderly used a bluish rinse or hair dye to tone down a particularly harsh gray color. Perhaps a little excess blue dye on the scalp was the culprit in this instance. Yet the judge's hair didn't have any lingering bluish color. Her fingers stilled on a small, approximately dime-sized, faded blue object. An eagle, she realized. A tattoo of an eagle. The tattoo was on the parietal region of the scalp, in line with but an inch or so above the ear.

Sylvia snapped a photo to send Jess via text, but she hesitated. Where had she seen a tattoo like that before? Memories of covering her dad's eyes while her mother and younger sister sneaked in with a surprise birthday cake rushed through her mind. She'd been twelve or thirteen. She'd noticed the tattoo and asked her father about it. He'd said the small tattoo was from his Air Force days.

Anyone could have an eagle tattoo. Though the similarity of size and location seemed a little more than coincidence. Perhaps the judge had been in the Air Force as well.

Sylvia shook off the moment of déjà vu and sent the text. Deciding not to risk that she'd overlooked anything else, she unzipped the bag. "Sorry, Judge, but I need another look to make sure you're not hiding any more secrets from me."

Sylvia never missed a detail like this one. Yet another indication of the difficulty she'd encountered lately in keeping her mind on work and out of the past.

She couldn't deny its existence anymore. It was time to deal with that past.

CHAPTER FIVE

Buddy Corlew tossed back the last of the beer and set it aside. He leaned back in his chair and glared at the pile of papers cluttering the desk in his home office.

"I hate this stuff."

What good was an accountant if he still had to do all this paperwork come March every year? He laughed. To hear his CPA tell it, if he kept up the paperwork year round he wouldn't have this mess as the dreaded tax deadline approached. She also reminded him that she had actually needed all this last month.

"Yeah. Yeah. Yeah." Buddy pushed back his chair and grabbed his empty longneck bottle. Facing this pile of disorganized work history required at least one more beer. Maybe he'd break out the hard stuff.

A distant memory abruptly elbowed its way through his frustration. "Maybe not," he muttered.

The last time he'd filled out any government forms while under the influence of his favorite eighty-proof he'd gotten hauled in for questioning. Apparently, it was frowned upon to make smart ass remarks in answer to questions from the federal government. He'd hired his CPA that very year. Buddy grunted and decided it was best not to get all worked up about the things he couldn't change. Life was a hell of a lot more pleasant when he focused on fixing the problems of his clients rather than his own. Not that he had any real troubles beyond paperwork.

Nah. His house was paid for. So was the sleek black Charger parked out front. He had a little cash in the bank and all the sweet babes he could handle. What else could a man want? His traitorous mind instantly conjured up the image of one babe in particular. A firm rap on his front door prevented him from going down that not so smart path.

He spent about two seconds considering whether or not he should find a shirt to drag on before answering the door. Deciding not to bother, he headed that way. Anyone who showed up at his house at this hour was probably a client who knew him well enough to have his home address. Or, he mused, the ex-husband of a client who'd found him through the only competitor in town dumb enough to stoop this low. Giving out a PI's home address to the wrong guy was like sanctioning a hit.

A couple more hard raps echoed through the house. "Hang on." He grabbed his snub nose as he passed the hall table and tucked it into the waistband of his jeans at the small of his back. Sounded like his anxious visitor was pretty pissed or damned scared. Either way, it could mean trouble.

Buddy moved to the window on the hinge side of the door and eased the curtain aside. Visitors were typically focused on the knob side of the door, allowing him a quick peek from this side without being spotted.

Sylvia Baron stood on his porch. Even if he hadn't been surprised to see her there he still would have lingered to get a good long look at her before opening the door. Damn. The woman was hot. Those legs of hers went on forever. The green skirt and white blouse failed to hug all her subtle, sweet curves, but he knew every damned one. Dark glasses hid her eyes, and she had all that silky hair twisted into a conservative up do of some sort. She presented an uptight, conservative image, but he knew better. Peel off the designer labels and drag her between the sheets and she was a wildcat. His body reacted instantly to the memories.

"Fool." He flipped the latch and opened the door. "Well hello, *Doctor* Baron." He braced against the doorframe. "Took you long enough to decide you wanted an encore."

"Please."

She set her hands on her hips and glared at him. He didn't have to see her eyes, he could feel them raking over him.

"I'd like to speak with you. Privately. If you're not too busy."

"Come on in." A whole list of potential issues was suddenly running through his mind. They both had gone a little stupid the night of Jess's wedding. He'd never had sex without using a condom...except that once. Surely a woman as sophisticated as Sylvia was on some sort of birth control. He suffered a twinge of panic.

"Would you please put on a shirt first?" She lifted her chin in that haughty manner she used to put people off. "I have no desire to look at your naked chest."

He shrugged. "So don't look."

She shot him a glare that warned she was dead serious. Rather than argue, he left her standing at the door while he went in search of a shirt. He grabbed the tee he'd tossed across the bed when he got home this morning and pulled it on. The sound of the door clicking to a close told him she'd come inside. When he swaggered out of the bedroom, she stood in the small entry hall, looking sorely out of place.

"You want a beer or something?"

She took off her sunglasses. "I'd really like to move straight to business."

Buddy rubbed the back of his neck, his uneasiness mounting. "Sure." He gestured to the living room. "We should probably sit down."

She settled in the chair near the front window. It was the one with the most direct path to the front door. Didn't surprise him. She looked ready to run.

Holy hell. Twenty-seven years. He'd never once had sex without using a condom until...*her.* The only good advice his drunken old man had ever given him was never ever to have sex without a condom. Even at the hormone-driven age of sixteen, he couldn't have sex without that sage advice echoing in his head.

"This is very difficult." She took a deep breath.

Buddy recognized he should say something, but he couldn't find his voice.

"I've been carrying this around for too long, and it's time I did what needs to be done," she announced.

He couldn't take it. "Just tell me what you want me to do." He exhaled a chest full of tension. He could do this. If Jess could have a kid, he could. Sure. Hell yeah. No problem.

Sylvia appeared taken aback or confused. "Isn't that generally your job? If I knew what to do, I certainly wouldn't be here." She tucked her sunglasses into her bag and clasped her hands in her lap.

Now he was confused. He swallowed, wished he'd gone for the hard stuff when he'd had the chance. "Why don't we start with exactly why you're here?"

"I'm here because..." She shifted in her chair. Crossed her legs, and then tugged at the hem of her skirt. "I'd like to hire you to look into a...situation."

Relief roared through him like a freight train. "Whew." He scrubbed a hand over his face. "That's a relief. I thought you were here to tell me you're pregnant."

Judging by the horrified look on her face he should have kept that to himself.

"You...?" She stared at his Eagles t-shirt, then his ragged jeans and bare feet. She laughed, but not quickly enough to cover the way her breath quickened and her cheeks flushed. "No. Absolutely not."

He grinned. "Yeah. Right. So, tell me about your *situation*."

She uncrossed her legs. Then crossed them again. Her edginess was killing him. Every time she crossed or uncrossed those gorgeous legs he remembered the feel of them around his waist.

"Let's get something straight first." She scowled at him with those dark as midnight brown eyes. "You are bound by privilege, Buddy Corlew. You cannot discuss this with anyone else. Are we clear?"

Whatever this situation was, it was big and personal. He leaned forward, braced his forearms on his knees. "You listen to me, Doc. I've been doing this for a while now. You think I'd have the reputation I do if I didn't know how to keep secrets?"

She cleared her throat as she clasped and unclasped her hands. "You can't even tell Jess."

Their gazes met and he saw the hurt there. Whatever this was, it was not only big and personal it was painful. "You have my word."

"All right." She nodded. "By the way, I appreciate your discretion about...that night."

He gave a nod. He didn't kiss and tell. As he waited for her to begin the silence settled around them. No need to push. They had all night.

"When I was twenty-two I found myself in a difficult position." She stared at her hands. "I'd just graduated college. I'd been accepted to medical school and I was very excited. I was in love with a young man with the same career hopes and dreams as I had." She met Buddy's eyes briefly. "Except his hopes and dreams didn't include a future with me."

Buddy flinched. "Most guys are real shits at that age."

She nodded. "I was naïve. I never saw it coming." She squared her shoulders. "In any event, I couldn't go to my parents. I didn't want to disappoint them and Nina had just been diagnosed with schizophrenia. They didn't need another problem to deal with, so I handled it myself. I told them I wanted to take a semester off in Paris and they agreed. With Nina falling apart midway through undergraduate school, I think they were terrified I might fall apart, too."

"But you didn't go to Paris," he guessed. It was easy to see what was coming.

She shook her head. "I spent the next six months in Sacramento. When I came home, I never told anyone what happened. You're the first person to know."

No wonder she was so uptight. She'd been carrying this burden all alone for a hell of a long time. He appreciated her trust more than she could know. "Just tell me what you need me to do."

She exhaled a big breath. "I'd like you to find my daughter."

CHAPTER SIX

"He was tortured," Senator Robert Baron said somberly. He gazed at those gathered and wondered if any one of them understood the implications of what those words actually meant.

This was no game...no mere threat or scare tactic. This was real and the intent was undeniably clear. This was the first time the four of them had been in a room together outside a social event in six years.

Six. There had been six of them when this began. Six brilliant young men determined to make their marks in this world. Too bad they hadn't considered the long-term consequences a bit more closely. At the time all that had mattered was achieving the greatness they each desired.

If only they had known then what they knew now.

"You called this meeting," Joseph Pratt fired back, "to tell us what we'll see on the news by this time tomorrow?" He sipped his scotch. "Considering

36

THE DYING ROOM

how many defendants he sent to death row, it's a miracle this didn't happen years ago."

Robert wasn't surprised by Joe's indifference. The former mayor had always been the last to see what was right in front of his nose unless it suited his purposes.

"You don't see the relevance between this murder, our old friend's sudden disappearance, and the release of his loyal assistant?" Surely they recognized what was happening here. Robert certainly did.

Craig Moore set his drink aside and cleared his throat. "Are you saying you believe that old bastard is somehow responsible for this?"

"I am," Robert confirmed.

"Really, Robert," Sam Baker shook his head, "the suggestion is absurd. How do we know Wilson Hilliard isn't dead? And that crippled assistant he had forty years ago is a crippled old man now. How can you believe he's behind Harmon's murder?"

"I've been briefed on the crime scene," Robert insisted. "We need to take this threat seriously."

Isaiah Taylor held up his hands. "What do you suggest we do? It's not like we can go to the police." He looked from Robert to the others, his gaze resting briefly on each face. "We all have secrets we'd like to keep. Who of us is willing to open this particular Pandora's box?"

"What we can do is watch our backs," Robert offered. "Of course, none of us wants to rehash the past with the public or the police. Be that as it may, we have to be smart. None of us wants to end up dead, either. I believe—"

Joe waved his hands back and forth, cutting Robert off. "Whoever did this," he argued, "the last thing we need to do is to panic and start spilling our guts. Frankly, I have enough trouble right now without one of you opening this can of worms."

Craig nodded. "I'm with Joe on this one. I have an election year coming up. I can't afford any scandals. We need to stop making more out of this than it is. Murders happen. Harmon made himself an easy target."

"If," Sam spoke up again, "Harmon's death had anything to do with...what Robert is suggesting, that doesn't mean any of us are in danger of the same end."

Robert held his temper. "How can you make such a conclusion? We were all there." He looked from one man to the next. "We all reaped the same benefit. We *all* made the same promises, and we all walked away."

"We're not the ones who saw that Wilson was committed to that institution," Sam argued. "We didn't ensure his assistant was charged with and convicted of embezzlement."

"No," Robert agreed, "we didn't. But we were there when the vote was taken. We all voted to make it happen—whatever the cost. Harmon was just the one with the means to put the necessary steps in motion. His assistant spent years at Bibb Correctional Facility. We are responsible, gentlemen."

No one argued with him this time.

They all knew he was right. The only question that remained was what in the world would they do now?

CHAPTER SEVEN

SHOOK HILL ROAD, MOUNTAIN BROOK, 9:40 P.M.

Sylvia sat in her car outside her family home for a while. She'd grown up in this massive house. To most who visited the place, it looked more like a museum than a home, but it wasn't like that at all. She and Nina enjoyed idyllic childhoods. Their parents doted on them and ensured they had everything they needed. Of course, need is relevant. Certainly, she and Nina had more than most, yet their upbringing had been rooted in respect for others, appreciation of all the things they had been blessed with, and their obligation to give back to society.

That picture-perfect childhood had been shattered to some degree by Nina's mental illness. Though Nina had stabilized sufficiently to finish her undergraduate work as well as law school, life had never really been the same. They'd all gone on, but that distinct wound had never fully healed. How could it? Each time they believed she was going to be fine, there would be a relapse and she'd fall apart again. Each time she fell apart, the family shattered a little more. Eventually, Nina had been lost to them for the most part. Would her recent astounding and ongoing recovery put those missing pieces back together? Sylvia wasn't sure.

Perhaps the guilt haunting her just now was prompted by watching all those around her move on with their lives while she stood absolutely still. On some level, she suspected that was the reason her mind insisted on questioning every single step she took lately. Like that ridiculous blue eagle tattoo. No matter how she attempted to dismiss it the idea of it continued to chaff like a new pair of shoes.

Images and sounds from the night she'd spent with Buddy tried to invade her thoughts and she banished them quickly. Buddy Corlew was the last person she needed in her life aside from his ability as a private investigator. Jess had mentioned on numerous occasions how good Buddy was at his work. Sylvia trusted he was equally discreet. So far, he hadn't fallen down in that area. She hoped her revelation didn't change his trustworthiness. There were no doubt gossip rags that would pay well for a story about the senator's secret granddaughter.

She sighed, the sound hissing in the silence. How would she explain her decision to her parents? Would she? If Buddy found...*her*, Sylvia would have to make the decision about revealing herself. There were many things to take into consideration first.

What if she—her daughter—was very happy in her life just as it was? She might not appreciate this sort of life-changing news. What if her adopted parents hadn't told her she was adopted? The idea of shattering her life was one Sylvia couldn't bear to examine.

She shook her head. "Take it one step at a time."

What if her daughter was dead?

The thought ached through Sylvia. Any time she had allowed herself to think about the baby she gave up for adoption, she'd always imagined her as having grown up in a wonderful, happy home. She'd be a junior or senior in college now. She might even be engaged or married.

What if she hates you for what you did?

This was the other painful question Sylvia had carefully avoided all these years. She had done the right thing at the time. On numerous occasions she had gone over those days and months. Her family had been in turmoil. Sylvia wasn't sure her parents could have dealt with more unsettling news. She had wanted to finish her education and to build her career. How could she possibly have been a good mother at the time?

"It was the right decision." Sylvia took a deep breath and opened the car door. She always made the right decisions—almost always anyway, she amended as those erotic images of the night she'd spent with Buddy Corlew flashed one after the other in her head.

"What a mess." She climbed the steps, suddenly feeling so damned weary. It was late and she'd had a long day. Turning around and going home was immensely appealing, but this was another of those things she had to do. She would keep her visit short. She hadn't eaten since lunch and wasn't sure she could summon her appetite. If her mother found out she would immediately start warming up leftovers.

After giving the doorbell a push, she shoved her key into the lock and opened the door. Though her parents insisted this was still home and she could pop in any time, she preferred giving at least a quick warning.

"Sylvia." Her mom smiled as she padded into the entry hall, her feet bare. "Please don't tell me you're just leaving work at this hour."

Louise Baron had graduated Summa Cum Laude from Vanderbilt University with a degree in Economics and History. Despite that accomplishment, she had never worked a day at anything other than being the senator's wife and the mother to their two daughters. Sylvia had never understood that about her mother's generation. Her mother had insisted that she loved her job as wife and mother and had no desire to do anything else.

Apparently, Sylvia had not inherited that gene.

Sylvia waved off her mother's concerns. "I had a meeting that ran late." She suddenly wondered what her mother would think of Buddy Corlew. Would she be mortified at his long hair and coarse ways? He certainly wouldn't be the sort of man with

whom the senator expected his daughter to be…
involved.

Sylvia dismissed the idea. She and Buddy weren't
involved. They'd had one night of hot, crazy sex.
Crazy being the operative word since they hadn't
used a condom. She barely stifled a groan. How
could she have taken such a risk? The barrage of
tests that followed had assured Sylvia that Buddy
had indeed been as clean of STDs as he'd claimed.
Thank God.

"You work far too hard, dear."

Sylvia blinked, grateful her mother couldn't
read her mind. "Is Daddy home?"

"He's watching the news in the family room."
Louise rolled her eyes. "I'd heard enough of
that nonsense. I've been curled up in the parlor
reading."

They discussed the latest recommendation from
her book club as her mother led the way to the family room. Before they reached the door, Sylvia heard
her father arguing with the commentator. He'd
always been quite vocal about his feelings, even
when it was just him and the news. He'd been known
to shred a newspaper from time to time.

"Robert, turn that television down," Louise
ordered. "Sylvia is here."

The senator looked up, smiled, and immediately
muted the program. "Is something the matter?" He
eased forward, lowering the footrest of his recliner.

Before Sylvia could answer, her mother piped
up, "I'll make some tea."

Sylvia sat down on the sofa. "I finished Judge Rutledge's autopsy today." Suddenly, she felt more mentally drained than she had since exams in medical school.

The senator raised his eyebrows. "Do the police have any leads on his killer?"

Sylvia shook her head. "There were no signs of breaking and entering. For now, they're assuming he knew his killer."

"He certainly made more than his share of enemies."

"That seems to be the general consensus," Sylvia agreed. "Have you spoken to any of your mutual associates?" Birmingham was one of Alabama's largest cities, but it was still a relatively small town when it came to the who's who. Most everyone knew everyone else.

"Over the past few years Rutledge more or less turned his back on those of us who had been his closest associates at one time. I imagine the usual crowd will attend his service out of respect." With that declaration, he shifted his attention to the news scroll.

Sylvia hadn't actually expected more than that and still she prodded. "Were the two of you in the Air Force together?"

A frown lined his forehead. "No. Why would you ask?"

She tapped her head, just above her right ear. "He has that same blue eagle tattoo. It's exactly like yours. I thought maybe you served together."

He shrugged. "He may have been in the service during the time I was away, I don't know. Either way, we were both young and reckless at one time. Many soldiers found themselves permanently marked after a night of drinking with comrades."

"I suppose you're right."

"I spoke with Nina's doctor today," he said, his expression brightening. "It was good news all the way around."

Louise arrived with the tea and homemade tea biscuits. Sylvia was grateful for the warm beverage. She hadn't realized how cold she felt inside until she cradled the cup. "When is she coming home?"

"May first." He exchanged a knowing smile with his wife as she got comfortable in her recliner. "We're very excited. She'll have a full-time nurse here at the house for as long as the doctor deems necessary. She'll be seeing her doctor at UAB twice each week, but the therapist in New York will direct her care for the next several months."

"That is excellent news."

"We're so grateful," her mother said. "We weren't sure this day would ever come."

Sylvia had spoken with her sister's lead therapist. There was some risk that her condition would deteriorate again but the prognosis was outstanding. "When she's ready, we'll host a long overdue welcome home party."

"I'm already planning," her mother said with a wide smile.

They talked for a while longer. Her mother insisted Sylvia try her new tea biscuit recipe. As she nibbled on the sweet cake, Sylvia's appetite roused. She ended up having a chicken salad sandwich. Her mother made the very best chicken salad with pecans and grapes. The woman did love to cook. Sylvia much preferred to dine out. She was rarely home during mealtime anyway. On the rare occasion when she was it was far easier to order from her favorite restaurant. Cooking for one was more trouble than it was worth.

By the time Sylvia said her goodnights, she felt back on an even keel. Somehow her daddy always had that effect on her. He steadied her. He had that effect on most people. Staying in an elected office for most of his adult life was proof positive that his constituents saw him as strong and reliable.

In her car, she checked her cell. Three missed calls from Buddy and one voicemail as well as a thank-you text from Jess. Not in the mood to speak to Buddy again, she drove home. He couldn't have any information already. Before she'd left his house he'd asked questions she wasn't ready to answer— questions not relevant to the job she'd hired him to do. One way or the other she would get that point across to him. This was a business relationship. They were not friends. They certainly weren't a couple. What happened that one night was never going to happen again...*ever.*

She drove through the quiet community of Mountain Brook until she reached her own home on Montevallo Road. Rather than park in the garage, Sylvia shut off the car in the driveway and stared at her home for a time. She'd bought this house the year she and Lieutenant Lawrence Grayson married. She'd been thirty-two at the time. It was her first and only marriage so she'd gone all out—a big wedding, a suitable home in the best neighborhood.

How had twelve years elapsed since then?

Honestly, even then she'd only married because everyone expected her to *settle* down. Her parents had liked Larry. What wasn't to like? He'd been a good man, a decorated cop. But he'd wanted children. Sylvia had not. She hadn't been able to have another child knowing what she'd done all those years ago. Eventually he'd turned his interests elsewhere, and they'd ended up getting divorced. His new wife had given him the child he desperately wanted. Unfortunately, she'd been murdered last year.

Life really could be ruthless sometimes. As much as she'd hated the *other* woman at first, Sylvia hadn't been able to hold the divorce against her. It was Sylvia's fault her marriage had ended. Her relationships since had all been about mutual gratification. A smile tugged at her lips. Detective Chad Cook had made her really feel again for the first time since the divorce, but he'd been young enough to be her son…not much older than the daughter she'd given away.

Chad had almost been killed by one of the followers of a vicious serial killer. Sylvia helped save his life. During his hospital stay she met his mother—a woman two years younger than her. Reality had hit home in that moment and Sylvia realized Chad needed to move on. He was a wonderful young man. He deserved a woman who wanted a future with him—a home and a family—not just hot sex.

"And then you went from bad to worse," she grumbled as she climbed out of the car. She still blamed the break-up with Chad for her night of pure insanity when she'd gone home with Buddy Corlew.

Sylvia unlocked her front door and quieted the security system. She closed the door and secured it, setting the alarm once more. As she turned from the door, the only sound was the soft tick of the antique grandfather clock her great-grandmother had brought to Birmingham from England. She dropped her keys on the hall table and headed for her bedroom. Halfway there she removed her heels and padded barefoot the rest of the way, her toes curling at the cool feel of the hardwood.

She grabbed the remote and turned on the television. There really wasn't anything she wanted to watch, but the noise chased away the silence of living alone. After skimming the cable channels, she settled on the local late night news. A deep sigh of relief slipped past her lips as she peeled off her dress. She tossed it in the dry cleaning hamper, and then dispensed with her bra and panties.

The cool hardwood turned to cold tile as she entered the bathroom and a shiver sent goose bumps spilling over her skin. She set the temperature on her spa tub and let it fill while she removed her makeup. The reflection staring back at her from the mirror wasn't so bad. She didn't look her age. Careful attention to the needs of her skin and good genes had helped. She worked out every morning, maintaining a lean and toned figure.

From the outside, one would never know she was so empty and...*lonely*. Sylvia closed her eyes and shook her head. Denying the truth was pointless. It was true. She was lonely. She opened her eyes and stared at her reflection. She had numerous friends, a fulfilling career, and financial security. Why wasn't that enough anymore?

Somehow all these weddings and babies had awakened a traitorous need to be the other half of something. *Husband and wife...mother and daughter.*

How utterly ridiculous was that? Sylvia Baron had always been perfectly content and fulfilled with herself.

Until now.

Now she was a jumble of uncertainty and urgent need.

She closed her eyes and thought of Buddy pulling her against him...touching her and kissing her until her body cried out for all of him. Somehow she couldn't turn that need off more than three months later.

Maybe she had turned *him* off with her request. After all, what hot-blooded southern male wanted a woman who'd given her child away and never looked back?

"Maybe you are as cold-hearted as your ex and his friends think," she accused the woman staring back at her.

Sylvia turned away from the mirror and climbed into the tub. She sank into the deliciously hot water, closed her eyes, and tried to relax. She banished the voices from the past and sought a calm, quiet place.

If only her mind hadn't found Buddy there…

CHAPTER EIGHT

DELL ROAD, MOUNTAIN BROOK, 11:15 P.M.

Jess tossed aside the forensic report on the Rutledge homicide scene. Bear, her yellow Lab who looked more like a small pony than a dog, lifted his head and gazed at her. "Sorry, boy." She scratched him behind the ears.

She was frustrated, that was all. The killer in this case had taken great care in not leaving identifiable evidence. The prints of the victim, his housekeeper, as well as his son and late wife had all been eliminated. Though his wife had been deceased for two years, her prints remained on the perfume bottles still sitting on the dressing table in her bedroom and anything else in the house that had been important to her. The housekeeper was never allowed to touch his wife's belongings and treasures with anything other than a feather duster. The judge insisted that those things remain exactly as his wife had left them. Jess believed the man had a bigger heart than most who knew him believed.

The son, Harvey, proved little help to the investigation. He and his father hadn't seen eye to eye, according to the son, since he graduated high school and decided to go into architectural engineering rather than law. Since his mother passed away, the son only came home for Christmas. He and his father spoke by phone occasionally and briefly, but saw each other only on that one day each year. If the judge had any enemies, the son had no idea who they might be or why any animosity existed. His father never mentioned any problems. All judges received threats at one time or another in their careers. Rutledge had suffered with plenty, including the attempt on his life, but none of the documented incidents were recent.

So far, those who knew the judge the best felt convinced that whomever had done this terrible thing was related in some way to a ruling he'd made on a case. No one could point to a specific case that stood out in his or her mind. Nearly all his rulings had been controversial, making most of them memorable.

Jess scowled at the pile of reports spread around her on the floor. How could the victim have had an enemy who hated him enough to take such a risk without anyone noticing that trouble was brewing? Entering a man's home and creating a scene like the one found in Rutledge's library took time and focus. Holding the judge hostage and worse in that very room required comprehensive planning and an equally comprehensive knowledge of the comings and goings at the judge's home. None of his neighbors had noticed anything out of the ordinary.

The killer not only knew the judge, he had watched him and his housekeeper for a good long while before executing his plan. The judge had apparently allowed his killer into his home without resistance.

For now, Jess would keep her team focused on the death penalty cases of the past decade. Since all death penalty cases from the judge's career had been plastered on that library wall, each one would be studied. One by one, relatives of each of the defendants were being interviewed and alibis confirmed. Jess heaved a weary breath. The trouble with that theory was that everyone they'd interviewed so far had an alibi.

Dan sat down on the floor next to her. Bear immediately shifted closer and rested his head against him. "It's time to call it a day, Jess." He removed her eyeglasses, folded them, and placed them on the coffee table. "You need rest. The baby needs you to rest. Even Bear is exhausted just watching you work."

He was right. She placed her hands on her enormous belly. "Sorry. I lost track of time." She'd promised him no more crawling into bed at midnight.

He smiled and her heart reacted. From the first time she laid eyes on him back in high school, she'd fallen for that smile and those dimples. And the blue eyes. Even now, more than two decades later, she melted just a little simply looking at him. Daniel Burnett completed her. She couldn't begin to count the number of times he had told her the same. He made her so very happy. She couldn't wait for the baby to come. The idea was still a little scary, but she believed without doubt that Dan would be an amazing father. His parents would be wonderful grandparents and her sister Lily would be the perfect aunt.

Jess aspired to be even half as good a mother as Dan would be a father.

He kissed her temple. "How about I organize all this for you? I'll leave it on your desk while you go get ready for bed."

Dan had insisted that all work was to be left at the office or kept in the home office. Jess had always created a case board at home. At her last place, she used the living room wall. With the baby coming, taping photos of victims and suspects on a common wall was not a good idea. She surveyed the wall of her office where Dan had installed an enormous white board. This worked just fine.

"You'll have to help me up." She turned to him and made a face. "Getting on all fours and crawling to the desk to help myself up isn't exactly attractive."

Dan laughed. "You might be surprised how attractive I would find you in any position."

"Ha ha. Now help me up."

Dan got to his feet and held out his hands. Jess put her hands in his and first moved up on her knees, then to her feet.

"Thank you. Oh!" She pressed her hand to her belly. "I guess the baby didn't like it that I got up and disturbed her sleep." Jess laughed as she placed Dan's hand to her belly. "Do you feel that?" The baby moving still amazed her. At first, it had been nothing more than those little butterfly wing flutters. Eventually, she'd felt the kicks and then it was the baby moving around. There wasn't a lot of room left these days so the baby's movements were particularly startling at times.

Dan's grin made her heart perform another of those happy little pitter-patters. "I can't believe *he* will be here in a mere twenty days."

"*She* will be here before we know it," Jess teased. They had this ongoing banter about the gender of the baby.

"A little Jess will be fine by me." Dan scooped up the reports.

Jess grabbed a pile and carried it to her desk. If she didn't help, Dan would be in here all night. He had a desk on the other side of the room that sat in front of the windows overlooking the backyard. Jess had wanted hers close to her case board. Besides, the gardens could be too distracting. Under the meticulous direction of Katherine, she and Dan had planted hundreds of bulbs in early December. Now those gorgeous tulips provided a river of color around the yard. The landscape lighting showcased clumps of brilliant reds and soft pinks as well as rich purples. She'd never had a flower garden much less a vegetable garden but they'd already planned out a small vegetable plot.

Eating healthy was more important than ever now. They were going to be parents. Setting a good example in all things was important. No more M&M stashes—at least not at home.

When her work piles were organized on her desk, Dan turned out the lights. "Did Lily tell you she found a magician for Maddie's birthday party?"

"That's great." Jess wrapped her arm around his as they headed for their bedroom. Bear followed close behind them. "Maddie seems so happy."

Four-year-old—soon to be five—Maddie was the daughter of the half-sister Jess and Lil hadn't known about until a few months ago. Amanda Brownfield, a serial killer herself, had ended up a victim of the infamous serial killer Eric Spears. Lily and her husband Blake had adopted Maddie. Between Maddie and Lil's college kids, Blake Junior and Alice, the baby had three sweet cousins and a loving aunt and uncle awaiting her arrival.

Not to mention one exuberant great aunt. Jess had resisted accepting Wanda Newsom back into her life, but she'd come around eventually. Wanda was the only blood relative Jess and Lil had left other than their children. They had learned a great deal last year about the parents they'd lost when they were children. Eric Spears, the depraved serial killer who had been obsessed with Jess, had unearthed all the family secrets and used them to taunt her. She shivered at the vile memories. Obsession was just one of the many faces of evil she had discovered about Eric Spears.

"You cold?" Dan hugged a protective arm around her.

"I was just thinking about Mom and Dad."

"And Spears?"

Jess hesitated and looked into Dan's eyes. She nodded. "Sometimes he still haunts my dreams."

"He can't ever hurt you or anyone else again."

He absolutely could not. Jess had put a bullet in his evil head. Since Spears had no family, the state had been responsible for his final arrangements. Jess had made sure he was cremated. She'd personally escorted his body and watched the entire cremation process. She had needed to see him burn. His ashes had been taken to the landfill and dumped like the garbage he had been.

She brushed her teeth while Dan drew back the covers. She'd taken her shower and pulled on her gown after dinner. She'd learned as the weeks of the third trimester passed that she ran out of steam early. It was best not to assume she could work late and then manage to go through the usual nightly rituals.

Dan helped her into bed, adjusting her pregnancy pillow, and tucking the covers around her. She watched as he rounded the big bed, pausing to give Bear a loving pat. Bear slept at the foot of the bed on a big, fluffy doggie pillow of his own.

A smile broadened her lips as Dan climbed in on his side, and then turned off the lamp on the side table. A nightlight in the bathroom allowed for those middle of the night trips—another third trimester perk.

"I'm thinking of putting Lieutenant Hayes in charge of SPU while I'm on maternity leave." Jess snuggled closer to Dan and felt her whole body sigh in happiness.

Though Hayes outranked him, Harper had been in charge while Jess and Dan were on their honeymoon. Hayes initial inability to fit in with the team had been the primary reason. He'd repeatedly ignored Jess's orders. While they were on their honeymoon, Dan had admitted that he'd instructed Hayes to keep an eye on Jess, going a long way to explain the lieutenant's un-team like behavior. To her surprise, Jess had laughed when Dan made the heartfelt confession. Dan had been so worried that she would be angry. She was pretty sure that was the reason he'd waited until they were on their honeymoon before fessing up. The truth was, Dan had been right to worry about her. She'd so desperately needed to stop Spears that she had taken far too many risks with her safety.

"Hayes has certainly earned your respect." Dan kissed her forehead. "He seems to work well with the team now. I think the surprise birthday party Harper and Wells planned for him says it all."

"I agree. Cook really likes him." Hayes had gone above and beyond to help Cook prepare for his detective's exam.

"I think putting him in charge is the right decision."

"This is nice."

"Which part?" Dan kissed her again, his lips lingering at her temple. "The part where I offer to kiss every inch of you or the new shower gel scent that makes me think of those long, hot nights in Barbados on our honeymoon."

Jess giggled. "The part where I can have the chief of police's ear any time I want it, like now in the middle of the night."

"Seriously?"

She turned her face up to his. "Actually, I really like that offer of you kissing every inch of me."

He growled as he brushed kisses along her cheek. "My pleasure."

He moved the body pillow aside and started a slow, lingering path down her throat. Jess closed her eyes and allowed the sweet sensations to chase away all thoughts of victims and suspects and murder.

Her time with Dan was far too precious to take for granted...even for work.

CHAPTER NINE

"The external examination of Jane Doe is complete," Sylvia announced for the audio recording of the autopsy. She sighed and surveyed the deceased once more before taking the next step. The elderly woman's body was discovered in Railroad Park one week ago. Her autopsy had been delayed by the two recent homicides, which included Judge Rutledge's.

Sylvia prepared to make the Y incision. Based on the external examination, she felt reasonably confident the woman had died of natural causes. However, the bump on the right side of her head as well as a bruise on her right forearm combined with her unattended death dictated the need for an autopsy.

The door behind Sylvia opened. "Dr. Baron?"

"Yes?" Sylvia snapped. The staff knew very well that she was not to be interrupted when performing an autopsy. She scowled at Tammy Lang, the receptionist, who dared to do so anyway.

"I'm sorry to bother you, but he says it's an emergency."

Sylvia placed the scalpel back on the table and removed the splatter guard and facemask. "He who?"

If her boss had called an emergency staff meeting, then he could fill her in later. Sylvia didn't bow to his or anyone else's demands in the middle of an autopsy. Or any other time for that matter. Dr. Martin Leeds was well aware of her rules.

"Mr. Corlew." Tammy shrugged. "He's waiting in your office. I told him you couldn't be disturbed, but he said he wasn't leaving until he spoke with you. Should I call security?"

Dear God. "No, that won't be necessary." Sylvia removed her gloves and squared her shoulders. "Thank you, Tammy."

Tammy nodded, her expression reflecting her confusion and curiosity. Far too wise to ask questions, she hurried away, the door closing quietly behind her.

Sylvia removed her disposable lab coat and left the autopsy room. On the way to her office she considered the various options for putting Corlew in his place. Obviously, he intended to have answers to his intrusive questions and had decided to throw his weight around to get them.

Well, she hoped whatever he had to say was worth it because she felt like pinning him on a cold steel table in an autopsy room and ripping open his torso from shoulders to pelvis. She had taken a huge risk sharing her secret with him. If he made her regret that decision he would absolutely wish he'd chosen otherwise.

Buddy stood behind her desk studying the diplomas and awards on the wall. She walked in and closed the door, the sound drawing his attention to her. For four of five seconds she only stared at him. Not once in her life had she been so enamored by a man so…rough around the edges.

He wore his usual fare. An unbuttoned shirt, he hadn't bothered to tuck into those well-worn, body-hugging jeans, exposed a skintight gray tee. Then there were those battered and somehow immensely sexy cowboy boots. But it was the long hair—longer than hers—that set him so far apart from any other man she'd ever had dinner with much less mind-blowing sex.

"I don't know what you pay your secretary," he said as he stepped away from her desk, "but you should give her a raise. She's a bulldog."

To regain some physical as well as emotional distance, Sylvia moved past him to stand behind her chair. Even putting both the chair and the desk between them failed to provide an effective buffer. "I was in the middle of an autopsy. Why are you here?"

He picked up the framed photograph from her desk. The picture of her with her sister was more than a decade old. *Happier times.*

"I thought of a few more questions I needed to ask you." He placed the photo back on her desk. "I called you last night and then again this morning, but you didn't call me back."

Her fingers squeezed into the leather of her executive desk chair. "I think I made myself clear about answering any other questions."

"Okay. So you're not going to tell me the father's name." His gaze zeroed in on hers, his smoky gray eyes making her instantly uncomfortable in her clothes. "Did you inform him before proceeding with the adoption?"

Tension trickled through her. "I did not. No. He made it clear he wasn't interested in me, marriage, or in children. There was no reason to tell him. The adoption was a private one that didn't include unnecessary questions or stipulations."

"Before I go any further," he warned, somehow seeming closer, "you need to think about the legal ramifications of what you did back then."

Anger ignited inside her. "Of what I did back then?" She jammed the chair against her desk and stalked around to the other side to confront him face-to-face. "Do you have any idea how difficult it was for me to come to you with this?"

He held her furious gaze without flinching. "I have a pretty damned good idea."

"Then why are you determined to make me regret my decision?" For years she had pretended *it* never happened. She had blocked the memories of her rounded belly and of the fierce pains of childbirth. And the cries...the sound of her daughter's first cries still echoed through her from time to time. She had blocked those memories just as she had any happy moments from her ten-year, ill-fated marriage. Sylvia Baron was an expert at burying feelings…at hiding the hurt.

His hands were on her arms and pulling her close before she could bat them away. "I never want you to regret anything you share with me."

If he hadn't murmured the words so tenderly… so honestly she might have been able to stay angry and push him away but he had and she could do nothing except lean into him.

"You did what you had to do," he whispered against her hair, those strong arms holding her so tight. "No one can fault you for that. I'm just not sure you're seeing past your emotions."

Sylvia grappled for her composure. She drew back from him, his touch falling away, leaving her feeling cold and empty. "This was not a snap decision. I've struggled with it for months."

"Everything about your life will change. The father could cause trouble for you personally and to your professional reputation. Before I go beyond the point of no return, I need to be certain this is what you really want."

Drawing in a deep breath, Sylvia steeled herself. "This is what I want. I'm prepared for meeting any legal challenges that may arise. If you choose not to take my case I would appreciate a recommendation for another investigator you feel is trustworthy and reliable." There. She'd said it. There was no turning back. This was the right thing to do. This was what she wanted to do. No question.

"Have you talked to your parents?" He stood firm with his questioning. "This affects them as well."

Sylvia folded her arms over her chest. He was not changing her mind. "I have not told another living soul except you." She searched his face. If she didn't know better she would think he was the one having trouble with moving forward. "Are you not up to the challenge of getting the job done?"

He hesitated and another burst of fury flamed through her. "Are you operating under the delusion that our one-night stand somehow gives you some stake in my wellbeing? Don't flatter yourself, Mr. Corlew. We had sex. Granted it was good sex—"

"Great," he corrected. "We had *great* sex."

She rolled her eyes. "I've had great sex with my vibrator. That doesn't mean I plan to start consulting it regarding difficult decisions."

He propped his hands on his hips. "Your vibrator? Really? Can your vibrator make you scream its name? Or beg for more?"

Heat rushed up her cheeks, but it was the heat that roared to life between her legs that truly infuriated her. "Are you taking my case or not?"

He stepped closer, nose-to-nose. "I'm on it, Doc. I will find her, and then I'll do whatever you want me to do. Just remember when the shit hits the fan that I warned you to think carefully before you started down this path."

All she had to do was tilt her head just a little and then lean in the slightest bit and their lips would touch. The thought of having his mouth on hers had her burning up…had her melting faster than sugar in hot tea.

"Got it. Now get out of my office."

He stared at her lips, licked his own. "Whatever you want."

He turned and walked away. Sylvia inhaled a ragged breath. Her whole body trembled with need as she watched him swagger to the door. If he'd held out one more second—

The door lock clicked.

She snapped to attention. He'd…*locked* the door!

Slowly, he turned to face her once more. Before she could find her voice he'd closed the distance between them and pulled her against his hard body.

"You might fool everyone else, but you don't fool me." He kissed her hard. The fingers of one hand dove into her hair, while the other found her breast and squeezed.

Her knees buckled. She whimpered. One skilled hand slid down over her hip. He squeezed her bottom while his mouth continued to plunder hers.

He backed her against her desk and she gasped, the sound lost to his hot, punishing kisses. Before she could summon the wherewithal to do more than whimper, he dragged the hem of her dress to her hips and spread her legs apart. A finger slid inside her, then another. She whimpered.

"God, you are so damned wet."

"You should leave," she said, the words panting out of her…her thighs trembling.

"Tell me you don't want me." He unbuttoned his fly, lowered the zipper. "Tell me that fire isn't for me." He stroked her possessively.

Speech was impossible...she could scarcely breathe...

He shoved his briefs out of the way and nudged her intimately. The battle was lost. She wrapped her legs around his waist and he dove into her. The sound of papers sliding across her desk and slipping to the floor only made her more desperate. His fingers lowered the zipper of her dress, following the curve of her spine. He dragged the fabric down her chest, exposing her satin encased breasts.

"You are so damned gorgeous." He ground his pelvis into hers, letting her feel how deep inside her he was. He slid his tongue between one lacy satin cup and her breast, then toyed with her nipple with his teeth.

She bit her lips together to hold back the scream. Her fingers buried in all that long hair as she lifted her hips to meet his slow, deep thrusts. Everything that was wrong in her life slipped away, leaving her feeling nothing but a desperate need for his touch... for all of him.

She came twice before he finished. Even then, she wanted more.

If only he'd simply zipped his fly and walked out when he'd finished, maybe she could have hated him for making her so weak. Maybe she could have cursed him for being a bastard.

He didn't.

Like everything else about Buddy Corlew, his tenderness after lovemaking was unexpected. As soon as he'd righted his jeans, he grabbed tissues from the box on her desk and cleaned her. Slipped her panties back into place and adjusted her bra and dress, lastly tugging her zipper back into place. Then he smoothed her hair and smiled down at her before dropping one last kiss on her lips.

"I'll call you."

"No." How she summoned the ability to utter the one word, she wasn't sure.

He hesitated at the door and stared expectantly at her.

She lifted her chin and met his gaze with the defiance for which she was known. "I don't want to hear from you again until you have what I'm paying you to find."

For three seconds that lapsed into five he merely stared at her. "Whatever you want."

And then he was gone. Sylvia passed a shaky hand over her face. Okay. *Pull yourself together.* She gathered the scattered papers and tidied her desk. When her respiration had evened out, she smoothed her palms over the skirt of her dress and headed to the ladies room.

This wasn't the first time she'd had sex in her office. There had been a couple of other incidents. This was, however, the first time she wasn't in control. Buddy Corlew made her lose control. No other man had ever been able to make that happen.

Ten minutes later, she was back in the autopsy room wearing gloves, splatter shield, facemask, and lab coat ready to continue. She stared at the elderly woman who had died alone in that park.

She didn't want to die alone. She didn't want to continue proving what people said about her behind her back. She wasn't entirely self-sufficient or completely heartless as they accused. She had feelings and needs. She wanted things...

She wanted to spend more time with the living than with the dead.

CHAPTER TEN

Jess tapped the photo of Reed Summers, the brother of the last prisoner to be executed under Rutledge's authority. "Let's question him again. He's the only one whose alibi we haven't been able to confirm."

"Even if we find the prostitute he claims he took home with him, can we rely one way or the other on her testimony?" Lori joined Jess at the case board.

Jess shrugged. "Frankly, I don't think we've interviewed our killer yet." Jess surveyed the row of faces, male and female. The list of close family and friends whose loved ones were sentenced to death by Judge Rutledge had been now narrowed down to a mere dozen. Yet, not one of those appeared to have sufficient motive in Jess's opinion. The sister of the bomber had moved to Florida to live with her daughter. She hadn't even realized Rutledge was dead much less murdered.

"I'm not feeling it either," Lori agreed.

Detective Chad Cook rose from his desk and swaggered over to join them. Jess smiled inside as she noted the limp he'd struggled with was almost gone now. The young man had worked hard to come back from almost dying at the hands of one of Eric Spears's followers.

"We're not even close." He braced his hands on his narrow hips and shook his head. "We're missing something by looking only at the people who had reason to hate the judge. What if the killer was expecting something he didn't get? Maybe the judge promised a ruling he didn't deliver and all this stuff about those he gave the death sentence is just smoke and mirrors."

The smile Jess had kept to herself slid across her lips now. "Very good, Detective."

Cook blushed. "I mean, the killer could be trying to throw us off his trail."

"His son was thousands of miles away at the time of the murder." Lori moved to the photo of the son.

"He could easily have hired someone to off his old man," Cook suggested.

"He could have," Lori agreed. "But, according to the family attorney, a half million dollar insurance policy goes to the grandson and all property and other assets go to the son. It's a fairly large estate but still not much of a motive for killing the judge considering Harvey is quite wealthy in his own right."

And there they were, back at square one without the necessary trinity: motive, means and opportunity. Jess hoped Sergeant Harper and Lieutenant Hayes gleaned something more from their interviews with the dozen remaining persons who had loved ones sentenced to death by Rutledge.

Jess reviewed the board once more. "Since the housekeeper and everyone else we've interviewed claim the judge had no friends, why don't we take a different route this afternoon? Let's make a list of his closest professional associates and see what we find there. Maybe we're looking for an attorney who'd had enough of Rutledge's style of justice. Or a clerk he treated badly one time too many."

"His wife has been dead for two years," Lori offered, "we may be looking for a scorned lover. There's Viagra in his medicine cabinet."

"Detective Cook," Jess turned to the youngest member of their team, "start with the housekeeper and let's find out if she failed to mention a girlfriend or a companion."

"Yes, ma'am."

Jess made her way to her desk and rounded up her sweater and bag.

"I have the list of professional associates." Lori flipped through the file she'd retrieved from her desk. "This lineup is interesting."

Tugging on the pink sweater that had quickly become her third trimester favorite, Jess mentally ran through the names she'd read on the list. "No doubt. On the rare occasions when the judge social-ized, he was certainly among the powerful and elite of the Magic City."

Birmingham's hierarchy hadn't changed much for as far back as Jess could remember. Most of the current upper crust had connections going back to those who changed Birmingham from a fledgling community off the map to the Pittsburg of the south. Dan's family was among those old money clans.

"Our former mayor and our victim go way back." Lori closed the file. "Isn't his trial coming up soon?"

Jess slung the strap of her bag over her shoulder. "It's set for May. Dan thinks he'll take a plea deal. His attorney turned down the one the DA offered last month." Former Mayor Joseph Pratt was charged with a number of crimes, not the least of which were misuse of funds and the abuse of power. Dan's career had almost been destroyed because of Pratt's devious conduct.

"We could start with him." Lori grabbed her bag and jacket and headed for the door. "He's on house arrest. I doubt he has anything better to do."

Jess couldn't deny the little burst of glee she felt at the idea. "Let's go make his day then."

As they reached the elevator, Jess settled her hand on her belly. "We have to stop for lunch on the way. This baby does not like to wait."

Lori pressed the call button for the elevator. "I cannot wait to start looking and feeling pregnant!"

Jess laughed. "You do remember that less than a year ago we were both totally focused on our careers. Babies and husbands weren't in our five-year plans."

The doors glided open and they stepped into the elevator car. Jess braced against the back wall and waited for the elevator to bump into motion. She'd learned quickly that sudden movements could be problematic to her balance these days.

"You started it," Lori reminded her. "The next thing I knew I had the fever, too."

"Guilty as charged." To this day Jess wondered if subconsciously she'd missed those birth control pills on purpose. Whatever the case, in just over two weeks she and Dan were going to be parents. "So, have you and Harper started discussing baby names?"

"We're making our lists. Once we've picked out our individual favorites, we'll negotiate."

Jess laughed so hard the baby jumped. "I'd like to be a fly on the wall during your negotiations."

Lori grinned. "Boy names will be easier. Since Chester is already named after him, we're thinking of my father or his for boy names. I think I'll win that negotiation."

Chet's son would be four by the time the baby was born. Jess imagined there would be a few awkward moments when Chet's ex heard the news. On the other hand, she had taken the announcement that Chet and Lori were getting married fairly well. Maybe this one would be as easy.

"Our boy name is a given," Jess said, "we'll name him after Dan. Selecting a name for a little girl hasn't been so easy. Dan wants to name her after me or at least to use my middle name."

"Are you okay with that?"

The elevator doors opened once more and Jess waited until they were outside to answer. The March wind whipped hard, making her wish she'd tucked her hair into a ponytail. "I'm not sure."

Jess's middle name, Lee, was after her father. Her parents had died in a car crash when she was ten, but last year she'd learned that most of what she'd believed about her parents had been fiction. Though her father had turned out to be one of the good guys, he had cheated on her mom. It was a long sad story that had shaken her and Lily.

They loaded into Lori's red Mustang. "I like the name Beatrice Irene."

"Is it a family name?"

Jess smiled. "My mother's middle name was Irene."

"Are you worried about offending Katherine?"

Dan's mother was so excited about the baby Jess was reasonably sure it wouldn't matter what they named the child. Still, she wanted to do this right. Family was important. She hadn't really realized just how much so until the past few months.

"Katherine's mother's name was Beatrice."

"I like it." Lori merged into downtown traffic. "It's elegant."

Jess agreed. *Beatrice.* She rubbed her belly. It was perfect.

CRESCENT ROAD, 1:30 P.M.

Joseph Pratt lived in a 1910 Craftsman style home that sat on a hillside overlooking prestigious Forest Park, one of Birmingham's historic communities.

His grandfather had built this house as a gift to his wife. It was a lovely home.

When the social niceties were out of the way, the former mayor looked directly at Jess. "I suppose you're here about Harmon's murder."

"We are." Jess settled her teacup on its saucer. "The two of you traveled in many of the same circles. You worked together on fundraising efforts over the years. You served side by side on various councils. I'm hoping you can provide some insight as to who might have wanted him dead."

Pratt sipped his tea before setting it aside. "Harmon lived by one rule: an eye for an eye. Justice was all that mattered to him. If you broke the law and had the misfortune of appearing in his courtroom, you paid the highest penalty allowed by law. I'm sure he left a very long list of enemies."

"We're considering those as well as any friends and close professional associates."

He laughed. "I see. Am I a suspect?"

"Should you be?" Jess turned the question back on him.

"Harmon and I began our careers around the same time. We were going to be the most powerful and influential people in the city. The movers and shakers who made things happen." He shrugged. "To a large degree we succeeded."

"Did the judge ever cross that line he so rigidly held others to?" They both knew Pratt had crossed a number of lines.

"You mean was he like me? Capable of doing whatever necessary to achieve his goals?"

Jess assumed the question was a rhetorical one.

"Any man who reaches a position of considerable power makes decisions that can weigh on his conscience. It's a necessary evil. In time, Dan will tell you the same, I'm sure."

Jess had wondered how long it would take Pratt to try to drag Dan into the muck with him. "Have you heard any rumors about the judge being involved with a female friend or companion?"

"Men like Harmon are very careful about their personal lives. If he was keeping company with a lady friend, she would have been a professional."

Jess hesitated. "By professional do you mean a companion who gets paid for her time?" There really was no delicate way to put the question.

"Certainly. There are a number of services in the city that are discreet. If Harmon was enjoying the comforts of a companion you'll find it was handled in a very businesslike manner. He was far too devoted to his wife to begin a relationship with another woman. Perhaps his companion had a boyfriend who wasn't happy with her job choice. I suppose, if such a scenario occurred, she could have been followed to Harmon's home by someone with criminal intent."

"We're considering all possibilities," Jess agreed.

Pratt stood. "I'm afraid that's all the time I have to share today, Chief. If you have any additional questions, feel free to call my attorney."

"Thank you for your time." Jess managed to get to her feet without grabbing onto Lori who'd already stood.

As they left the room, Pratt commented, "Dan was wise to pass on the offer to be the city's next mayor."

Jess glanced at him. "He's quite happy as the chief of police."

Pratt nodded. "The more power a man possesses, the more temptation he faces. You remember that, Jess, and Dan will be fine."

Neither Jess nor Lori spoke again until they were ensconced in her Mustang, and Pratt's address was in the rear view mirror. "That was strange," Lori said.

"Very." Jess mulled over Pratt's final comments for a moment. "How many high-end escort services are operating in Birmingham?"

Lori considered the question as she navigated traffic. "Three I can think of." She glanced at Jess. "But only one a man like the judge would patronize."

"That's our next stop," Jess announced. "Let's find out if any of Rutledge's death row alum have friends or family employed by one of the high-end services. Maybe this wasn't the first weekend the judge had been all tied up."

The idea that the judge would break the law by hiring a call girl would have made his killer even angrier. A judge who regularly sentenced defendants to the harshest penalties should have held himself to the same standard.

Maybe being a hypocrite had carried a higher penalty than the judge had anticipated.

CHAPTER ELEVEN

Buddy ordered his usual. Like the song said, it was five o'clock somewhere. He needed a beer. Hell, he probably needed something a whole lot stronger but a beer would have to do.

He had all sorts of contacts in the world of private investigations. He even had a few a wiser man would avoid. Occasionally, a case required the kind of expertise only someone working outside the law could provide. Finding Sylvia's daughter required a little bending of the law. Nothing too drastic, just the proper connection in Sacramento. He'd found a guy he thought might come through for him. No worry there.

It was the other part that bugged the hell out of him.

Dan Burnett walked in and looked around. He spotted Buddy at the table in the darkest corner farthest from the door and started that way. Dan

80

and Buddy were the same age. They'd been fierce football rivals back in high school. As quarterbacks, Dan had represented the best at his fancy private school, and Buddy had given him hell from the public school on the other side of the tracks. In recent months they had become friends, sort of. They both loved Jess, and they both cared about Sylvia. Though Sylvia was a year older, Dan would have been in high school with her. He'd known her his whole life. Hell, he'd married her younger sister a decade or so ago. One of several failed attempts to forget Jess.

Dan would surely have some idea who the father of Sylvia's child was.

The chief of police took a seat at the table and sent a pointed look first at the beer and then at Buddy. "You having a bad day, Corlew?"

Buddy motioned for the waitress. "Let's just say it could be better. What're you having?"

Dan grinned. "Maybe I'll join you."

Stella, the waitress, paused at the table. "You want another one of those?" She pointed to Buddy's Corona?

He shook his head. "Bring one for my friend."

Stella winked. "Anything for Birmingham's top cop." She sashayed away.

"I took the afternoon off," Dan said. "I have some shopping to do."

Buddy grinned. "Spoiling that baby already, are you?" Dan and Jess were going to be incredible parents. The kid was one lucky little urchin.

"Actually." Stella arrived with the beer and Dan thanked her. "This gift is for Jess. There's this mother and child necklace I want to give her when the baby's born. I've been looking all over for just the right one and I finally found it. I'm picking it up today."

Six or seven times Buddy had gone over how he would approach the subject and now that Dan was here, he wasn't so sure where to start.

"You have something on your mind, Corlew?" Dan knocked back a slug of his beer.

No use putting it off any longer. "I need some information on a friend of yours." He leaned forward, braced his forearms on the table. "But this has to stay strictly between the two of us."

Dan's eyebrows reared up. "I don't keep secrets from my wife, Corlew. She has issues with secrets. The last one I kept from her, when I had Hayes keeping an eye on her, cost me three nights in the guest room after we got back from our honeymoon."

Danny boy was right about that. Jess would kick both their asses. "Okay, but tell her she'd better not say a word to Sylvia."

Dan frowned. "Sylvia? What does she have to do with this?"

Buddy had two options here. He could tell Dan Sylvia's secret or he could spill his own. "She…" He slouched back in his chair and blew out a burst of frustration. "I got a thing for her, man." He moved his head from side to side. "I can't shake it."

Dan nodded slowly, a frown furrowing its way across his brow. "You're saying that you like Sylvia? You're interested in her...*romantically*?"

Buddy had never allowed a woman to get so far under his skin. Not once. He'd never been married—hell, he'd never been engaged. He had no desire for kids or any of that home and hearth baloney. Sylvia made him want to stake a claim. The thought of her with another man made him see red. He couldn't keep her out of his head long enough to focus on a damned thing. Over the years, his pals had told him this would happen one day. Love was like a drug, once you stumbled upon the one that tripped your trigger you were addicted.

"Yeah," he confessed. The admission didn't hurt as much as he'd expected it would. "She's all I think about." Saying the words out loud somehow lifted the elephant off his chest and let him breathe a little easier.

Dan chuckled. "April fool's day is not until tomorrow, Corlew." He reached for his beer again.

"Part of me wishes this was a joke, but it's not. I need your help, Danny boy. I gotta figure this out."

"You're serious?"

Buddy nodded. "As a heart attack."

Dan was the one bracing his forearms on the table and leaning forward this time. "Are you two seeing each other?"

"We had this moment." He couldn't believe he was spilling his guts like this. "That night...after your wedding. I guess we both tried to pretend it was nothing, but then…it started again." Just thinking about this morning had him sweating. God Almighty, he wanted that woman every minute of every day.

Dan nodded. "All right, so how can I help?"

Buddy shrugged. "I'm way out of my league here. I know Sylvia was married once to Larry Grayson." He knew the lieutenant from his days on the BPD. Grayson was a veteran cop with only a slightly better pedigree than Buddy. Rumor had it that Sylvia only married Grayson so people would stop wondering when the senator's oldest would get married. The marriage had ended when Grayson turned his attention to another, younger woman. "Since that didn't work out, I'm wondering if there was someone before that who maybe stole her heart. Maybe she's already had the love of her life and isn't interested in finding anyone new. Like you and Jess, you know? If that's the way it is, I'd like to know before I get in any deeper."

Dan held up a hand. "You have to forgive me. First, I can't believe we're having this conversation, but secondly, and more importantly, I'm having trouble with the idea that the infamous womanizing Buddy Corlew is smitten. Maybe it's Sylvia who should be worried."

"Trust me," Buddy assured him, "I'm the one who's in way over his head."

Dan studied him for a moment. "Sylvia was very focused on her education back in school. We lost touch during our college years since I was in Boston with Jess."

Damn it. Buddy had forgotten about that. "I guess you don't know who she was involved with in college."

"As a matter of fact, I might." Dan glanced around as if he feared being overhead. "I remember my mother mentioning that Sylvia and Benton Murdock were an item."

Buddy's gut twisted. "You mean the eldest son of Winston Murdock, as in the governor of Alabama?" Holy shit.

"That's him. I think they dated most of her senior year in college, but the next thing I heard he'd married someone else. The daughter of some Texas oil tycoon."

"You're sure there wasn't anyone else?" Buddy's heart felt as heavy as a load of bricks. Now he understood why Sylvia wouldn't tell him the name of the father.

"If you really want to know more, you should ask my mother. She kept up with everyone who was anyone back then." He laughed. "I think she still does."

"I don't think your mother would like the idea of Sylvia and me together. She'd probably rush over and warn the senator."

Dan shrugged. "I can start a conversation with her. See what I can find out."

"I'd appreciate it. This is new territory for me." *Damned scary territory.*

"Sylvia has always kept her personal life close to the vest. She's a very private person, Buddy. With her family being such a prominent one, it's the only way to maintain some degree of normalcy."

Buddy finished off his Corona. He set the bottle aside. "Thing is, I wasn't looking to fall for a rich woman. I don't need her money and I damned sure don't need the grief that goes with the name."

Dan nodded his understanding. "When Jess and I first started our relationship, my mother was livid. She wanted the right girl for me. Someone like Sylvia, from the right family, etcetera. When it comes to falling in love, money and pedigree are irrelevant. A person can have a relationship with and even marry a person for all the right reasons, but that doesn't mean they'll be happy. There's no rhyme or reason to true love. Jess and I were in love and no matter how hard we both worked to prove we didn't need each other, nothing was ever going to change that fact."

Dan was right and Buddy was doomed. However he looked at it. No matter how he tried to pretend. He had it bad for the woman. She wasn't his usual type, but for the first time he didn't care. He knew for a fact that Dr. Sylvia Baron didn't usually go for guys like him. Yet, if his instincts were on target, she had it pretty bad for him, too. There was no faking the way she came alive in his arms…the way she surrendered to him.

What she was asking of him could very well tear her apart in ways he wasn't sure she was prepared for. But it was what she wanted and he couldn't refuse her.

Even if it tore them both apart.

CHAPTER TWELVE

Joe Pratt threw the damned remote at the television. It bounced off and shattered on the floor. One of these days the damned Coleman bitch would get what was coming to her. He'd hoped when the city learned she'd hidden her secret life as a lesbian she would be finished here. But the fools had forgiven her. Just as the fools had in Sodom and Gomorrah.

"This city is going to hell."

His life had already gone to hell. In the past six months, he'd been forced to resign as mayor, his wife had left him, and his son wasn't speaking to him. All because he had played the game.

He stomped to the bar and poured himself another scotch. How was a man supposed to make it in this world if the devil kept throwing obstacles in his way? He'd never done one damned thing that wasn't for the greater good. He'd followed in his father's footsteps, ultimately rising far above those accomplishments. He had served this city and helped it to flourish as never before.

Where had the sacrifices gotten him? Charged with unspeakable crimes and alone.

"Bastards." He downed a hefty serving of his favorite drink. His own wife had turned on him as if all the years he had devoted to her meant nothing. His attorney had warned him the bitch was determined to have this house. It was his family home, not hers. He shoved his hand into his pocket and removed his keys. She expected him to give her half of everything. Disgusted, he threw the keys against the wall. Just his luck the damned things slid behind the bookcase. Didn't matter. He wasn't allowed to leave the property. He made a disgusted sound.

At any rate, he'd have to hunt up his spare set to lock the door before he went to bed. Or maybe he'd locked the door when he came inside. He couldn't remember. He'd been far too angry. A man couldn't even have a drink on his own front porch without some lowlife reporter sneaking through the shrubbery.

"Screw it." He didn't give one damn anymore.

His life was destroyed. One of these days, the blind fools would realize that men like Daniel Burnett were not the answer to their dreams. Burnett was too damned self-righteous, too damned good to do the necessary evils that life sometimes required. Few men were prepared to make the sacrifices Joe had made.

And that wife of Burnett's…Jess had showed up in Joe's town and brought the devil himself with her. The damned serial killer who'd followed her here had been responsible for the murder of dozens of citizens, and still Jess was the darling of Birmingham. The way she and Burnett stayed in the news with their every move documented as if they were royalty made Joe sick.

The favored couple would never make it. Just wait until real trouble hit the city. Those two would be worthless. The citizens would be clamoring for Joe then. But he'd be in prison…rotting away for doing nothing more than what was necessary to get the job done. This city prospered because of his sacrifices.

How dare *she* come here to question him about the murder of an old friend! Harmon Rutledge had known what it took to serve this state and this city. Like Joe, the judge had sacrificed more than anyone would ever know. Men were no longer forged the way he and Harmon had been. Most of them turned into the kind of indecisive namby-pamby morons Baron and the others had become. The very idea Jess and her minion would show up at his home infuriated him. Furthermore, he was still fuming that Robert had come up with the ridiculous theory that Wilson Hilliard was somehow responsible for the judge's death. The man was grasping at straws.

"They can all go to hell." He poured himself two more fingers of scotch before stumbling out onto the back patio and staring up at the moon. His ancestors had helped build this city with their own blood, sweat, and tears. "So much for loyalty."

"What would you know about loyalty?"

Joe whirled around, almost lost his balance. He tried to see who had spoken. Whoever it was lingered in the shadows beyond the moonlight's reach. "Who's there?"

"A ghost from your past, Mr. Mayor."

Joe tried to place the voice, the man sounded vaguely familiar. "If you have the nerve to come uninvited onto my property, at least have the guts to show yourself."

A tall thin man stepped out of the shadows. His movements were stilted. Not a young man, Joe decided. The long face nudged at Joe's memory but he couldn't place it.

"You probably won't remember me, Mayor Pratt." He held up what appeared to be a cell phone and snapped a photograph.

Joe blinked at the flash. Another damned reporter! Bastards. "What do you think you're doing?" Joe reared back and puffed out his chest. "I suggest you delete that photograph and get off my property before I call the police." Joe swayed in spite of his best efforts to hold himself steady. The idea that this reporter was wearing rubber gloves joined the other whirling thoughts in his head.

The man was suddenly standing right next to him. "I don't think you will, Mayor."

Joe tried to back away but the man's iron grip on his arm held him close. "Unhand me!"

"Come inside, Mayor. We wouldn't want your neighbors to be disturbed. We have much to discuss."

Joe tried to fight him. He kicked at his leg and hit something hard like steel. His glass crashed onto the stones. He opened his mouth to shout but a cloth closed over his face. The pungent smell overwhelmed him. He tried not to breath but it was too late...the deadening fumes filled his lungs.

The sound of his heels dragging on the stone patio followed him into nothingness.

CHAPTER THIRTEEN

Lori Wells scrubbed her face and added a layer of moisturizer. She studied her reflection. *Wow.* Anticipation rushed through her. She was going to be a mother. She hadn't expected to be *expecting* in this decade. Jess was right when she said that not even a year ago Lori had been totally focused on her career.

She lifted her hand and admired the gorgeous engagement ring Chet had given her last September. He'd made her the happiest woman in the world with his heartfelt proposal. Now, to be carrying his child was a dream come true. Her mother was so excited. Her sister couldn't wait to be an auntie.

"You okay?"

Chet moved up behind her and Lori's breath caught. He smiled at her in the mirror and her heart picked up its pace. "I was just taking care of all those little extra details that keep me looking like the woman you want to marry," she teased.

His arms came around her waist and he nuzzled her neck. "You're perfect just the way you are. No extra details necessary."

Lori turned in his arms and smiled up at him. "No one has ever made me feel as cherished as you do." Chet Harper was the most gorgeous man she had ever laid eyes on. More importantly, he was a kind and generous man as well as a loving father to Chester. He was a good cop and she loved him with all her heart.

"I plan on spending the rest of my life making you feel that way." He brushed a kiss across her lips. "Hmm, you taste good."

She giggled. "You like my toothpaste, do you?"

He pressed his forehead to hers and grinned. "I love everything about you."

"I guess you'll still love me when I'm big and fat."

"You will never be big and fat to me, no matter what size you are."

Lori had to laugh. "You sure know how to say all the right words, Sergeant Harper."

He lifted her into his arms. "I have all the right moves, too, Detective."

Lori laughed as he carried her to their bed. They bounced down on it together and she sighed. "When we get old and one of us dies, you think the other will end up all alone like the judge?"

Chet frowned. "What are you talking about? Chester will be there for us." He rubbed her tummy.

"And we'll have this one. Our children won't ever desert us that way. We'll be such good parents they'll want to be there for us."

She stroked his strong jaw. "I hope so. I can't imagine ignoring my mother. I will always be here for her."

"I'll be here for her, too."

Chet's parents were deceased, but he treated her mother as if she were his own. Lori appreciated that more than words could properly articulate. "She loves you like a son."

Chet braced his forearms on either side of her head. "Good cause I adore her."

"Jess and I interviewed Tina Templeton. She denies any connection to the judge."

"I don't know why you didn't let Hayes and me take care of that interview."

Laughter burst out of Lori. "No way were we going to have you guys interviewing the premiere madam of Birmingham."

"Alleged premiere madam," he reminded her.

"Whatever." Lori banged at his chest. "You know who she is."

Chet laughed. "Every male over the age of 14 knows who she is. Did you really expect her to admit dealings with a person who is now a homicide victim?"

"Hey, why not? Unless she has something to hide, of course." Lori couldn't help being mesmerized by the beautiful woman. At fifty-seven, she'd been involved in or operating an escort service under the law's radar for almost forty years. The most intriguing part was her ability not to get caught. The fact that her service catered to the rich and powerful and was very discreet probably helped. Her employees were well trained and all damned gorgeous.

"She has plenty to hide I'm sure," Chet countered, "but I doubt her sins include the judge's murder."

Lori ran her fingers through his dark hair. "Whoever killed the judge did a hell of a job of not leaving behind any evidence."

"We'll get him." Chet rolled onto his side. "We always do."

Lori turned on her side to face him. "What're we going to do when the baby comes?"

"If you want to stay home for a while or until he or she graduates high school that's fine by me. We can manage on one income."

They were lucky when it came to finances. "It's a big decision, but right now I can't imagine giving up my career. I love being a cop. I worked hard to get where I am."

"You did," Chet agreed. "Is the chief still planning to come back to work?"

"Definitely." Lori traced a path down his chest. "Katherine keeps telling her that when she holds that baby in her arms, she may change her mind."

"Is that what you think will happen with you?"

She looked deep into his dark eyes. "Yeah and it scares the hell out of me. I'm not sure how I feel about putting my career on hold even for a couple of years."

"Whatever you decide works for me. We'll be good parents whether we're both working or not. Your mom would love nothing more than to retire and take care of her grandchild."

"She sure has made that loud and clear." Lori had to smile. Her mother would be an amazing grandmother. "Like you said, we have plenty of time to decide."

"We do."

"I made another decision just now." Lori slid her finger into the waistband of his boxers. "These have to go."

"Yes, ma'am."

He kissed her long and deep and Lori melted into the sensations of making love with Chet. Whatever decision they made about the future, it would be the right one.

Then she stopped thinking at all...

CHAPTER FOURTEEN

Holding her breath, Jess leaned down to get a closer look at the victim's face. "There's some bruising around his mouth." Other than that small amount of discoloration and the fact that former Mayor Joseph Pratt was tied to a chair in his study, he might have simply been asleep.

The chair had been turned to face the wall on the side of the room farthest from his desk. His wrists were secured to the wooden chair arms with nylon rope in a very similar manner as the judge's had been. The legs of the chair had been used for binding his ankles. As with Judge Rutledge, a wider nylon band worked like a safety belt to fasten his torso to the back of the chair. The stench of human waste and urine permeated the room.

"The newspaper clippings tell quite a story," Lori said.

Jess straightened. Rubbing her aching back, she stepped closer to the wall where framed photos of Pratt with various other politicians had been removed and a collage of newspaper articles about Pratt's career as Birmingham's mayor had been created.

"All of it bad," Jess pointed out.

Unbeknownst to his constituents, the mayor had spent most of his career doing what was best for himself and his close friends. Of course, he had accomplished a fair amount of good for the city, but the greater part of his endeavors and achievements had been self-serving. Jess wanted to feel bad that he'd spent his final hours of life being forced to face his nasty deeds, but somehow she didn't. Maybe it was because one of Pratt's final acts as mayor had been an attempt to destroy Dan's career. Not to mention his callous efforts had posed a serious threat to Dan's personal life.

"Looks like we're dealing with the same killer as the one in the Rutledge case," Lori suggested.

"No doubt." Jess considered the staging of the victim once more. "Same type and color nylon rope. Same knots. Same *brag* wall of photos and clippings collected over time." She gestured to the newspaper clippings plastered to the wall. "The question is what did both ex-Mayor Pratt and retired Judge Rutledge have in common that triggered a motive for murder?"

Every violent act committed was prompted by motive. In Jess's experience, the sooner the motive was uncovered the sooner the killer was revealed. Find the motive, find the killer. If Pratt and Rutledge were victims of the same killer, then the two victims shared a common thread that apparently linked their lives and/or careers. Rutledge's rulings may have seemed heartless or simply wrong to the family members and friends of convicted criminals, so revenge was a reasonable motive. Jess couldn't quite see a similar motive for Pratt's murder. His vile deeds had only recently been revealed to the public. It would take some digging to uncover any suspects carrying a murderous grudge against both Rutledge and Pratt.

Lori checked her phone. "Lieutenant Hayes is talking to the wife now. He was able to catch her before she saw the news."

"Good." Before Jess arrived at the scene reporters had already descended on the block. Birmingham's finest had done a great job clearing the area, but it hadn't taken long for an ambitious reporter to slip through and determine the probable victim. Pratt had been the focus in the news for months now. In the beginning, his devoted wife had been at his side. Eventually, news broke that she had left him. Still, the two had a long history. The news was no doubt shattering for her as well as their son.

"Is the ME on the way?" Jess was surprised Sylvia wasn't here already. Lately everyone moved faster than Jess did.

"She should be here by now." Lori checked her phone again. "I can call her."

Jess shook her head. "Let's give her a few more minutes. She may have run into a traffic issue." Though Harper had gone through the house before

Jess arrived, she wanted to have a look around herself. "Let's take a walk through while we wait for Sylvia."

Crime scene techs had arrived and were going through their protocols. Pratt's computer as well as his cell phone would be taken to the lab, and phone records would be ordered. Harper, the first detective on the scene, was now interviewing neighbors. Jess and Lori moved through the house, room by room, the first floor and then the second. Harper had found no indications of forced entry during his search. Though all windows remained locked, the front door, as well as the one leading onto the patio, had been unlocked. As with Rutledge, the lack of forced entry suggested the victim knew his killer. Although they had discovered broken glass on the patio outside, there was no other indication of a struggle. There was no way to know as of yet if the broken glass had anything to do with the murder.

Pratt's attorney, Marvin Siniard, had discovered the body. He and Pratt had an appointment this morning at eight. Since the front door was unlocked, Siniard had rung the bell and entered the house as was customary for their appointments. Harper had interviewed Siniard only briefly since he'd had to leave to be in court. Jess would interview him again later.

Her cell burst into the old-fashioned ring tone she hated. She hesitated on the upstairs landing and dug in her bag for it. One of these days she was going to change that annoying sound to something more pleasant. The only reason she'd kept it this long was because it was so different from everyone else's. No one wanted it, which made Jess's ring tone unique in an irritating sort of way.

Dan calling.

She smiled as she answered the call from her husband. It still warmed her to think of Dan as her husband. They'd been in love since high school, and then spent two decades apart before finding each other again.

"Hey."

"Hey to you, too," Dan replied. "Are you feeling better?"

The lower backache that started last night just wouldn't go away. It wasn't unusual at this stage of pregnancy, just annoying. "I feel a little better now that I'm moving around."

Lori went through the upstairs rooms a second time. She wouldn't go back down the stairs again until Jess was ready to do the same. Her team took extra good care of her. These days Jess sincerely appreciated the extra backup.

"You should be taking it easy, Jess. The doctor said—"

"I know what the doctor said," Jess caught herself and added, "sweetheart." Dan was only trying to help. "I'm fine. If I need to sit down, I will." She would be taking enough time off work in the coming months. No need to start now.

"I'm certain you will," Dan replied patiently. "What're we looking at?"

"Same MO as the Rutledge homicide." Jess knew Dan would have preferred to come to the scene personally, but his attorney had advised him to steer clear of anything related to the former mayor until his case was adjudicated. Then again, she supposed the Pratt case was closed as of now anyway. "No indications of forced entry. No readily discernible cause of death. He was home alone. The front and rear doors were unlocked. The ME isn't here yet, but I would estimate that Pratt's been dead seven or so hours."

"I'd like to hear more frequent updates on this one, Jess. Have Detective Wells keep me in the communications loop. We may have a vigilante out there who's targeting persons he feels wrongly wielded the power of their positions."

Jess had a very bad feeling that was exactly what they were looking at. Though Pratt's misdeeds were a matter of public record now, Rutledge had never been accused of wrongdoing. The killer could decide to target any public figure whose actions he perceived as wrong, making Dan and numerous others potential targets.

At this point, revenge was the only viable motive. Lori had learned from Rutledge's private physician that he had recently been prescribed Viagra to help protect against heart issues related to the Doxorubicin prescribed for his prostate cancer. So a scorned lover or escort appeared to be off the table.

"I'll make sure you're kept in the loop," Jess promised as she smoothed a hand over her belly. "You just watch your back. We don't know this killer's ultimate objective."

"I'll call a briefing with the folks who might be potential targets. For now, I don't see any point in suggesting a serial killer or a mass murderer to the media. Let's make absolutely certain these two homicides are connected first."

"Will do," she promised.

"Be safe, Jess."

"You, too."

As Jess dropped her phone back into her bag, the front door opened. Sylvia stepped into the entry hall and looked around before a forensic tech showed her to the body. Maybe it was her imagination, but to Jess her friend looked harried and shaken. Jess wished she would share whatever was going on with her. Being so visibly off her game was completely out of character for the brash, tough as nails deputy coroner. Maybe her distraction had something to do with Buddy. Jess's old friend had confessed to Dan that he had a thing for Sylvia. Jess still found the idea surprising. When and how had that happened? Talk about opposites attract.

Before Jess reached for the railing and started down the stairs, Lori was at her side. "I didn't find his car keys."

Pratt's keys were nowhere to be found, which was odd since his car was in the driveway rather than the garage. The man was on house arrest. "Have another look around downstairs," Jess suggested. "As soon as Sylvia gives the okay, check his trouser pockets a little more closely."

"On it." Lori took the final step down and set to the task.

Finding the keys was relevant in terms of determining whether or not Pratt had possession of them when the killer entered his home. Jess leaned toward the theory that the victim knew his killer. Breaking and entering likely hadn't been necessary. Jess headed for the study. Sylvia had already begun the process of determining approximate time of death. The small incision below the ribcage allowed her access to the liver. Liver temperature was an incredibly accurate way to gauge time of death.

Despite her harried demeanor when she'd arrived, Sylvia was dressed impeccably. The lavender skirt and jacket were no doubt tailor made for her tall, slender figure. The matching high heels made Jess regret having given hers up months ago. Oh well, she had other priorities now.

"Time of death was between two and four this morning," Sylvia announced. She looked at Jess and presented a weak effort at a smile. "Good morning."

"Good morning." Jess fished out her notepad and pencil and jotted down the information. "You look especially nice this morning." The lavender was a good color on Sylvia.

"I have a business lunch," Sylvia said, playing off the compliment.

The truth was, Sylvia always looked nice. It was the distracted expression she wore and the atypical sense of being in a rush that were so out of place.

"We should have lunch soon," Jess suggested. "I'd like to plan a baby shower for Lori. I could use your help."

"Sure." Sylvia focused her full attention on the body.

"I'll call Gina and figure out a good time."

Sylvia made an agreeable sound without looking Jess's way again.

"Well, I'll leave you to it." Jess headed back to the entry hall.

Whatever was eating at Sylvia she had no intention of sharing it—at least not right now. Life was so much simpler when Jess had been too focused on her career to have real friends. Maybe she'd demand an explanation from Buddy.

"The keys weren't in his pockets," Lori announced as she joined Jess.

"Let's find out what time the attorney will be free." Jess had a long list of questions for him though she was confident he wasn't their killer.

"Hayes called. He said the wife is particularly upset because she and Pratt had exchanged heated words over dinner last night regarding the divorce settlement. Otherwise, she had no idea who might have wanted to do anything like this."

Jess felt for the poor woman. Losing a loved one—even an estranged one—with hurtful words as the final exchange made the loss even more painful.

Whether it was the pregnancy or just the fact that she was getting older, Jess had spent a lot of time thinking about her relationships lately. She and Aunt Wanda had made amends after a lifetime of estrangement. The most surprising part was that Jess had come to see that she actually *liked* Wanda.

Life was full of surprises.

Joe Pratt had faced a startling one last night. No matter how powerful a man thought he was and how many friends he thought he had, the past always caught up with him and it was rarely pretty.

CHAPTER FIFTEEN

"Thanks, DeeAnn." Buddy held up the book he'd just paid sixty bucks for and gave the bookstore owner a wink. He'd come to the bookstore as soon as he'd gotten DeeAnn's call.

DeeAnn Garner owned and operated The Book Shop, a bookstore that offered a few extra services like providing communications options for those who didn't want to leave a paper or electronic trail. Besides being the owner of the shop, DeeAnn was one damned fine woman. Buddy liked her, but lately he'd been too hung up on another woman who was so far out of his league he had no chance in hell of catching up. Sure, he could light her fire easy enough, but making a woman happy between the sheets was way different than pleasing her on an intellectual level. Or, in this case, even on a social level. What the hell was he doing falling for a rich chick—a senator's daughter at that. Jesus Christ. A damned medical examiner. Buddy groaned inwardly. He was so screwed.

Oblivious to his dilemma, DeeAnn blushed. "My pleasure, Buddy. Just let me know if you need anything else."

He heaved a big old sigh. Why hadn't he played it smart and set his sights on this sweet, prim little blonde? *Cause you're an idiot, Corlew.* "Sure thing, doll."

DeeAnn giggled as Buddy walked away. He waited until he was out of the store and in his Charger before he thumbed through the book. The note, addressed to #10—his secret ID number—was tucked neatly in the center of the paperback copy of *Little Women.*

Let's have a beer. I got what you need.

"That didn't take you long," Buddy muttered. He'd asked a good friend to look into the adoption of Sylvia's daughter. Since the legal proceedings had taken place more than two decades ago and in another state, he'd needed an assist. His friend had the right kind of connections.

No private investigator knew it all or could handle it all, but the best PIs found and maintained the right contacts. Contacts were key in this business. Buddy had cultivated a number of contacts during his days in the BPD. The more important ones he'd discovered in this gig. A good PI couldn't always be a good guy. Sometimes his work required crossing certain lines, like the one he'd had a contact bulldoze right over to find Sylvia's daughter.

"That's why you get the big bucks," he grumbled as he slowly backed out of the parking spot and drove just around the corner to his favorite watering hole.

The Garage Café was a vintage joint with a rustic vibe. Buddy was a regular so he knew the people behind the counter. Trust was another essential element in his business. He trusted the folks who operated The Garage. So did several of his contacts.

Buddy spotted the one he was meeting today. He slid onto the stool next to him. "I wasn't expecting to hear from you so soon."

"I ordered you a cheeseburger." Rob Johns jerked his head toward the kitchen. "It's lunch time, you know. You don't eat, you can't do your best work."

"Yeah, yeah." Buddy hitched his head toward the bartender, and then turned to Rob. "Tell it to your kids."

Rob grinned. "Everyday, man. Everyday. I got three in school, you know."

Buddy grunted. He didn't see how the guy kept his sanity with three kids. The bartender, Casey, left a Corona in front of Buddy. He took a swig before asking, "So, what's the lowdown out in Cali?"

Rob shrugged and reached for his beer. "I got the 411 on your college girl, only she ain't no college girl anymore. She graduated early. Evidently she's some sort of brainiac."

Buddy didn't see a file or a briefcase or any damned thing else he might be carrying a report in. What he had spotted was an attitude he recognized all too well. "What's your bump in price? I don't have all day. I have stuff to do."

"I figure a rich client's kid is worth double the usual run of the mill offspring. You got an issue with a price adjustment, or maybe a nice tip?"

Buddy laughed. "Nah. I would've done the same thing. In fact…" He took a long draw from the bottle and made a satisfied sound. "I was thinking though, about those photos your ex hired me to take of you when you were cheating on her."

Rob's eyes narrowed. "You trying to blackmail me, Corlew?"

Buddy shook his head. "No way, man. I'm just showing you how things can have a different value under the right circumstances. I didn't charge you for taking those extra kinky pics out of the mix."

"She still sued me for divorce," Rob argued. "What's your point?"

"My point is, I know a city councilman who could make your life hell if he found out you'd screwed around with his wife. Especially in some of those positions." Buddy grinned. "I didn't charge you a dime for keeping your fat out of the fire."

Rob waved him off. "Man, that was two years ago. What're you doing bringing up the past?"

"Sometimes we need to remember the past so we know the right way to go in the future." Buddy was a fine one to be spouting advice. As true as that was, he wasn't about to be taken to the cleaners by this guy. It wasn't as much about the money as it was about making sure he didn't get any ideas about the future potential of the info he now possessed. Protecting Sylvia was too important to let this guy get a whiff of fear.

Rob grinned. "I guess you got a point. Let's enjoy our lunch while I fill you in and we'll settle up afterwards."

"Works for me."

On cue the bartender dropped two plates loaded with cheeseburgers and fries on the counter in front of them.

After downing a few bites, Rob started talking. "Finding the people who adopted her was easy. I tracked down the private service your client used first, and then I located a retired file clerk. It cost me five G's to get her to give me the name."

"Reasonable under the circumstances," Buddy allowed.

Rob tore off another bite of his burger. Buddy did the same, his patience thinning a little. He'd never known the guy to beat around the bush, but he was damned sure doing exactly that today.

"The young lady graduated from UCLA. She's a nurse. Graduated at the very top of her class. Some of the Facebook posts from her friends suggested she could have done anything she chose. Her friends were all complaining that she didn't continue on to med school with them. Evidently, she dropped pre-med and switched to nursing at the end of her second year in college."

"I guess she just decided she didn't want to be a doctor. So what about the couple who adopted her?"

Buddy hoped the kid had lived a happy life so far and had been treated well. Sylvia already punished herself enough for giving the kid up. He could imagine how she would suffer if her daughter had been treated badly.

"Rich folks. In their early fifties when they adopted her. The father was a heart surgeon. The mother was a pediatric surgeon."

"Was?" Buddy frowned. "Both parents are deceased?"

Rob nodded. "The father had a heart attack. The wife had a heart attack trying to save him. They both died right there in their living room and the daughter found them."

"Damn." He shook his head.

"Hell of a thing," Rob agreed. "Bad for the kid. That was a couple years ago, around the same time she changed her career path. I looked back a few years on her Facebook. It seemed like her parents were not only in a stressful field but they were involved in all kinds of humanitarian work. They went to foreign countries and helped the needy rather than take vacations. The kid worked right alongside them until she went off to college. The parents retired five years ago and had been spending a lot more time overseas."

"Sounds like a hardworking family."

"Maybe too hard," Rob said. "Sounds like a lot of stress to me. Maybe the kid decided she didn't want that much stress in her life."

"Maybe so." Buddy knew how it felt to hold another person's life in his hands. Though he'd never had to take anyone's life when he was a cop, he'd come close. Those few seconds had felt like an eternity. Trying to save someone's life would be a similar desperation. Doctors, especially surgeons, he supposed, faced intense situations every day. In recent years going overseas, even to serve the communities there, could be a dangerous business. "Kid still living in Cali?"

Rob downed the last of his fries. "That's where things get interesting. As soon as she graduated, she closed up the family home place in Sacramento and took off."

"Did you find her current address?" Buddy found himself holding his breath...for Sylvia.

"This is the part you're not going to believe."

Buddy shook his head. "If you tell me the kid is dead—"

"No. No." Rob held up a hand. "She's *here*."

Another of those deep frowns furrowed Buddy's face. "In Birmingham?"

Rob moved his head up and down in a slow, firm nod. "She hired a West Coast PI and tracked down her biological mother. Whoever the dad is, she didn't find him, but she knows who your client is, Corlew. She's been watching her for the past two months. She works at UAB Hospital."

A new kind of tension stirred in Buddy. He tossed payment for their lunch on the counter. "I'm ready to settle up now."

Rob tossed back the last of his beer. He followed Buddy outside, retrieved the file and his itemized bill from his car, and handed both over to Buddy.

"This—minus the price bump—will be in your bank account before the end of the day," Buddy assured him.

"Nice doing business with you." Before climbing behind the steering wheel of his sedan, Rob added, "I want those pics burned or shredded."

Buddy waved him off. "Consider it done."

When he'd dropped behind the wheel of his Charger and had the doors closed and locked, Buddy opened the large envelope that held Rob's reports and the photos he'd taken. He scanned the summary report. Buddy wouldn't deny being grateful finding the girl had been this easy. The problem was, any time something was this easy there was trouble.

If Miss Addison Devers wanted to know her biological mother, why not talk to her after she'd found her? Buddy could understand some amount of uncertainty, but this went way beyond simply taking some time to take stock or to shore up her courage. This was almost stalking. Had she been following Sylvia around? Buddy studied the photo of Addison. She was a heartbreaker just like her mother. The girl—young woman—could be a runway model. She had the same long legs and killer figure her mother had. Her hair was a darker brown, almost black, and the eyes were different. Addison's were a cool gray.

Heaving a disgusted breath, Buddy shook his head. Since his conversation with Dan, he'd done his research on Benton Murdock. The guy had the same almost black hair and those pale gray eyes.

Addison also had a chin dimple that matched the one Murdock sported in all his media pics. At least now Buddy knew.

Murdock was married with two kids in college. The man had political aspirations. Buddy wasn't sure how well he would take having a secret from the past revealed. Since Sylvia had never listed him as the father, Addison wouldn't have had any way to locate him.

Addison had leased a loft apartment in Five Points. She'd been hired after her first interview at UAB. She drove a BMW convertible. A snazzy little red one. Sylvia's daughter was not only alive and well but right here in the Magic City.

Was she looking for a relationship with her mother or to get a little revenge for having been given away at birth?

He had a few good contacts at the hospital. Maybe he'd find out just what Miss Addison was up to and maybe even have a chat with her.

Buddy placed the photos and reports back into the envelope. Having a client who meant something more than a paycheck made things complicated.

Unfortunately, this was about to get a hell of a lot more complicated.

CHAPTER SIXTEEN

Jess placed Joseph Pratt's photo on the case board. Lori immediately stepped in to add relevant data beneath the photo. There was a lot they knew about Pratt. Jess shifted her attention to the photo of the judge. The same could be said for Rutledge. Yet, with all that they had gleaned about the victims from research and interviews, there was no smoking gun or clear motive for their murders.

All aspects of the crime scenes indicated the murders had been carried out by the same killer. Where was the connection? More importantly, what motive fit both crimes?

"What did you two have in common that put you in the same crosshairs?" Jess muttered, mostly to herself.

Harper rounded his desk and moved to her side. "I'm thinking they were part of a secret group that screwed over the wrong guy and that guy has been waiting for the perfect opportunity to have his revenge."

DEBRA WEBB

"Except," Cook spoke up from his desk, "everyone we've interviewed claims Rutledge rarely left his home during the last two years." He pushed out of his chair and strolled up to stand next to Jess. "Wouldn't this secret group have meetings or something?"

Jess wasn't sure the good old boys club was what the sergeant had in mind, but she had a feeling he was on the right track. "Maybe this secret group had a falling out and stopped having meetings."

Lori glanced over her shoulder. "You guys have watched way too many movies." She offered the marker. "But if you want to put your thoughts on the board, you might start with civic organizations and fundraising committees the vics had in common. I'm sticking with the theory that our killer is someone who feels wronged by both vics."

Harper reached for the marker. "I'll put my money on a secret club." He walked up to the board and added his theory to the other data already listed.

Before Jess could voice her own ideas, the door to the SPU shared office space opened and Hayes breezed in. He took a moment to assess the case board before closing the door behind him.

"Where've you been?" Cook asked. "You didn't make it to Cappy's for lunch."

"Sorry." Hayes pushed aside the lapels of his designer suit jacket and tucked his hands into the pockets of his trousers before joining the group at the case board. "Lunch is on me next time."

Cook shrugged. "Works for me."

"You're late," Jess reminded the lieutenant. They had all agreed to meet back at the office at one. She had been impressed with his team attitude the past few months. Hopefully, this wasn't the first sign of a regression.

"I have a very good defense, Chief." He held out his hand to Harper. "May I?"

Harper passed him the marker. "You find a lead?"

Hayes grinned. "I did." He wrote the name Ronald Durham on the case board. "I don't have a photo just yet, but this one is a game changer."

"Tell me about him," Jess prompted, anticipation lighting in her chest. They badly needed a big break on this case.

"One year before he retired," Hayes capped the marker and tossed it back to Harper, "Judge Rutledge received a number of threats, including having his tires slit and his windshield smashed."

"There's no record of any threats in the past seven years," Lori countered.

"He didn't want an official case opened," Hayes explained. "His wife was very ill and he didn't want her seeing anything about it on the news. So he handled it off the record. A couple of retired BPD detectives found the guy responsible—one Oden Pitts. He had a couple of outstanding warrants so it was easy to get him off the street. Pitts claimed that Durham paid him to give the judge some trouble."

"Who's your source?" Lori asked, still visibly skeptical.

"Willow Andersen. She's just hung her shingle over on Seventh Avenue. Her first job out of law school was as a legal clerk for Rutledge."

Lori walked over to Hayes and tugged at his shirt collar. "Did you check out her new office over lunch?"

He cleared his throat and adjusted his lipstick-stained collar. "No comment."

Lori shook her head. Cook and Harper struggled not to grin. Jess didn't care where he'd had lunch or who had been on the menu. "Where is this Oden Pitts?"

"Dead," Hayes answered. "Car accident last summer."

"What about Durham?" Dammit. They needed a break here.

"Donaldson Correctional Facility." Hayes grinned. "You want to take a guess at who put him there?"

Now they were getting somewhere.

DONALDSON CORRECTIONAL FACILITY
BESSEMER, 3:30 P.M.

It was always a pleasant experience to visit a maximum-security institution, particularly one that specialized in controlling hard to manage violent offenders. Rapists, killers, the worst of the worst were housed here.

Inside, the cold concrete floors went on forever. The clang of steel doors punctuated the somber silence. Jess took a seat at the austere metal table and flipped to a clean page in her notepad. This was the end of the line for many of those unlucky enough to find themselves inmates of Donaldson Correctional Facility. The man they'd come to visit today was no exception.

Lori paced the floor. "If you go into labor while we're here, you could end up having your baby in the prison infirmary."

As a friend, Lori was not happy with Jess's decision to conduct this interview personally. "Think what a story it'll make for our grandchildren one day."

Lori tossed her a look. "I know you did not just say that."

Jess flashed her a smile. The steel on steel jangle of the door being unlocked drew her attention as it opened with a whine. Two guards, one on either side of the shackled inmate, led him into the room. His ankles were constrained, as were his wrists. The wrist restraints were additionally secured to the belly shackle at his waist. When he took the seat opposite Jess, he was further chained to the massive hook in the floor that would prevent him moving more than a few inches in any direction. Jess would be the first to admit that the extensive security measures allowed her to breathe easier. When it came to inmates with nothing left to lose, it paid to be prepared for most anything.

"We'll be right outside the door. Let us know if you need anything else, Chief," Officer Simmons, the lead guard, said as they left the interview room.

Lori took a position a couple of feet behind Jess. Their weapons and cell phones as well as their bags remained at the check-in desk. All Jess needed to conduct this interview was her badge and her notepad. Well, and her pencil.

"Hello, Mr. Durham. I'm Deputy Chief Jess Burnett from the Birmingham Police Department."

Ronald Durham cocked his head and openly studied Jess. He was only thirty-five years old. Ten of those years had been spent right here on death row. Ronald had been convicted of killing his grandmother for her social security check. At the time, he'd been an addict desperate for another hit of his drug of choice. Today, he was the only prisoner still on death row who had been sentenced by Rutledge.

"You here for the meditation, Chief?"

Jess smiled. A few years ago the prison, named after a corrections officer slain here, had started a centuries old meditation program. According to all reports, the program was transforming violent inmates into much calmer men. Maybe she could use a little meditation in her life but so far she hadn't found the time. She spent too many of her days and nights tracking down men like Durham so they could be put in places like this, and have all the time in the world for meditation.

"Actually, I'm here to talk to you about Judge Harmon Rutledge."

"The judge who made sure I would spend the rest of my life here." Durham laughed. "Yeah, I heard the old bastard finally got his. I can die happy now."

So much for the calming effects of the meditation program. "You have, what? A hundred or so days left before you're scheduled for execution?"

"One hundred and one."

Durham carried the scars that told the story of his life. A particularly ugly one dissected his left cheek and disappeared beneath his collar. There were others, mostly hidden by his jumpsuit. He was a victim of child abuse. A criminal with a long rap sheet of violent crimes that had landed him behind bars numerous times even before he committed murder. According to his version of the story, killing his grandmother had been easy since she'd overlooked the abuse he'd suffered his whole life. In his mind, *the old bitch had it coming.*

"You made certain threats against the judge," Jess reminded him. "You hired people on the outside to do things to intimidate him. Maybe this time, you decided to have a more permanent revenge."

He shrugged. "I could have. I have my resources and he did send me here to rot." Durham leaned forward.

Jess braced against the urge to draw away.

"This place is the bottom of hell. It stinks of evil and death. Everything in here is rotting from the inside out. Those twenty-four cells they got for guys like me, we call them the *dying rooms.* You know, like those orphanages in China. We're tossed in there like unwanted trash and then we're left to die. The sooner the better. If we don't die before the scheduled date, then they send us to hell with a lethal cocktail. I hope the judge got that kind of send-off. I hope he saw just a little bit of what it's like to stare at the same walls…the same memories of what you know you did…before he died."

Jess scribbled a few notes on her pad before meeting those eerie gold eyes once more. "You did a very good job of describing my crime scene."

He grinned. "I guess my dream came true."

"You've had one visitor in the past year besides your attorney." Jess cocked her head and studied the man. He knew something. She was certain of it. "He was here this past Monday. I'm sure you remember him. Tall, slim man?"

Durham shrugged. "Just another writer wanting to do my story."

Oh, yes. Mr. Durham was lying. The way he averted his eyes when he made that last statement told the tale. "Really. Did this writer," Jess turned back a page and glanced at her notes, "Al Hitchcock, have a real name?"

"Like I said, I didn't know him. Never seen him before in my life." This time he looked straight at Jess when he spoke. "He came to see me. He had an interest in my history. That's all I know."

"I see." Jess surveyed her notes once more. "You withdrew your appeal this week."

"I did."

Jess watched his face very carefully for any reaction. "Couldn't keep a decent lawyer? Or did you give up fighting for your life? It takes a lot of courage to keep banging your head against that same brick wall. I guess you decided to give up on winning."

"Like I said, the meditation did the trick." He made a bored face. "I'm through pretending I was wrongly accused and sentenced. I did a lot of bad things. I killed my own grandmother. Even if the bitch deserved to die, it was wrong of me to take her life."

Too bad he couldn't muster up any regret in his expression or his tone. "When did you complete the meditation course, Mr. Durham?" The ten-day course was held four times per year. According to Durham's medical jacket, he attended the program this time last year.

"What difference does that make?" He made another of those negligent shrugs. "Ain't a man like me allowed to change?"

"Certainly. I'm simply trying to work out how you suddenly came to feel you deserved your sentence and the timing of the withdrawal of your appeal. There's quite a gap there. If your meditation experience opened your eyes to the truth, then why wait a whole year to drop the appeal."

When he only stared at her, Jess went on, "I mean, that's a huge decision. I'm sure something new happened—an epiphany of some sort—that motivated you to make the decision."

He laughed. "You got me, Chief. When I heard the news about Rutledge, I dropped the appeal. I was so happy I wanted to celebrate." He looked down at his shackles and then back at her. "You know how it is. You don't always get everything you want."

"But you got one thing, didn't you, Mr. Durham?"

"You accusing me of something?" He leaned forward again. "You know, you are one sexy lady cop. I could—"

Before Jess could blink Lori had rounded the table, grabbed him by the collar, and jerked him back. "Answer the question, Durham."

"Hmmm. I love strong women. We could have a threesome." He flicked out his tongue in a vulgar manner. "Guess this is my lucky day. Did you know you're never hotter than you are when you're pregnant?"

"Enough," Lori growled close to his face. "I wish I had my nine millimeter and I would wipe that smirk off your ugly face. Now, answer the question."

He glared at Jess as if she should do something about her detective. She did the shrugging this time. "What can I say? She's likes keeping me happy."

Lori released him and Durham stretched his neck to the right and then to the left before responding. "You want to know if I had anything to do with the judge's death." He shook his head. "I wish I could claim it and you better believe if I could I would. I'm on death row. It ain't like I got anything to lose. I would shout it until these nasty ass walls rung with the glory hallelujah sound of it. But no. It wasn't me."

"Still, you've heard rumors," Jess suggested. He was far too cocky and informed to have heard nothing. He knew the damned crime scene, for Heaven's sake. "Maybe your Mr. Hitchcock told you a little something about it."

"I heard it was one of the judge's own." Durham grinned. "Or maybe it was that crazy ass serial killer who spent all last year chasing after you." He leaned forward again. "Maybe the ghost of Eric Spears is back just to make sure you don't get bored...or lonely."

Jess stood. She'd heard enough for today. "Thank you, Mr. Durham."

"Can't take the heat can you, Chief?" he shouted at her back as she strode to the door. "I see why killers go for you. You got an aura about you, Chief. It's tempting as hell. Makes a guy want to do anything just to get your attention."

Before Jess could urge her to let it go, Lori had returned to the table and leaned down to Durham.

"I'm sorry. Did you say something, asshole?" she demanded.

When he opened his mouth—no doubt to sneer something disgusting—Lori slammed his face onto the table.

"Oops." She groaned as blood poured from his nose. "You should be more careful, Durham. You could hurt yourself."

He screamed profanities as they left the room. The lead guard turned to Jess. "Have a nice day, ladies. I apologize for Durham's behavior. He's been known to slam his face against whatever's handy."

"I've learned to expect the unexpected, Officer Simmons," Jess assured him.

She waited until they had collected their personal items and made their way to the parking lot before she spoke. "Durham is not our guy."

"The way that guy likes to brag, he'd be telling the world just like he said," Lori agreed. "Unless Chet and Hayes have any luck with the few names left on that list of family members, we're back at square one."

Jess paused at the Mustang and gazed at Lori across the roof. "Let's find out who this Al Hitchcock is. I think maybe we've been focused on the wrong list."

"We're going back to the friends and associates scenario? Maybe the members of a secret club?"

"I can't see any other direction to go. All we have to do is figure out which one despised Rutledge as well as Pratt enough to plan and commit their murders within mere days of each other."

Jess opened the door and eased into the seat. For her comfort, Lori had installed a seat belt extension. These older model vehicles were not third trimester friendly.

"If our killer is working off some sort of list," Lori started the car, "we could have another body within the next twenty-four hours."

"That's what worries me." Jess didn't say out loud the part that truly terrified her. Both men had been movers and shakers in Birmingham. Men of position and power. Dan met those criteria.

She had to find and stop this killer fast.

CHAPTER SEVENTEEN

"I'm leaving first thing tomorrow morning on a flight to Mexico," Craig Moore declared as he paced the floor. "My family thinks we're going on a surprise spring break vacation."

Yesterday, these same men would have considered the congressman's move an overreaction, but Joe's murder had changed everything. Whoever was behind this lethal plot, he was clearly not finished.

"I think sending your family away is a good idea," Robert said aloud when the rest of those seated around his study only sat there looking shell shocked. "Louise is going to New York for a few days, but I'll be staying here. I refuse to run from this."

Craig dropped his gaze as he returned to his chair. He obviously understood that Robert saw his actions as cowardly. They had made this mess. Running away from it was not the answer.

"I'll send my wife to Denver," Isaiah Taylor spoke up next. "I'm staying here as well. Whoever is behind these murders, however, won't find me such easy prey. I've hired a private investigator from Mobile to come to Birmingham and see what he can find." When questioning gazes landed on him, he added, "He'll be discreet. We can't just sit here and do nothing."

"My wife left for Montgomery this afternoon," Sam Baker confessed. "As soon as I heard the news, I came up with a reason for her to go visit our son. I'm with the two of you," he said with a glance at Taylor and then at Robert. "I'm staying. But I don't need a private investigator or the police digging around in my affairs. I'll take care of this myself."

"We must be vigilant," Robert insisted. "We can't do as Joe did and let our guards down. We're fully aware what's happening now. If the killer comes into my home, I'm going to be ready for him."

"If he comes into my house, he's a dead man," Sam echoed. "He's not destroying all I've built. The only way to handle this is to contain the threat." Sam looked from one man to the next. "If we run, we're only prolonging the inevitable. If we go to the police, we're going to have to explain what happened forty years ago and, frankly, I have no desire to see that part of my past in the news."

Unfortunately, what happened forty years ago wasn't the problem…it was the things they had done since to repay the gift they had accepted forty years ago.

Robert saw no need to remind anyone of what they already knew.

Sam was correct. The only option was to contain and neutralize the threat.

CHAPTER EIGHTEEN

After Sylvia went through the cleaning ritual, she smoothed lotion on her hands. Today had been a long one. She'd finished the autopsy ahead of Joseph Pratt's half an hour ago. It was late and she was exhausted, but she intended to have a quick coffee and then move onto his preliminary examination.

Dr. Leeds, her boss, had checked in on her a couple of times the past two hours. He'd been fielding calls from the city's elite, the media, and the state investigators on Pratt's pending case all afternoon. Nothing like a little extra pressure.

In the break room, Sylvia inserted a pod into the coffeemaker, placed her cup under the dispenser, and waited for the Colombian dark roast to brew. She'd wanted to inspect Pratt's body more closely as soon as she'd returned from the scene this morning, but Deputy Chief Black of BPD's Crimes Against Persons had been here waiting on his victim's autopsy. She'd given him all she could today. Like everyone else, he had no choice but to wait for the toxicology results. Not that anyone needed those results to determine the victim's manner of death. One shot to the face had done the job. Apparently, the son-in-law had grown tired of his wife spending so much time taking care of her invalid mother.

Men could be such bastards. Sylvia exiled the image of Buddy Corlew that immediately invaded her senses. The man was nothing but trouble. She should never have allowed herself to get involved with him. Not for a single night much less an encore. How was it possible that she had such a weakness for him? Where was her usual control? He was nothing like the men she typically dated. He was brash and crude and he wore his sexuality too openly and boldly.

She felt suddenly warm just thinking about him and sex.

"You are a disaster, Sylvia," she muttered as she added French Vanilla creamer to her coffee. She usually took it black, but tonight she needed a change of pace. The thought made her cringe. The last time she'd decided a change of pace was in order, she'd ended up in bed with Buddy. A shiver swept over her skin. She couldn't sit at her desk in her own office without thinking of the way he'd ravaged her there.

She drank her coffee and tried to dismiss Buddy as well as her lack of restraint. Another of Birmingham's high-powered elite was dead. Though Pratt had taken a substantial fall from grace as of late, he'd been a major force in the shaping of

Birmingham during the past two decades. He'd no doubt made plenty of enemies along the way. At one time, her father and the former mayor had been good friends. Just as the two had also been friends with Judge Rutledge at one time.

"Dr. Baron."

Sylvia shook off the troubling thoughts and met the expectant gaze of the medical clerk who supported her office. "Yes."

"I believe you've been expecting these labs." She passed the file to Sylvia. "The tox screen results for Rutledge."

Sylvia perked up. She was quite anxious to learn Rutledge's cause of death. Something had certainly made his heart stop beating. Since there were no visible physical reasons for the arrest, she felt confident she would find the culprit inside this file.

"Thank you, Cindy."

Setting her coffee aside, Sylvia scanned the results. Her eyes snagged on the offending chemicals and her breath caught. Midazolam, Pancuronium Bromide, Potassium Chloride. The three drugs generally used in lethal injections for the executions of those on death row.

A very disturbing scenario started to form, sending Sylvia rushing to the morgue room where Pratt's body was being prepared for her to proceed with the autopsy. "Let's do the labs now."

Her assistant, Bonnie Gonzalez, who was already annoyed that she would be here another three or four hours at least, made a face. "Whatever you say."

Under other circumstances Sylvia would have reminded her who was in charge, but just now she had no time to explain her request. If her concerns were correct, Jess had a serial killer on her hands.

"I want the specimens at the lab tonight." Another unhappy look shot Sylvia's way. "Whatever it takes, I need those results back sometime tomorrow."

While Bonnie grumbled under her breath and drew the necessary labs, Sylvia pulled on her gloves and lab coat and moved to the head of the steel table. She started the search at his forehead, but it took only a moment to find the pale blue eagle right where she'd found Rutledge's.

And her father's.

SHOOK HILL ROAD. MOUNTAIN BROOK. 9:40 P.M.

It was late. Her mother was likely already in bed. The senator wouldn't be. Sylvia didn't have to see the light on in his study to wonder. He would be up. Every night before going to bed, he spent an hour or so watching the news around the world. It was part of his job he'd always insisted. A man in his position needed to know what was going on in the world from the eyes of the public.

Sylvia let herself in without ringing the bell. She didn't want to wake her mother. Her father would hear the notification from the security system. Fortunately, he hadn't yet armed it for bedtime. Thank God her parents hadn't added a security system to their home until after she'd gone off to college. Half her allowance had gone to Nina anyway for keeping her mouth shut about her comings and goings. Not that Sylvia ever got into any real trouble. She hadn't. Like most teenagers she'd yearned for freedom and independence. When it wasn't forth coming, she'd taken it by sneaking out after her parents were in bed.

Maybe now it was her turn to check up on her father. Her entire life she had looked up to him as the epitome of truth and integrity. She was forty-four years old and still his high moral standards never ceased to amaze her. He was such a rare breed.

Unless he'd been hiding a terrible truth all this time. Sylvia thought of Jess and the horrors she'd learned about her own father. Sylvia had been certain her father kept no secrets from his family. None that mattered anyway.

Apparently, she had been wrong.

"Sylvia, have you been working late again tonight?" Her father met her in the hall outside his study. He was already dressed for bed. It would be another hour or more before he joined her mother.

"I need to speak with you."

He frowned. "Of course. Would you like something to drink? Have you had dinner?"

She shook her head. "I'm fine. I just—"

"Nonsense." He caught her by the elbow and guided her toward the kitchen. "Your mother made that wonderful potato soup I love so much. There's plenty left."

This was the way things always were. If she showed up late, her father or mother insisted she eat. It was part of being a parent, she supposed. By the time she'd settled on a stool at the kitchen island, her father had warmed a bowl of soup. The sudden resurrection of her appetite helped in her decision to hold off a few minutes more on the questions she needed to ask.

For a time she ate in silence, her stomach suddenly realizing she'd neglected it today. Nothing new, she mused. She rarely ate when she should. Her world, her every waking moment, revolved around her work. *Look where it has gotten you.* Yes, she had an enviable career. She had a beautiful home, a luxurious car. Her wardrobe would make any woman she knew swoon.

Those things were her life and somehow that realization made her sad. As much as she loved her family and her family loved her, she felt so empty lately. Weddings and babies had inundated her with doubts and regrets. Now this murder case had suddenly intruded on the part of her life she considered impeccable and impervious. Her childhood had been idyllic. Her family, other than Nina's illness, had always been happy and close.

She pushed her bowl aside and looked at her father. "I need you to tell me the truth, Daddy."

Another of those frowns lined his handsome face. "Why wouldn't I tell you the truth? For Heaven's safe, Sylvia, what's this about?"

"You know what it's about. The judge and the mayor."

"Ex-mayor," he pointed out.

"Pratt had the eagle tattoo just like the one Rutledge had. Just like the one you have." She stared directly into his eyes, her heart aching. "Please tell me what the connection is."

He chuckled. "I've dedicated my entire life to this city, and to this state. Are we really going to sit here at this hour and have an unpleasant discussion about a mistake some old buddies made too many years ago to talk about?"

"So Pratt and Rutledge were in the Air Force with you." She held her breath.

He shrugged. "I believe Pratt was in the Air Force, but he wasn't stationed with me. Rutledge was a Marine."

Feeling as if she were in shock, Sylvia watched as he busied himself with cleaning up her bowl and spoon. He carried both to the sink, rinsed them, and loaded them into the dishwasher. The whole time he chatted about his military days as if she hadn't pointblank asked him about the tattoo.

"Men do impulsive and foolish things when they're young, Syl." He faced her once more and braced his hands on the cool granite counter. "Would you like coffee?"

Sylvia drew in a deep breath. "What I would like is a straight answer. Is there a connection between those tattoos and the two murder victims? For God's sake, you could be next."

He waved her off and made a dismissive sound. "That ridiculous tattoo means nothing. You're making far too much of this. Don't you think that Jess would be following that lead if she thought there was anything to it? She is the one in charge of investigating the case. You've told me many times how good she is at solving cases. Look how she handled the Eric Spears's case. And Nina. Why Nina would be dead now if not for Jess."

So this was the way it was going to be. "Jess hasn't added the tattoos to her investigation because I haven't told her everything yet. I was waiting for you, Daddy. I wanted to hear the truth from you first." Sylvia stood. "But I guess that isn't going to happen." She reached for her bag. "If my hunch pans out," she went on, knowing full well she should be keeping her mouth shut, "these two men were executed in the same manner as a prisoner sentenced to death by the State. Is that how you want to go, Daddy?"

Sylvia walked out of the room without looking back. The blasted tears burning her eyes made her want to scream and stamp her foot. Instead, she did something she had not done in decades. She paused midway down the entry hall, removed her shoes, and slipped back toward the kitchen. She eased back against the wall and listened. Her father had already picked up the kitchen phone and entered a number. Moments later, he spoke.

"We need to talk." Pause. "No," he argued. "This won't wait. The police are going to start asking questions. We may not be able to avoid a different step than the one we discussed today."

With her heart in her throat, Sylvia left her childhood home.

Her father, the man she had loved, respected, and attempted to emulate her entire life, had lied to her.

Worse...he was in serious trouble.

CHAPTER NINETEEN

"So this tall man just showed up at Mrs. Dority's door?" Jess glanced up at Dan who was so generously massaging her shoulders. She had been alternately pacing the floor and sitting at this desk in her home office for better than three hours. Eventually, the chair had won out.

Mrs. Dority was the mother of Meredith Dority. Meredith had worked with Mayor Pratt years ago when Dan had been the liaison between the BPD and the mayor's office. The two had been married briefly during that time. Sadly, Meredith was murdered by one of Eric Spears' followers last September.

"She said," Dan repeated, "he showed up at her door about eight-thirty this evening. Detectives Wells and Harper are over there now taking her statement."

Jess huffed. "I would have preferred to do that myself."

142

"I knew you would," Dan confessed, "that's why I called Harper while you were still in the shower and sent him and Wells over there."

Growling her frustration in spite of those magic hands, Jess checked the time. "One of them should be calling me any minute."

"I have every confidence." Those wonderful fingers stopped in their work. "How about a cup of hot cocoa?"

Jess looked up at him again, feeling a little contrite now. "I would really love that, but I hate to put you to so much trouble at this hour."

Dan smiled. "No trouble. You do what you have to do and I'll be back shortly." He paused at the door. "Marshmallows?" he asked with a wink.

She grinned. He knew her well. "Please."

Jess watched him go. She felt bad that he refused to go to bed without her, but she couldn't stop replaying that interview with Durham. She was exhausted, there was no doubt about that part, and still her mind wouldn't stop going back to the undeniable fact that Pratt's and Rutledge's murders were connected. The killer had obviously put the word out so that men like Durham would hear the news. The tall thin man who'd visited Durham on Monday had to be involved somehow. If only the prison camera had gotten a better shot at his face. Damn it! Now, a man matching that same description showed up at Mrs. Dority's house. This was no coincidence.

Turning her attention back to the computer, she flicked a few keys and summoned the search results for the *dying rooms*. Her heart sank when she clicked on the images of the children. How could a rage killer like Durham compare himself to the innocent children left in such deplorable conditions? According to the reports, many of the children were simply left to die in the government run orphanages. How could a government be so cruel to its own people? She shuddered.

Forcing herself to continue reading, she slowly began to see the connection Durham appeared to be drawing to his own ugly history. Many of the children were abandoned by their families, for reasons Jess couldn't begin to understand. Some of the children were unwanted because they were the wrong sex, female. Others were sick or physically challenged in some way. Her chest ached and her stomach churned at the horrors. The children ended up in horrible conditions, some suffering slow unthinkable deaths. According to Durham's psych eval, he'd been tossed aside by his mother when he was born with clubbed feet. He hadn't known his father, and his grandmother had allegedly abused him as a child. His allegations to the prison psychiatrist included beatings, starvation, and sexual abuse. In his mind, he'd been abandoned as surely as those children in the reports Jess had just read. He'd been abused and, essentially, left to die more than once.

The difference was that Durham had survived to adulthood. He'd had choices. The children in these reports had none.

"Here we go," Dan announced as he returned with a steaming cup of cocoa on an heirloom silver platter his mother had given them.

Jess closed the window on the computer screen and blinked in hopes of clearing the horrific images from her eyes. There were some things a person could never *unsee*.

"Thank you so much." She placed a soft kiss on his handsome jaw as he leaned down to place the cocoa in front of her. "Where's yours?"

Before he could answer, the doorbell rang. Bear growled, scrambled to his feet, and raced off to bark at the front door. Dan frowned. "I'll get back to you."

Jess hoped everything was okay with his parents. She imagined his mother would have called if his father had taken ill. Though Dan Senior seemed to be doing well these days, he had a history of cardiac episodes. She supposed it could be Lori or Chet reporting in, but mostly likely they would call. The sound of Sylvia's voice eased the tension nudging Jess. Not Dan's parents. Thank God.

Was there bad news about Nina? The new worry gnawed at Jess until Sylvia walked into the room with Dan and Bear right behind her.

"I knew you were still working," Sylvia explained. "I saw the light." She gestured to the window that overlooked the backyard. Their house sat on a corner lot. Anyone driving up the side street would see lights on in the rear of the house.

Jess pushed out of her chair. Her cocoa was too hot to drink anyway. "Looks like I'm not the only one working late." She hesitated at the corner of her desk. "Unless this is about something else."

It was then that Jess noticed just how pale Sylvia's face was. Her eyes brimmed with tears. "Maybe you should sit down," Jess suggested.

Sylvia stood there not saying a word.

"Two more hot cocoas coming up," Dan announced, breaking the awkward silence.

Jess ushered Sylvia to the sofa near the window. "Thanks, sweetie," she said to Dan when he lingered by the door. "Sylvia would love a cup."

When it was just the two them with Bear curled at their feet, Jess clasped Sylvia's hands in her own. "What's going on?"

Sylvia seemed to snap from the trance she'd drifted into. "I thought my life was…" She shrugged. "I don't know. Okay. I don't have any financial worries. My career is great. My love life is…" Sylvia shrugged again. "Sometimes really great. But, you know," she turned to Jess, "I really believed things were damned good considering the state of the world. Sure, we've all done things in the past we regret, but lately I've been dwelling on a decision I made half a lifetime ago." She shook her head. "I've been all wrapped up in ancient history and I didn't see that there was something terribly wrong here and now."

"Take your time," Jess offered, "and tell me what's going on."

"I received the tox screen back on the judge." Sylvia pulled her hands free of Jess's and clenched them in her lap. "The cause of death was cardiac arrest. He was administered a lethal injection of the same three drugs used to execute prisoners on death row."

Jess felt the new tension stir and start to climb up her spine. "Pratt?"

"I believe we'll find the same. I've put an extra rush on the testing, but I won't be able to confirm until the results are back."

Jess rubbed at the worry lines across her forehead with the back of her hand. "If we're dealing with the same killer in both cases, as my team and I suspect, I doubt he's finished."

"That's what I'm afraid of." Sylvia wrung her hands a little harder. "Pratt has the eagle tattoo on his scalp. Same size, color, and location as the one I discovered on Rutledge."

"Both belonged to the same good old boys' club," Jess added. Birmingham might be one of the most progressive cities in Alabama, but some things hadn't changed a whole lot. Women like herself and Sylvia fought hard to attain a level in their careers enviable by most, female or male. In Sylvia's case, it hadn't hurt that she was also a senator's daughter and wealthy. And still, neither she nor Sylvia belonged to that club.

"Should I be offended?" Dan asked as he returned with two more cups of cocoa. He set one on the coffee table in front of Sylvia. Before Jess could ask, he brought hers over.

"Thanks, sweetie." Jess sipped her cocoa. "Sylvia may have uncovered another connection between Rutledge and Pratt."

Dan pulled Jess's executive desk chair around her desk and closer to the sofa. "I'm listening."

"Both the victims had the eagle I was telling you about." Jess hadn't thought much of the tattoo. Rutledge had been a young man at one time. Young men often did wild and impulsive things. There was no reason to suspect it was connected to any aspect of the case.

"Have you found an organizational connection related to the tattoo?" Dan lifted his cocoa but hesitated before taking a sip. "I can't think of any clubs or organizations that use a single blue eagle as a logo."

"Whatever it is," Sylvia spoke up, "Daddy has one."

At least now Jess knew what it was that had Sylvia so upset.

"After I saw the one the judge had," Sylvia explained, "I remembered seeing Daddy's when I was a child. I asked him about it and he said he'd gotten it while he was in the Air Force. When I mentioned the matching one I discovered on Rutledge's body, Daddy pretended to know nothing about it." She stared at her cocoa. "I went to see him tonight. After finding the same thing on Pratt, I wanted answers. I demanded to know the truth."

Jess waited through a tense moment of silence.

"He lied to me." Sylvia exhaled a heavy breath. "He looked me in the eyes and told me there was nothing to it. He said some nonsense about old buddies making a mistake a long time ago."

"It's possible he could be right," Jess said even as her instincts warned that he had indeed lied to Sylvia.

She shook her head again. "When I left he called someone. Whoever he called, he said they had to talk. That the police were going to start asking questions."

"If our killer has a list, as we suspect, the senator could be on it." Jess could definitely see how terrifying that prospect was for Sylvia.

"I'm worried, Jess. I've never known my daddy to lie to me. Who would he be protecting?" She closed her eyes and shook her head. "I can't believe he's keeping something like this from me."

"We all have secrets," Jess reminded her. She glanced at Dan. "Most of us anyway." Jess and Dan had made a promise to each other on their wedding day that they would never keep secrets from one another. "Is it possible your mother would know about whatever this is?"

"I don't think so." Sylvia visibly forced herself to sip the cocoa.

Jess doubted she had bothered with dinner. "Have you had dinner? Would you like a sandwich or something?"

"I had a bowl of soup with Daddy while I worked up the courage to confront him."

"I can't imagine the senator keeping a secret related to the murder of two men," Dan said. "He, Pratt, and Rutledge respected one another. There must be some aspect of this you don't know that will explain everything."

Sylvia squared her shoulders. "I hope so. Either way I'm taking a few days off work."

"I can understand you might want to be close to your father right now." Jess would do the same. "I'll speak to the senator tomorrow. Maybe he'll come clean with me."

"I want to help with the investigation," Sylvia stated.

Jess was confused. "Why take a few days off then? You're the ME on this case."

"I want to be with you every step of the way on this one. I don't want to be stuck in the morgue. This is a high profile case, Martin will take over if I make the request." Sylvia gave a nod as if the decision was made. "We'll consider it a ride along. I'm sure your team won't mind."

"But you're already a part of the team by doing exactly what you do."

"I won't take no for an answer, Jess. This is my daddy we're talking about. I have to be a part of every step."

Jess looked to Dan. She actually didn't have an issue with Sylvia being involved, she supposed. As chief of police, the buck stopped with Dan. "I'm game, if you don't see a problem."

"If Dr. Leeds is agreeable, then so am I."

"Martin Leeds wouldn't dare say no to me," Sylvia informed Dan.

"I'll expect you at the office by eight in the morning," Jess warned.

"I'll be there." Sylvia's relief was palpable.

The baby kicked Jess hard. She jumped and pressed a hand to her belly. "I think someone's trying to tell me something."

Sylvia set her cup aside. "I should go and let you get to bed." She stood. "I'll see you in the morning."

Jess nodded. "I'll be there. Night."

The sound of Dan's voice reassuring her as he walked Sylvia out made Jess feel warm inside. He was such a good man. She rubbed circles on her belly. This baby was going to be a very lucky child.

Jess got to her feet and gathered the cups onto the platter Dan had used to serve. She shuffled to the kitchen with Bear right on her heels, rinsed the cups, and placed them into the dishwasher. As she straightened away from the dishwasher, one of those harsh twinges twisted in her lower back. She groaned.

"Hold on, little one," she said softly. "We have a couple of weeks to go yet."

Her cell rang and she forgot all about back pain. She hurried back to her office and snatched it up. *Lori calling.* "Hey, Lori. How'd it go with Mrs. Dority?"

"The guy showed up at her door. She wouldn't open it since she didn't know him. He told her he understood and that he had a message for her."

Jess hoped this was something that would provide a direction in the case instead of simply more questions.

"He told her the man who had put her daughter in harm's way had paid for his evil deeds and that she could rest easy now."

"Pratt." Jess nodded. "Did her visitor introduce himself?" Not that it would have mattered. He would likely have used another alias. Al Hitchcock certainly hadn't been his name. They had tracked down every A. Hitchcock in the greater Birmingham area. There were only three. None were tall and thin and only one was Caucasian.

"Al Hitchcock," Lori confirmed. "She described him. He was the same guy who visited Durham."

The image they'd viewed of the visitor to the prison filled Jess's mind. "Well, I think maybe we've got our guy. We just don't know who he is or exactly what his face looks like."

Lori laughed. "It's a start."

"That it is. Thanks, Lori. See you in the morning."

Jess ended the call and headed for the bedroom. She was beat. Dan caught up to her in the hall. "I turned off the lights in the office." He wrapped his arm around her waist, not an easy feat these days. "I'm going to get you to bed. You look ready to collapse."

Jess smiled. "I won't argue with you, that's for sure."

Dan guided her to the bathroom and let her take care of essentials while he turned back the covers. When she had brushed her teeth, he helped her into bed, gave Bear a goodnight pat, and then massaged her feet for a few minutes.

By the time he slid between the sheets next to her, she was barely awake.

"I love you, Jess."

"Love you, too."

Maybe tonight she wouldn't dream of murders and serial killers.

CHAPTER TWENTY

Buddy had been parked on the street for a couple
of hours now. The New Orleans style lofts he had his
eye on were located atop the restaurants and shops
along Cobb Lane. According to his source, a sweet
little X-ray tech over at UAB, Addison Devers had
rented a loft at this address when she first moved to
Birmingham. Buddy had watched her drive away in
that sporty little red BMW ten minutes ago. Since she
wasn't on shift until tonight, she'd either gone shopping or out with a friend. Either way, he intended to
get a handle on her intentions.

Her lease on the loft extended another four
months. Addison apparently intended to stay a
while. What he didn't understand is why she hadn't
attempted to make contact with Sylvia. She'd had
more than enough time to get the lay of the land.
By now, she was fully aware that her mother and
grandparents were wealthy, prominent people in

the community. He doubted her goal was money. She'd inherited a hefty sum from her parents before deciding to give most of it away.

His cell vibrated with an incoming text. He checked the screen. *Got her.*

Rosey Cunningham, Buddy's most trusted colleague in the business. Rosey would tail Addison and keep an eye on her while Buddy did a little exploring. He sent a response to his colleague. *Don't lose her.*

Buddy climbed out of his Charger and strolled up the block. He moved closer and closer to her door, but he didn't go straight to it. Instead, he popped into one of the shops and bought a framed print. By the time he was moving toward the door once more Rosey reported that Addison had entered a restaurant downtown.

Buddy climbed the stairs leading to Addison's apartment. Rosey would let him know if she left the restaurant. Between now and then, Buddy intended to cross a line he rarely stepped over these days. He eased his conscience with the assurance that the effort was for the greater good.

When he reached the door with her number on it, he set the print aside and removed a lock pick from his pocket as if it were a key. A little toggling and the tumblers cooperated. He opened the door, didn't hear or see a warning that she'd bothered with a security system. Even better, there was no dog.

Inside, he closed and locked the door. For a rich girl, Addison's taste ran along the lines of minimalistic. The loft was one large space with a single interior door that likely led to the bathroom. Nothing on the walls. She wasn't exactly a neat freak. A tee he suspected she used for a nightshirt lay across the unmade bed. A bowl and spoon in the sink suggested she'd had cereal for breakfast. Plenty of wine and yogurt in the fridge along with a half empty quart of milk. A half-eaten cheese ball. The few cabinets were mostly empty except for a small set of stoneware, a few cans of soup, and a box of cereal.

A laptop and a stack of papers waited on the table in the center of the room. Buddy pulled out one of the chairs and sat down. He opened the laptop. No password. "Yes!"

The screen went directly to a Google search page. Buddy checked her history and saw where she'd been doing research on the Baron family. He tapped the necessary icon and went to her email account.

He shook his head. "Honey, you have got to stop assuming that your private life can be kept private behind nothing more than a single locked door."

Addison had emailed back and forth with a couple of women who appeared to be friends from college. The thread of several conversations revolved around her move to Alabama. Addison had shared her quest with her friends. She was curious more than anything. Before their deaths, her aging adopted parents had urged her to find her birth mother and form a relationship. Addison had ignored their advice until after she graduated. Once school was no longer her focus, she'd had no choice but to make a decision one way or the other. Since her arrival in Birmingham she had discussed her biological mother with her friends.

"Hmmm." Buddy was pleasantly surprised by her emails. Addison considered her mother beautiful and intelligent. She couldn't decide how to approach her. Then, she'd met a guy and gotten a little distracted.

Buddy's phone warned he had a new text. He read the update from Rosey. *Lunch with male friend.*

With a grunt Buddy composed a response. *Send me a pic of the guy.*

For the past five weeks, Addison's emails had been more about Mr. Wonderful as she called her new beau. Buddy rolled his eyes and backed out of her email account. He closed the laptop and for a couple minutes moved around the room, checked drawers, rifled through the wardrobe rack. Nothing out of the ordinary. Another buzz of his cell and he checked the screen. A pic of Addison Devers giving a guy a hug expanded on his screen.

"Holy hell."

The guy in the photo was Detective Chad Cook, Sylvia's former boy toy.

BIRMINGHAM POLICE DEPARTMENT. 12:45 P.M.

Buddy waited until Cook hurried out of the department's parking garage. As soon as the guy hit the sidewalk Buddy pushed away from the wall. "Running behind, Detective?"

Cook stalled. For a moment he look startled, and then he relaxed. "Hey, Mr. Corlew. Yeah." He gestured to the building where the rest of his team no doubt waited for him to return from lunch. "I'm a little late getting back from lunch."

"I need a few minutes of your time, Cook."

He glanced at the BPD building. "Sure. Okay. What's up?"

"You got a new girlfriend?"

He grinned before he could school the expression. "I do. She just moved here from southern California."

"Let's take a walk, Detective."

"I should…ah…get to the office."

"We're headed in the same direction anyway. If I slow you down, you tell your boss I held you up."

Cook shrugged. "Okay."

"How'd you two meet?" Buddy watched the young cop's gaze narrow. "I'm not trying to get all up in your business, it's just that you know Jess and I are really good friends. With the baby coming I'm keeping an eye on anyone who gets close to Jess or any of her associates. After what happened with Spears you can see how she would be concerned about that kind of thing."

Realization dawned on the young detective's face. "Oh, man. I didn't even think of that. I should apologize to the Chief for not telling her about Addi."

"Actually," Buddy dodged, "you don't need to do anything like that. I'm taking care of the background checks quietly and without any fanfare."

Cook laughed and pointed a finger at Buddy. "I see. Chief of Police Burnett hired you to do this and he doesn't want the Chief to know. I gotcha. She'd probably be pissed."

Buddy put his hands up in surrender. "You got me." Then he dropped them back to his sides and laughed. "What we do to keep the women in our lives happy."

"I know what you mean." Cook grinned. "But Addi's different. She's thoughtful and confident. We don't play games with each other's feelings."

Damn. Buddy hated to see the guy get hurt like this. The relationship sounded serious. "How long have you two been seeing each other?"

"About six weeks but we've officially been dating for one month today. That's why I'm late. She has to work tonight, so we had lunch together to celebrate our anniversary."

"How'd you say you met?" Buddy paused at the intersection.

"She came on staff with the surgeon who took care of my leg. I met her when I went back for my six-month follow up. We just hit it off."

The length of time the two had been seeing each other gave Buddy pause. He couldn't see it taking a month for Addison to get whatever she wanted from her mother's former lover. Maybe their relationship was happenstance.

"So you got past the breakup with Dr. Baron?" The traffic light changed and the two crossed the street. Buddy didn't miss the fact that Cook still had a bit of a limp. Guy almost lost his life to Eric Spears's obsession with Jess.

"Yeah. She's an amazing lady and all, but she…" He glanced around as they hit the sidewalk on the other side of the street. "Sylvia wasn't interested in anything but sex. I kind of want to settle down and have a family."

Buddy ignored his body's foolish reaction to Sylvia's name and the word sex in the same sentence—even one coming out of another man's mouth. "Aren't you a little young for a family?"

"I don't think so. My mom and dad got married when they were younger than me." He shrugged again. "I love kids. I've been saving for a house since I graduated high school. I don't know, maybe I'm old-fashioned."

Buddy clapped him on the back. "Old-fashioned can be a good thing, Cook. Don't let anyone tell you different."

"Thanks." The guy ducked his head.

"So is this the one? Does she want to get married, too?"

Cook considered the question for a bit. "We have a lot of the same goals and ideas on what family means. I think she really feels something for me but nobody's mentioned the L word yet." He grinned. "I did take her to meet my parents last Sunday."

"Wow. This sounds serious." Buddy frowned. "So what brought your girl all the way to Alabama?"

"She lost her parents a couple years ago. She doesn't have any family left. As soon as she finished her nursing program, she wanted to come here and find her roots."

Buddy shot him a confused look. "I thought you said she doesn't have any family left."

"She was adopted. Her birth mother lives here."

Buddy scratched his head. "You don't say."

Cook nodded. "She hasn't worked up the nerve to talk to her yet, but she knows who she is."

"Do you know who she is?" Buddy didn't see how that was possible.

"She's keeping that to herself for now. Addi really wants to break the ice with her before she brings anyone else into the picture. I can understand. She's not ready to share such a tender spot just yet. You know what I mean? She's just getting used to the idea of having a different mother from the one who raised her. She needs space to deal with this on her own. If she told me about her mother and I knew the woman, I might say or do something that would influence how this goes down. Neither of us wants to make the next step any more complicated than it's already going to be."

The guy had no idea just how complicated the next step was going to be for both of them. "She sounds like a nice girl."

"She really is, Mr. Corlew. She cares about people. The people who raised her taught her to be kind and giving. She's amazing."

Buddy gave him another clap on the back. "I've held you up long enough. Thanks for giving me the lowdown on your lady."

"Sure thing."

Buddy watched Cook hurry away. Damn but this guy was about to get his heart broken. No matter how nice Miss Addison Devers was, she would not want to continue a relationship with a man who'd made love to her mother.

This was not going to end well.

CHAPTER TWENTY-ONE

"The senator is doing an outstanding job of dodging me," Jess complained as she ended the call that had gone to voicemail.

Sylvia frowned. "I told you he's hiding something." She shook her head and turned back to the case board. "Whatever it is, I'll bet my inheritance it has something to do with these men."

Jess moved around her desk and studied the list they had spent the morning narrowing down. "Two are dead by the same MO, making them a given. We just need to figure out how the tall thin man is connected to them."

Pratt's computer had revealed nothing useful. His cell phone records, on the other hand, had proven most helpful. Since those records were already a part of the ongoing case against him, getting an update from his carrier hadn't been a problem. During the past week, Pratt had spoken to the same people on several occasions: Senator Robert Baron, Samuel Baker, Isaiah Taylor, and Congressman Craig Moore. All the digging Jess, Lori, and Sylvia had done this morning had connected Rutledge's name to the group as well as the names Wilson Hilliard and Alexander Carson—the movers and shakers consistently in the headlines and who had frequently associated over the past four or so decades.

"Congressman Moore is in Puerto Vallarta on spring break with his wife and daughter," Lori pointed out. "That leaves Senator Baron, former Mayor Wilson Hilliard, former Alabama Attorney General Samuel Fitzgerald Baker, former Alabama Supreme Court Justice Isaiah Aaron Taylor, and steel magnate Alexander Carson."

Sylvia moved closer to the board to study the photo of Moore. "Who has spring break this early? At Brighton our breaks were scheduled with Mountain Brook Schools' calendar."

Lori grinned. "One of the other hoity-toity private schools in the city."

"I guess I walked right into that one," Sylvia mused. She moved on to the photo of the tall thin man taken from his visit to the prison. "So this may be our guy."

"He's the only suspect we have just now," Jess admitted. She considered the seven men whose names they feared were on the man's list. "Since Mr. Carson doesn't have the eagle tattoo," Jess said, "let's take him out of the group for the moment."

Alexander Carson was the father of Elliott Carson, a victim in a series of murders Jess and her team had worked last summer. He remembered Jess and was happy to be interviewed. He agreed without hesitation to Sylvia's examination of his scalp. The same went for Isaiah Taylor. His son had been a victim of the same killing spree. He had agreed to an appointment with Jess for two this afternoon. Hilliard hadn't been found as of yet and Baker was dodging Jess as the senator was. Baker didn't like Jess. He'd taken offense at her investigative tactics when his son was murdered and hadn't forgiven her even though she'd brought the killer to justice.

The door opened, drawing their collective attention in that direction. Chad Cook entered the room.

He grinned. "Afternoon, ladies." He nodded toward Jess. "Chief."

Jess raised her brows at him. "I'm not a lady?"

His face turned beet red. "Sorry, Chief. Course you're a lady." He shuffled over to his desk as if in hopes of dodging anymore embarrassing moments.

Sylvia strutted right up to him. "Chad Wade Cook, I know that look you're wearing."

His face brightened to a more crimson shade of red. "Excuse me?"

Sylvia's gaze narrowed. "Do you have a girlfriend?"

Jess exchanged a look with Lori. And here she'd been so happy that Sylvia and Cook didn't seem to hold any grudges after their breakup nearly five months ago.

Jess opened her mouth to intervene but Cook spoke up. "I do." He grinned. "She's almost as pretty as you."

"That's wonderful!" Sylvia gave him with a quick hug. "I am so thrilled. Please tell me she's your age."

"Two years younger," he confirmed. "She's a nurse over at UAB. I met her when I went to see my doc the last time. She's new in town and has her first job."

Sylvia turned to Jess and Lori. "Why didn't anyone tell me this?"

"This is the first I've heard of it," Lori said, hands up stop sign fashion.

"That makes two of us," Jess piped up.

Chad was the one holding his hands up now. "Okay, you guys don't go ganging up on me just because I'm the only male in the room."

After a good laugh, they got back down to business. Hayes was keeping surveillance on Senator Baron, and Harper was at the morgue following up on Pratt's autopsy.

"The only one we haven't been able to track down," Jess returned to the case board, "is Wilson Hilliard."

"Former mayor, investment banker," Lori said. She went to her desk and sat down at her computer. "I may have something from some of the feelers I put out before lunch." She tapped a few keys. "Yep. Let's see," she leaned closer to the screen as she read, "Wilson Hilliard. Seventy-nine. He had a stroke and was in a state operated institution for the mentally ill until six months ago."

"He was in a mental institution?" Jess indicated the line-up of photos. "What happened to him after he left the institution? He was among the richest men in Birmingham in his day. Where's his family?"

"I can tell you a little about Wilson Hilliard," Sylvia propped a hip on the edge of Jess's desk.

"We're all ears." Jess took the extra chair that sat in front of her desk.

"Wilson's father and grandfather were the ones who helped launch the development of iron ore in Birmingham. The Hilliard family had money. Big money and major influence. They invested heavily in the production of iron ore as well as in railroads, and, as you both know, the Magic City was born."

"How did he end up in a state facility?" Most with means preferred a private facility.

"I'm getting there," Sylvia explained. "For decades, the Hilliard family grew richer and richer. Then the crash happened. More and more steel production went overseas and the bottom fell out of things here. Hilliard and his father lost everything their forefathers had built. His father committed suicide. Wilson managed to get by for a few more decades with his investment banking. He even survived a couple of crashes there, but then he had a stroke and dropped out of society all together. Until today, I hadn't heard his name in years." She shrugged. "I thought he was dead."

"What about a wife and children?" Surely there was someone Jess could track down to find the man.

"His wife died when I was in high school," Sylvia said. "They never had any children."

Jess glanced at her watch. "We should head to the appointment with Mr. Taylor." She stood and turned to Lori. "Lori, you and Cook locate Mr. Baker and keep an eye on him until—"

"Until," Sylvia cut in, "Jess and I finish with Taylor. I'll make sure Baker sees us then." She smiled at Jess. "There isn't a Baker in this county who would dare turn down a request from Senator Baron's daughter."

"Looks like having you on the team is going to be more advantageous than I realized," Jess said hopefully.

"I have my skills." Sylvia grabbed her bag as well as Jess's. She made a face. "Christ, what do you carry in here?"

"Don't go there," Lori suggested as she and Cook headed for the door. "She might tell you."

CANTERBURY ROAD, MOUNTAIN BROOK,
2:10 P.M.

Isaiah Taylor resided in a stately home near Jemison Park. Though the entry hall and great room were quite opulent, the home had a comfortable, lived in feel about it. Maybe it was the owner more so than the home. Seventy-six, tall and fit, Taylor's dark hair was heavily streaked with gray but it didn't detract from his good looks one little bit. Like the son he'd lost last summer, he was a very handsome man.

Once the pleasantries were out of the way, Jess turned to business. "Mr. Taylor, we appreciate your time this afternoon."

He gave a nod. "As I told you on the phone, my son's murder might still be unsolved if not for your hard work, Chief. I am more than happy to help." He shook his gray head. "Frankly, I'm stunned by the news of Joe and Harmon's murders. They both made their share of enemies, who hasn't, but to be murdered?" He moved his head from side to side again. "It's difficult to believe."

"Sir, beyond their successful careers, Mayor Pratt and Judge Rutledge shared a distinct mark." Jess hoped he would be as amenable about having his scalp examined. "We believe this has something to do with the reason they were selected as victims."

Taylor looked confused. "What're you saying, Chief?"

Before Jess could respond, Sylvia blurted, "She's saying they both had a small eagle tattoo. We need to know if you have one."

Jess sent Sylvia a look she hoped reminded her who was in charge here. The fact that Taylor at first looked startled and then stared silently at the two of them was answer enough to the question.

"I take it you have the same tattoo?" Jess ventured. No use beating around the bush.

He drew in a deep breath. "I do."

"May I—" Jess and Sylvia started at the same time.

At Jess's sharp look, Sylvia snapped her mouth shut. "May we have a look, sir? Just to confirm we're talking about the same mark."

"Why not?" The resignation on his face told Jess he'd hoped to avoid this moment.

Sylvia reached into her bag and withdrew a pair of gloves.

"Will you tell me how you came to share this mark with the victims?"

While Sylvia fingered through his hair, Mr. Taylor held very still. As soon as she gave Jess a nod, he began to tell his story.

"It was a very long time ago. I'd graduated from law school, I had a wife and a new son, and my career hadn't taken off as I'd expected."

Jess pressed a hand to her belly. "Having a child changes everything."

"Indeed." He gave a somber nod. "My family was one of some means, but not wealthy by any stretch of the imagination. I suppose the worst part was that I graduated at the top of my class. I knew I had the intellect and the skill, I only needed the opportunity."

Jess remembered those days. She'd worked extra hard to ensure she made her way into the FBI's intern program. She'd spent nearly two decades there before returning home to the man she'd always loved and joining the BPD. Some things were just meant to be and Jess was absolutely certain this was where she was supposed to be.

"Wilson Hilliard was at the top of his game in investment banking at the time," Taylor went on. "He asked for a meeting with me late one night after a long day at the law office where I had yet to make partner." He smiled, the expression faint. "Wilson said he recognized the fire and determination in me. He wanted to help me become what he knew I could be. He said the exact words I'd been harboring in my heart: *All you need is an opportunity. You're going to be the power in this city.*"

He fell silent for a moment before continuing. Thankfully Sylvia kept her lips sealed as did Jess.

"You see, Wilson had the influence and the power. The man had connections like no one else. Knowing what I know now, I suspect he built those connections the same way ours came about. Every man has a price, Chief. If not in dollars, in desire for something else he doesn't possess. Wilson made sure the right doors opened for me. He put in a word for me where needed and, eventually, I became a Supreme Court Justice of Alabama. It was the proudest day of my life next to my son's birth. I was so very thankful my father lived to see that day."

"So this tattoo," Jess offered, "it was Hilliard's way of marking you somehow?" Hilliard certainly wouldn't be the first power hungry man to mark his followers.

Taylor nodded. "Oh yes. The eagle represents power, influence, and greatness. He wanted to make sure we remembered where our success came from.

The location for the tattoo was his way of ensuring we never tried to distort or remove it."

"What did Mr. Hilliard ask in return for his help?" Jess held her breath.

"There's always that," Taylor said sadly. "At one time I would have ignored that question—the whole concept for that matter. Who cared what it cost? It was worth it, wasn't it?"

Jess understood the question was a rhetorical one.

"Occasionally, he would make it a point to meet with me and discuss a vote coming before the Court. He never asked, but I knew what he wanted. Frankly, what he seemed to want was what I felt compelled to support. It all seemed perfectly right and just for many years. But then, when his financial world started to crumble, he asked for favors with which I didn't agree."

When he remained silent a little longer than the last time, Jess prompted, "What did you do?"

"At first, I thought about doing as he asked. But, eventually, I refused him. When he threatened to expose me, I tendered my resignation citing health reasons. I would not taint the office."

"How did Mr. Hilliard react?"

"I don't know what he might have been capable of doing, but a debilitating stroke prevented him from taking any measures against me."

"When was this?" Jess asked.

"Ten years ago. His finances were in tatters by then. The last I heard he was institutionalized. I believe Judge Rutledge made sure that order was signed."

Well, well. The pieces of the puzzle started to come together. "Were you aware that others had this same tattoo? That Pratt and Rutledge, for example, had likely received the same sort of support from Hilliard?" Jess was reaching, but it was the only logical conclusion.

"Not at first." He braced his elbows on the arms of his chairs and clasped his hands together as if in prayer. "Who would want to share such a thing? Each of us prefers to believe we arrived at our career pinnacles on our own merit."

"But eventually you did," Sylvia nudged, speaking for the first time since Taylor began.

Taylor looked at her. "Have you spoken to your father?"

"Yes. He wouldn't tell me how the tattoo came about or who else might be involved."

"We had decided to attempt to take care of this ourselves, but," Taylor smiled sadly, "as soon as he called and told me the police would be asking questions, I made the decision to cooperate if approached. As much as I'd like to believe we could handle this ourselves, I'm not so sure now."

Jess and Sylvia shared a look. At least now they knew who the senator had called last night. Rather than ask how they had intended to resolve the matter Jess held her tongue in hopes he would keep talking.

"There were six of us that I know of," Taylor went on. "Besides Joe and Harmon, there was your father, Sam Baker, and Craig Moore. Wilson told us all the same thing, we were going to be the most powerful and influential people in Birmingham. I believe our hard work and abilities were part of it, but there's no denying he ensured our careers advanced the way we'd hoped."

He fell silent a moment before going on. "The six of us have pretended his support never happened, but we all knew. As soon as we learned the details of Joe's murder, Craig took his family and went to Mexico. He's the youngest of us and has a young family. I could hardly blame him. I sent my wife to stay a few days with our daughter in Denver. Sam's wife is in Montgomery. I spoke to Robert last night," this he directed to Sylvia, "he said he couldn't leave because of you. Apparently, your mother is headed to New York to visit Nina."

Sylvia looked to Jess again. "Mother called this morning and said she was going to see Nina. I didn't think anything of it other than being glad she would be gone."

"Mr. Taylor," Jess moved in a different direction, "if Mr. Hilliard had a stroke and spent the past decade institutionalized, who might be seeking revenge in his name? Perhaps against the folks he believes abandoned Mr. Hilliard?"

"Robert and I have been over and over this. We can't figure it out. Wilson had no family left. He's the last of the Birmingham Hilliards—if he's still alive. I can't imagine who would be doing this on his behalf."

"What about close friends?" Sometimes the bonds of friendship were deeper than blood. Jess had seen friends kill for friends many times in her days as an FBI profiler.

"Sadly," Taylor responded, "I don't believe the man had a single friend. He had a couple of dedicated employees."

"Let's start with those loyal employees," Jess suggested.

"One was a woman, a secretary. Patsy or Patricia, I think. The other was his personal assistant, Bernard Kinslow. He was quite tall, very trim. He was convicted of embezzlement and sentenced to prison several years ago. It's my understanding he was released some months ago."

Anticipation welled in Jess. She removed a copy of the Al Hitchcock photo from her bag. "Is this the personal assistant?"

Taylor took the photo and looked at it closely. "It could be. Of course, I haven't seen him in years and the face is difficult to see, but it's possible."

"Anything you can recall will be helpful," Jess urged.

Taylor lifted a finger. "Wait." He studied the photo more closely. "He wore braces. I think perhaps he had polio as a child."

Jess popped up from her seat. There was something she had to do, and it wouldn't wait. "May I use your restroom?"

"Of course." Taylor glanced at her belly and smiled. "Down the entry hall and on the left."

While Taylor and Sylvia discussed her father, Jess went into the hall. For once, she didn't need a bathroom. As soon as she was out of hearing range, she called Lori.

The instant the detective answered, Jess said, "Have you spoken to Baker yet?"

"Oh yeah," Lori assured her. "I spoke to him, but he refuses to allow us to remain on the property. We're sitting out here on the street which is a good thirty yards from the house."

Jess rubbed at her forehead. "For heaven's sake, doesn't he realize he may be in danger?"

"Maybe he's in denial."

More likely he was hiding a lot more than he or any of the men involved wanted to confess. Jess had watched Taylor's face as he spoke. He chose his words carefully and, she suspected, he left out a great deal. "Do the best you can."

"You got it."

"And, Lori…"

"Yes?"

"The tall thin guy is our man. His name may be Bernard Kinslow." Jess briefed her on the details Taylor had passed along.

"I'll see what I can dig up," Lori promised.

Jess exhaled a heavy breath and made the next call. This one to Lieutenant Hayes. The news from him was no different. The senator refused to allow

Hayes inside the house or on the property. He insisted that he had his own security.

Frustrated, Jess shook her head and returned to the meeting with Taylor. There were some things that were simply beyond her control.

The trouble was, she was reasonably confident whoever was killing off the city's most powerful people was well aware of how the men on his list would react. Worse, she feared the killer was about four bodies shy of being finished.

CHAPTER TWENTY-TWO

Bone tired, Sylvia drove along her street. Her father refused to listen to reason. He'd sent her mother to New York to see Nina and he'd urged Sylvia to go. As if she would leave him at a time like this. She'd wanted to stay the night at the house with him, but he had insisted she go home. He was fine. He had alerted his personal security team—which he rarely called upon. What was he thinking? Two men bearing those damned eagle tattoos were dead. The lab had confirmed that Pratt had received the same lethal cocktail as Rutledge. Her father just didn't seem to get it or he was in denial. He could be next! Sam Baker had behaved equally badly. Both men were acting like fools.

He had basically confirmed what Taylor said when Jess questioned him. To Sylvia it sounded as if the two had decided what to say. The congressman continued to be unreachable, and Sam Baker refused to discuss a situation he insisted had nothing to do with him.

Her head pounding, Sylvia turned into her drive. The headlights of her Lexus highlighted a black Charger and she stalled. She groaned and eased into her drive, her headlights forming a spotlight on Buddy Corlew sitting on her front steps.

Just what she needed to finish off this trauma-filled day. She supposed it was possible he'd found her daughter. Surely he knew better than to show up otherwise. Then again, after their last meeting she wouldn't be surprised by whatever he pulled.

"Who are you kidding, Sylvia? You surrendered to the man." It was a first for sure. She rammed the gearshift into park and emerged from the car. She slammed the door and hit the fob to lock it as she walked purposely toward the front steps.

"You're home late," he said as he stood.

"I've had one hell of a day, Buddy. Unless you have news for me, I would suggest you get back in that hotrod of yours and go do whatever it is you do at night."

There. She'd gotten that all out without pausing or even stumbling over a single word. She could be firm with him. So what if the sex was great? There were other men out there—ones who wouldn't make her feel so out of control.

"I have news."

She had hoped he would find answers for her. She really, really wanted to know. Suddenly, she wasn't so sure of what she wanted. "You couldn't call me in the morning? It's late, Buddy. I'm exhausted."

Rather than wait for an answer, she marched past him to the door. She jammed her key into the lock, but before she could turn it he was right behind her...against her and somehow all around her at the same time.

"We have to talk tonight."

The sound of his voice made her shiver in spite of herself. "Very well." She twisted the key and opened the door. As soon as she had silenced the security system, she closed the door behind him. No need to lock it, he wouldn't be here that long.

It wasn't until they were inside that she noticed the portfolio he carried. Her heart started to pound. So he really did have something for her. "Have a seat." She gestured to the living room. "I need wine."

She tossed her keys on the table and dropped her bag to the floor, then strode straight to the kitchen. Every ounce of willpower she possessed was required to keep her composure from slipping. All these years she had wondered...regretted. Now she would know. She wasn't ready for this.

Moving methodically, she placed two stemmed glasses on the counter before going to the fridge and selecting her favorite wine. Her fingers fumbled as she tried to handle the corkscrew. She should buy one of those new ones that made opening a bottle of wine easy but they seemed so cheesy.

"Let me."

As always, Buddy was next to her, whispering gentle reassurances. She held her breath when his hands brushed hers. He took the corkscrew from her and had the bottle open in seconds. When he'd poured a generous portion into each glass, he set the bottle on the counter.

They drank the wine in silence. He apparently understood that she needed fortification for what came next. When she sat her empty glass on the sleek stone counter, he emptied the bottle into it.

Sylvia didn't argue with him. She took the glass and went to the living room. Kicking off her shoes, she sat on the sofa and waited for him to take a seat. He reached for the portfolio he'd left on the coffee table and then sat down beside her. She turned her glass up and drank long and deep.

She licked her lips. "All right. Let's have it. Is she alive?"

He nodded. "She's very much alive." He removed an eight by ten photograph of a woman dressed in scrubs walking along the sidewalk. "This is Addison Devers. She grew up in southern California."

Sylvia reached for the photograph. Buddy took her wine and set it aside. It was a good thing since she would likely have dropped it. Her hands shook. "She's beautiful."

"She is very beautiful. Just like her mother."

Sylvia glanced at him. Her hands shook harder so she placed the photograph on the coffee table. "Is she a doctor?"

Buddy shook his head. "A surgical nurse. She graduated at the top of her class."

Sylvia nodded slowly. "So she's smart."

"Extremely smart. She started out in pre-med, but then shifted to the nursing program at UCLA and graduated with all sorts of awards."

"I don't understand. Why is she a nurse if she was in pre-med?"

"From all reports, she was planning to follow in her adopted parents' footsteps. They were both surgeons, but they died and she changed her mind."

"What do you mean she changed her mind?" This didn't make sense. "You don't just change your mind about something so important because nature takes its course and someone you care about dies."

"It wasn't that simple. The folks who raised her were good people, Sylvia. When they retired they spent most of their time in foreign countries where the need was greatest. After an extended stay overseas two years ago, they came home to spend the summer with Addison and the father had a heart attack. If that wasn't bad enough, the mother had one trying to save him. They died together and Addison was the one who found them."

Sylvia blinked to hold back the tears but they fell anyway. "That's horrible."

"I guess that's when she decided she didn't want to be a doctor and became a nurse instead." He shrugged. "Once she graduated, she donated nearly everything she inherited except her childhood home toward setting up hospitals in the very places her parents gave so much of their time. For sure, their deaths set her on a different path."

Sylvia pressed a hand to her chest. She tried to slow her heart. "She sounds like a very compassionate young woman."

"Everyone I spoke to raved about her."

"How did you get people to answer your questions?" Sylvia was sure he had his ways, but this was her daughter they were discussing.

"I posed as the head of hospital security. I told them I was running a background check on a new employee."

"So she has a job? At a hospital in California?" Though she had no right, the news made Sylvia proud.

"She's a surgical nurse. *Here*, Sylvia. She has a loft in Five Points."

"What?" Sylvia grabbed her glass and had another long swallow of her wine. She cleared her throat and stared at him. "What do you mean she's here?"

"She hired a PI to find you. She's been in Birmingham about two months."

Sylvia launched to her feet and paced the room. Her daughter was here. Looking for her. Sylvia stalled. "Does she know who I am?"

Buddy nodded. "The PI gave her a full background on you and your family."

"She's been here two months?" This made no sense. She finished off the wine and set the glass down. The room spun just a little.

Before she even swayed Buddy was at her side. "You need to sit down."

She didn't argue as he ushered her back to the sofa. "Have you spoken to her?"

"No. I did watch her for a while. I wanted to know who she talked to, that kind of thing."

"She has friends here already?" Sylvia had never made friends quickly. She hoped her daughter hadn't inherited that inability.

"She has."

Pride welled inside her. "You need to set up a meeting, Buddy. If she came here to find me, she may be unsure how to approach me." Sylvia had a reputation for being unapproachable. The Baron name at times intimidated people. She leaned forward and braced her head in her hands. "Oh my. I drank that wine entirely too fast."

Buddy propped his elbows on his spread knees. "Before we do anything, there's something else you need to know."

Sylvia raised her head. The room whirled just a little. "What do you mean? You just told me she's brilliant and a humanitarian. Why wait? She sounds wonderful, and she's here because she wanted to find me." He was confusing her.

"You asked about her friends," he began.

Sylvia nodded, afraid to say a word. Whatever else there was to know, she needed him to spit it out.

"She's met someone since moving here. A guy. They've been seeing each other for about a month now."

Impatient, Sylvia made a get-on-with-it signal.

"It's Chad Cook, Sylvia. Your daughter is dating Cook."

The conversation in the SPU office today suddenly replayed in her head. Chad had met someone...a nurse. "Oh my God."

"I don't think she realizes that the two of you used to be—"

"No. She couldn't. We stopped seeing each other months ago." Sylvia's stomach churned. Dear God, she'd made another terrible mistake that would end up hurting her daughter.

"I compiled the information about her into a report." He gestured to the portfolio. "When you've had a chance to look it over, we can talk again. What happens from here is up to you."

Sylvia stared at the portfolio. Her daughter was here. She was beautiful and smart and clearly apprehensive about approaching the woman who gave birth to her.

Reality washed over her like a tidal wave.

Not just the woman who gave birth to her...the woman who gave her away.

Sylvia turned to Buddy. Her lips trembled so hard she could barely get the words out. "She has every reason to hate me." Tears flooded out of her. "She'll never forgive me and I can't blame her."

Buddy pulled her into his arms. "It'll take time, that's all."

Sylvia sobbed so hard she couldn't breathe. Buddy held her tight and whispered reassurances to her.

How would she ever explain herself? There was no excuse. She had chosen selfishly.

And that was unforgivable.

CHAPTER TWENTY-THREE

Sam Baker was furious. He felt like a prisoner in his own home. He had ordered that lieutenant off his property this afternoon only to have him park at the end of his drive. As if that wasn't frustrating enough, the manager of the golf course had called to let him know that a Sergeant Harper was sitting in a golf cart at the back of the Baker estate. Of course, the manager had been concerned and wanted to know if there was anything he could do.

Rumors would spread like wildfire. Sam shouldn't care and perhaps he didn't. If he were completely honest with himself, he would confess that very little mattered to him anymore. He'd retired last year after Scott's death. His other sons hardly spoke to him anymore. Except his wife. No matter what he'd done, Clara still adored him and he adored her. She was the one person he could always count on.

As soon as he'd realized the seriousness of the situation, he'd sent Clara to Montgomery. She hadn't argued, but he had seen the worry in her eyes.

She needn't worry. To a large degree his life was over anyway. He had no desire for the police to know any more than they already did about this matter. He would personally handle whatever came next. Wilson, the poor bastard, was completely disabled or dead. Unless his ghost was back to have his revenge, it could only be someone from the institution who'd learned his darkest secrets during his lengthy stay there. Or perhaps it was his longtime errand boy. The notion that Kinslow was carrying out his own revenge wasn't completely outside the realm of possibility. The man might be physically challenged but Sam felt confident he'd understood exactly who was behind his prison sentence.

Kinslow wouldn't be so young now. Perhaps sixty, and riddled with physical frailties. Chances were he had a price. Sam would simply pay it and be done with this unholy business. He imagined Rutledge had been too self-righteous to do such a thing and, of course, Pratt had nothing to pay—his assets were all frozen.

Well, Sam had no problem paying the piper for the dance that had solidified his career. In fact, he'd taken fifty thousand dollars from the safety-deposit box at his bank this very day. He had tucked a .22 pistol into his sock at his ankle. Kinslow could be bought or he couldn't. Either way, Sam was prepared.

Let the trouble come. Every man had his price. Sam would find it, even if it meant emptying the safe hidden in the floor beneath his desk.

He checked all the doors once more as well as the security system. Brandy would be nice before he headed to bed. He padded down the hall, pausing to straighten a painting. He'd commissioned paintings of all his sons as well as himself and Clara. They were beautiful. He enjoyed walking past them each time he went to his study. When he entertained a colleague it was nice to show off those elegant paintings as they made their way to his lavish study.

What good was money if one couldn't flaunt the benefits of possessing such large sums of it?

Sam knew his study by heart. He stepped into the quiet darkness and moved straight to the bar. He flipped on the light behind the bar, highlighting the rich details of the wood and the ornate mirrors and stained glass. He'd had this one-hundred-year-old bar shipped all the way from Ireland. He loved it and, more importantly, his friends and colleagues were envious of it.

He poured the brandy and drank it down, and then poured another. He set the bottle aside, and a light across the room came on. He whirled around expecting that his wife had tricked him and decided to stay or that the police had somehow...

Not his wife or the police.

The man was moving toward him even as Sam's brain digested the details of what was happening.

He was tall and thin. Shock held Sam frozen as he recognized the rubber or plastic gloves on the man's hands, making his intention abundantly clear. His hair was cut too short to identify the precise color, but his eyes were dark sunken pools in a pasty white face. He wore a suit, but it was the high top leather shoes and the shiny metal of the braces visible at the hem of his trousers that drew Sam's attention.

"Do you remember me, Mr. Baker?"

Sam nodded, understanding settling over him. "Yes, I do." He did his best to shake off the shock and to gather his composure. "I've been expecting you."

The man didn't stop until he was standing toe-to-toe with Sam. He wished he'd remembered the gun at his ankle the instant he saw Kinslow. Sam swallowed the last of his brandy and reached out to place the glass on the bar. "How did you get in here? The police are right outside."

"You have a rather large estate, Mr. Baker. It was easy enough to evade the two officers attempting to keep watch beyond your property lines. Turning off your security system and getting through your locked door was simple. I spent six years in prison with a man who could break into the White House if he chose. It's amazing what you can learn when you have plenty of time on your hands."

Sam struggled to regain his composure once more. "How...how is Mr. Hilliard?"

Kinslow smiled. "Funny that you ask, Mr. Baker. Mr. Hilliard sent me to collect. I'm sure you remember there were certain compensations expected. Unfortunately, my time is short so we'll have to get on with the collection. I would have preferred to spend some time, you know, to do a good job for Mr. Hilliard as I did with Judge Rutledge and Mayor Pratt, but the timetable has been pushed up. There's no time to be as thorough as I'd like with you."

Sam nodded. This was good. Progress. "All right. What would Mr. Hilliard like? I'm prepared to pay whatever price he desires."

"He'd like your life."

Sam tried to raise his hands to defend himself but it was too late. The man pressed a cloth to his face and pulled him against his body before Sam could react.

"But first," Kinslow growled against his ear, "he'd like me to remind you of all that he gave you and all that you allowed to be taken from him."

Sam tried to scream. He kicked and failed his arms, but the thin man was far too strong.

"He wanted you to know," Kinslow continued, "how it felt to endure those hideous shock treatments and to be abused by a person charged with your care." Kinslow held him tighter still. "He wanted you to know what it is to be utterly terrified."

As his ability to hang onto consciousness slipped from his grasp, Sam wished he had allowed that damned detective into his home. He wished he didn't keep the shutters closed on the windows of his study…he wished he could tell his wife and sons how much he loved them and how sorry he was for the mistakes he had made.

His body refused to struggle anymore and the lights around him faded to darkness.

CHAPTER
TWENTY-FOUR

Jess would be glad when this killer was caught and this case was behind her. She much preferred riding to work with Lori or another member of her team. Sylvia was in a mood this morning. Or maybe Jess was the one in a foul mood. Either way, Sylvia hadn't said a word beyond 'morning' since Jess climbed into her car. It was bad enough to start the day off with a murder, she didn't need the silent treatment as well.

As they arrived at the crime scene and Jess reached for the door handle, Sylvia finally spoke. "Jess, wait."

"She speaks." Jess turned an unapologetic look in her direction and immediately felt contrite. "I know you're worried about your father." Who wouldn't be? They now had their third victim in this case.

193

Senator Robert Baron was on the same short list as the three victims. All they had was a photo of a tall thin man, possibly Bernard Kinslow, who had been Wilson Hilliard's personal assistant. And who, unfortunately, could not be found. The address listed on his prison release papers was bogus. He had no current driver's license. He was out there somewhere preparing for his next kill.

"I am very worried about Daddy, yes." Sylvia stared forward where crime scene tape was being strung around the Baker home and cops had fanned out to protect the perimeter. "Buddy came to see me last night."

Jess hadn't taken the Buddy-Sylvia thing too seriously when Dan told her about it. Buddy always had a new woman, or two or three, in his life. Sylvia played the field a little herself. Jess was under the impression she had no desire for a complicated relationship.

"Are the two of you seeing each other?" Jess asked when Sylvia didn't appear compelled to say more.

Sylvia exhaled a big breath. "Sort of." She turned to Jess then. "We've had sex a few times and...we seem to connect." She shrugged. "But that's not why he came by."

Jess shifted in the seat. Her lower back was still nagging at her today. She'd even resorted to wearing tennis shoes in hopes they would help. She wouldn't win any fashion awards but at least the shoes were brown like her slacks. The sweater was one of her favorites. It hugged her round body gently. Maternity clothes had come a long way since Lil had been pregnant.

Sylvia looked at her hands. Jess loved her French manicure. She couldn't remember the last time she'd taken the time to get a manicure. Dan was helping with her pedicure needs but he didn't trust his skill with a fingernail polish brush enough to do her fingernails. So she cut them short and left them bare. She really needed to change that.

"Whatever's going on, you can tell me, Sylvia." Hopefully, before detectives started knocking on the windows asking why she and Sylvia were still in the car.

"I didn't really go to Paris before med school." She lifted her gaze to Jess's. "I spent a semester in California to have a baby."

Stunned, Jess snapped her mouth shut. She hadn't meant for her jaw to go slack. "Oh," was all she could manage to say.

"No one else in this world knows except Buddy and whoever he hired to help him find her."

For heaven's sake. "You have a daughter?" She'd be what? Twenty-two or three? *Wow! Just…wow.*

Sylvia nodded. "Her name is Addison Devers. She's twenty-two and a surgical nurse." A shaky smile slid across her lips. "She's beautiful."

"This is amazing." Jess shook her head. "So, where does she live? Was she raised in California?"

"She was, but the people who raised her are dead. She recently decided to look for me." Sylvia's lips trembled. "She's *here*, Jess. In Birmingham."

"Oh my God!" Jess squeezed her friend's hand. "You have so been holding out! Have you spoken to her?"

Sylvia shook her head. "It's not that simple. She came here two months ago. She found a place to live and a job, but she hasn't approached me."

"She's probably nervous and uncertain."

"I suppose so. With this murder case," she stared out the windshield again, "I'm not sure now is the time to approach her."

"I don't know," Jess countered, "waiting might not be the right thing to do either." She couldn't imagine how difficult this was for Sylvia.

"She's dating Chad."

Taken aback, Jess had to close her sagging mouth once more. "Our Chad?"

Sylvia nodded. "She's a nurse for the surgeon who took care of his leg. That's how they met."

"She's the woman he was talking about in the office yesterday."

"She is."

OMG. Jess kept that to herself. "Here comes Lori. We'll talk about this later."

Sylvia managed a smile and nodded. "We will."

They emerged from the car and met Lori at the front steps. "The ME estimated time of death at between two and four this morning. No visible cause of death. The same ligature and Taser marks as the other two victims. No visible bruises. Baker was apparently worried. He had a .22 stuffed into his sock. For all the good it did him."

"Who's here from my office?" Sylvia asked.

"Toni James."

Jess nodded. They had worked with James before. "The officers on surveillance last night didn't see or hear anything?"

Lori shook her head as they stepped through the front door. "Nothing"

"No indications of forced entry?" Jess knew the answer before she asked the question. They paused in the entry hall to pull on shoe covers and gloves.

"The walk-through door in the garage as well as the one between the garage and the kitchen appear to have been left unlocked. We believe the killer came in that way and left that way as well. Evidence techs are crawling all over the place inside and out."

"He probably left through the golf course," Jess speculated. "With all those trees forming a border between the public space and the residences, staying in the shadows wouldn't be difficult." A two-man surveillance detail not allowed to come on the property could only do so much.

"I was thinking the same," Lori agreed.

Baker's home was large and grand. Jess hadn't expected anything less. She surveyed the entry hall as they entered. "Anyone call the wife?"

"Chief Burnett let me know he was making that call," Lori explained.

Suited Jess. No one liked making those kinds of calls. Dan knew the Bakers. Jess was glad he'd made that decision. "Bring me up to speed on what we're doing here?"

"Cook is interviewing the neighbors," Lori said, "Hayes is in the den taking a statement from the housekeeper who found him. Chet is trying to track down anything on our persons of interest." Lori gestured forward. "The body's in his study."

"Any luck learning the status and whereabouts of Wilson Hilliard or where Bernard Kinslow is holed up?"

"Not yet. I did, however, track down the secretary who worked with him for most of his career. Patricia Phelps passed away last year."

"Has anyone from the institution where Hilliard was a patient been able to identify who signed him out six months ago?"

"The administrator recalled Hilliard's departure and remembered that the man who signed him out was very tall and slim, and that he had a limp. He used the name Hitchcock and introduced himself as Hilliard's nephew."

Now they were getting somewhere. "See if you can track down the last physician who cared for Hilliard at the institution. Maybe he knows the physician who's treating him now."

"On it."

Dr. Toni James was just stepping away from the body when Jess and Sylvia entered the study.

"Detective Wells gave you my preliminaries?"

"Yes. Thank you." Jess flashed her a smile.

"Looks like that baby's coming any day." Toni smiled. "Hopefully not at a homicide scene."

"Two weeks and four days," Jess confirmed. "Definitely not at a homicide scene."

As Sylvia and Toni discussed the body, Jess took a quick look and then moved to the collage the killer had created on the wall. Like the other scenes, he had arranged photos and newspaper clippings about Baker and the most controversial cases he prosecuted as well as articles about his rise to power.

The killer evidently wore thick gloves. He hadn't left the first print at any of the scenes. Since it hadn't rained in a week or so there were no shoe prints outside any of the other victims' homes. No security cameras that took photos. No neighbors who heard or saw anything. Jess expected the same here. Still, they would go through the steps and hope he'd made a mistake this time.

She touched the first newspaper clipping and then the next. Some were decades old yet they looked extremely well taken care of. Who else besides a friend or family member—and there were none—would keep such meticulous records? As Hilliard's personal assistant, Kinslow must have been immensely dedicated.

He was their killer. Jess was convinced. They just had to find him.

She hesitated. Their attempts to find Kinslow would typically be focused on locating family and friends and finding a residence or a vehicle registered to him. None of those options were available. Kinslow had no known family and no address. Yet, he'd taken Hilliard somewhere when they left the institution. The two had to be somewhere. A place suitable for an elderly, disabled, and perhaps very ill man. Hilliard had been an investment banker. Despite having lost all his money, he might still own a small house or two somewhere in the city.

Jess surveyed the study. Kinslow murdered each of his victims in their personal study or library. Most were retired already or had home offices, so he'd selected that space for their *dying room*. A place where the victims had likely executed their duties from home. Duties that came with the positions Wilson had helped them attain. That, too, was telling. This was personal, but it was also business.

Lori appeared at the door, and Jess joined her in the hall. "I have the name of Hilliard's last known physician. I just sent his name and address to your cell."

"Sylvia and I will head that way. Check in with the senator's surveillance detail. I want eyes on him at all times."

"I'll drive over and check in with them in person."

"Good idea." Jess glanced back to see if Sylvia was still tied up with Toni. "Call Chet and ask him to look for a house or any property owned by Hilliard. Maybe all his assets weren't liquidated. An investment specialist would know how to hide resources."

"Will do. I'll touch base with you after I check in on Senator Baron."

"Stay safe," Jess warned. "Just because this guy seems to prefer striking after dark doesn't mean he won't change his MO." Lori was pregnant. She had to take special care of herself.

Lori laughed. "I seem to recall someone I know hating when people told her to take it easy out there in the field."

Jess rolled her eyes. "Go and be safe anyway."

Sylvia emerged from the study. "What next?"

"We take a look around, and then we leave the scene in the capable hands of Hayes and Cook and the forensic folks." She hoped Baker's computer and cell phone records gave them additional clues. They needed all the help they could get.

"I called Daddy."

Jess glanced at her. "Lori just left to check on him."

"He swears he won't leave the house and that everything's locked up tight."

The past few days had taken a toll on Sylvia. Her face was uncharacteristically pale and she was visibly tense. If the murders weren't enough, there was the business with her daughter. *Wow.* Jess still couldn't believe Sylvia had kept that kind of secret all these years.

"Would you rather be with him?" Not that Jess considered the idea a good one but she knew how she would feel under the same circumstances.

"He won't have it." Sylvia shook her head. "I swear, Jess. My gut tells me these men are behaving so stubbornly because they don't want us to know their secrets."

"I'm certain of it. It takes sacrifice to achieve great power. Sometimes those sacrifices are outside the lines. As proud as your father is, I doubt he wants you or anyone else to know he crossed a line of any kind."

"I just can't imagine any other reason for his determination to face this alone. Yet, I can't imagine him crossing any lines, either." She sighed. "He said if I came near the house he'd call Dan to come and pick me up."

It wasn't funny, but Jess had to laugh. "Dan would do it, too."

Sylvia shot her a look. "He'd try."

Jess laughed and finally Sylvia joined her. They needed a good laugh even if the forensic folks didn't get it.

Sometimes a person just had to laugh…this was one of those times.

CHAPTER TWENTY-FIVE

Sylvia couldn't believe she'd fallen apart and spilled her guts to Jess. She sighed. Oh well. It was done. She wasn't herself.

Her daughter was in Birmingham.

Addison. According to Buddy's report, her friends called her Addi.

Sylvia closed her eyes for a moment. She had a daughter who was twenty-two years old. An accomplished daughter. How would she tell her parents... her sister? Another sigh whispered from her lips. Her friends.

Then there was the issue of the father. Benton Murdock. Arrogant bastard. He was married and had grown children. He wouldn't be interested in Sylvia or Addison. Still, her daughter would want to know.

Sylvia stood. She could not sit here waiting a moment longer. At least they weren't stuck in the waiting room with all those coughing and sneezing patients.

Jess looked up at her. "Sometimes waiting is what we do."

They'd been waiting to see this doctor for forty-five minutes. Sylvia understood that he'd been called to the hospital this morning, but they were trying to stop a killer here!

"Chief, the doctor is back and can see you now."

Sylvia whirled around at the receptionist's voice. "It's about time," she murmured for Jess's ears only.

"Welcome to my world, Dr. Baron." Jess smiled. "How does it feel to be on the other side for a change?"

"Enough said."

Dr. Bryan Sowell stood as Sylvia and Jess entered his office. "I apologize for the wait, ladies." He gestured to the two chairs in front of his desk.

"The patients come first," Jess replied with a smile.

Jess's patience never ceased to amaze Sylvia. She wanted to shake the man and demand answers, not exchange pleasantries.

"Then I'm sure the two of you will forgive me when I tell you that I don't have a lot of time now. I have a lobby full of patients waiting."

"We'll get right to the point, then," Jess suggested. "Wilson Hilliard was your patient until six months ago."

Dr. Sowell nodded. "I haven't seen him since that time. Has he passed away?"

"We're not sure, doctor, but what I can tell you is that finding him may save lives. Three men are dead already and time is of the essence. These are exigent circumstances. Anything you know may help save the lives of others. That's why we're here. Can you tell me about his condition when you last examined him?"

He settled behind his desk. "I understand your situation though I doubt what I can tell you will be of much help."

"Whatever insights you have may prove more helpful than you can imagine."

"Mr. Hilliard was my patient for about two years. A stroke victim, he was bedridden, but his mental acuity remained quite high. I could never understand why he was committed in the first place. I filed a complaint with the institution. I believe Mr. Hilliard was abused during his extended stay there. Of course, I couldn't prove it and the complaint was dismissed." He sighed. "Unfortunately, six months ago he was diagnosed with advanced pancreatic cancer. I turned his care over to an oncologist but then I heard he had refused treatment and been released."

"Without proper treatment he should be deceased by now," Sylvia suggested.

"Most certainly," Sowell said. "If he is still alive, he will be in very bad condition. He would need pain meds to control the unbearable pain."

"No other physician requested his records?" Jess asked.

"No records on Hilliard were ever requested. I'm sorry." He shook his head. "I have no idea what happened to Mr. Hilliard after he left the institution."

Jess stood. Sylvia followed suit.

"Thank you, Dr. Sowell. We appreciate you taking the time to answer our questions."

Sowell nodded. "I hope you find him. I'd hate to think of him out there suffering."

As soon as they were outside, Sylvia turned to Jess. "Where to now?"

"Now we—" her cell burst into that wonky old ring tone, cutting her off. "Hey, Sergeant."

Sylvia tried to read between the lines of Jess's side of the conversation as they crossed to her car. Once seated inside, she stopping trying to figure out all the un-huh's and yes's and sent her father a text. He replied immediately that he was doing perfectly fine. Sylvia wanted to scream. It was clear where she'd gotten her stubborn streak.

"Thanks, Sergeant. We're heading that way." Jess ended the call and turned to Sylvia. "Wilson Hilliard owns two small houses under an old company name, Hill Enterprises. One is vacant and scheduled for teardown, the other currently has utilities connected and is our destination."

"Enter the address into my GPS," Sylvia suggested as she started the car. Maybe this was the lead they needed to end this nightmare.

THE DYING ROOM

Sylvia stood on the street with Jess and Lori as Sergeant Harper and Chad moved in on the bungalow that was in disrepair. The small blue house looked vacant to Sylvia. No vehicles in the driveway. The lawn had grown knee deep last summer and was then left to die in winter. The tall dead grass and weeds now looked more like an abandoned hayfield. The other houses along the block were in considerably better condition. Sylvia was surprised this one wasn't scheduled for demolition.

BPD officers had evacuated the homes nearest this one and had barred each end of the block. Jess and Lori had insisted Sylvia pull on a bulletproof vest. She was grateful she'd chosen slacks and a light wool sweater today. This vest would not have worked with any of her dresses or suits. Jess, on the other hand, looked quite chic in her maternity sized vest. Sylvia sighed. Why was this taking so long?

As if she had spoken aloud, Jess tucked her weapon back into her bag and turned to her. "All clear. We can go in."

Sylvia hurried to keep up with her strides. For a woman nearing the end of gestation, she moved quickly. "Is Kinslow here?"

Jess shook her head. "Only Hilliard. And he's alive."

The rickety porch led to an interior that appeared to be in somewhat better condition but gave the impression the residents were hoarders.

Decades old wallpaper was peeling from the walls. Doors that had once been white were a faded shade of gray. Jess passed Sylvia shoe covers and gloves. Harper called out: *Stay calm, sir, BPD!*

"Smells putrid in here." Jess held a gloved hand over her nose and mouth.

"It is," Sylvia confirmed. "What you smell is death." She met Jess's gaze. "It's the cancer."

The house had only four rooms and a small bath that Sylvia didn't dare enter. Hilliard lay in a bed in the larger of the two bedrooms. The smell was nearly unbearable. Sylvia didn't have to lift his sheets to know a number of his organs were failing him.

"I've been expecting you," Hilliard said, his voice weak as Jess and Lori entered the bedroom.

Sylvia remained by the door. She could hear and see all she needed to from right here. The man's skin was yellow with the poison his body was no longer able to handle. He looked nothing like the photos they had viewed of him taken as recently as twelve years ago. He was hardly more than skin and bone. His insides were rotting no matter that his heart continued to beat.

"Deputy Chief Jess Burnett," Jess said, showing her badge. "This is Detective Lori Wells. We're calling an ambulance for you, sir. Until it arrives, we need to ask you a few questions."

Watching Jess and Lori work was like observing a carefully choreographed dance. Lori was already making the call before Jess said the words. Harper and Chad were going through the other rooms looking for evidence. Hayes remained at the Baker scene to oversee activities there.

"Don't bother with the ambulance. I'm dying." A dim smile lifted the man's chapped lips. "You just missed Bernie. We've already said our goodbyes."

"Where is Mr. Kinslow?"

"I wouldn't know." Hilliard closed his eyes. "He was always such a dependable assistant. He knew exactly what to do without me having to say a word. I never had to worry."

Jess turned to Lori. "Get the surveillance detail at both locations on the line. I want visuals on both residents."

Sylvia stepped aside as Lori left the room. Had Jess just asked her to get a visual on Mr. Taylor and Daddy?

Sylvia stepped into the room as Jess spoke again, "Mr. Hilliard if you're aware of Kinslow's whereabouts and intent, that makes you an accessory."

Hilliard didn't answer. He was still breathing but was either opting not to respond or had slipped into unconsciousness.

Sylvia moved to the bedside table and surveyed the array of bottles. "There's no physician or pharmacy listed on any of these meds. He probably ordered them online." She shook the bottle of oxycodone. "I don't know how many were in here, but it's empty now." There were several empty bottles with the same label. "Oxy," she told Jess. "He may have purposely taken an overdose."

"Damn it." Jess turned around. "Where is—?"

"The paramedics are here," Lori said from the door.

Sylvia wasn't sure there was anything anyone could do at this point.

As they cleared out of the room for the paramedics to take over, Lori said, "Mr. Taylor called."

Jess briefed the paramedics before turning back to Lori. "Has he heard from Kinslow?"

"He's meeting with Senator Baron right now and the two of them have decided they'd like to make a statement before turning themselves in."

"Turning themselves in?" Sylvia echoed. Confusion mixed with the underlying fear that had been haunting her since this thing started. "What does that mean?"

Lori shrugged. "That's what he said."

"Maybe police protection is looking a little more appealing now," Jess suggested. To Sylvia, she added, "No offense."

"None taken," Sylvia assured her. "I couldn't be more relieved."

"We'll leave Sergeant Harper and Detective Cook in charge here," Jess said as they stepped out onto the porch. "Check with the surveillance detail at the senator's home and confirm Taylor's arrival."

"On it." Lori headed for her Mustang.

"We'll be right behind you," Jess called after her.

When they reached her car, Sylvia asked, "What do you think Kinslow will do once you've foiled his plans?"

"I don't know," Jess admitted. "I'd prefer to be taking him down right this instant, but I can live with simply moving his intended victims out of reach. Sometimes you just have to go with what you've got."

Sylvia was beginning to understand that sometimes the small victories were the most important.

CHAPTER TWENTY-SIX

"I know how you got onto the property," Robert said, "but what I can't figure out is how you got into the garage and then into my home."

"I didn't want to do this," Isaiah Taylor repeated. He shook his head and then looked away, unable to face Robert. "It's just as well, this has to end."

Robert wished there was something he could say to his old friend. Isaiah Taylor was a good man. He was only guilty of making the same bad decision Robert had made all those years ago. Like Sam, Joe, and Harmon, they had believed they could contain this situation, but they had been wrong. Kinslow had managed to slip past Taylor's surveillance detail. He'd walked right into Taylor's home and warned that unless he was able to finish this today, he would disappear. Then one day, when they were least expecting him, he would come back. Only next time he would come after their loved ones. He'd already proven how very capable he was.

Isaiah was correct. This needed to end.

Kinslow laughed, the sound lacking any sort of humor as he turned from his work on the wall across the room. "You all have housekeepers. Overworked, underpaid women who go home exhausted from trying to please." He shrugged. "I followed them. Took their keys, made copies, and placed them back on their key rings before they ever noticed they were missing. It was simple." He picked up another newspaper clipping. "You see, they don't have houses with fancy alarm systems." He laughed again. "All but one had the security codes to your homes written down in their wallets." Shaking his head, he turned back to the wall. "You should be more careful who you trust with your secrets, gentlemen."

"What do you want from us?" Isaiah demanded before lapsing into quiet sobs. "Just tell us what you want."

While his old friend pleaded with their captor, Robert tugged at the restraints securing his wrists. There would be no escaping these bindings. He sighed. Perhaps he should have listened to Sylvia and Jess. Pride had gotten in his way. He didn't want his daughters and his wife to know what he had done. How would he have ever looked them in the eye again if they learned he wasn't the hero they thought him to be?

No. It was better this way. His family would never be safe until this ended. It had to end here and now.

"Suffering a few regrets, Senator?"

He looked up as Kinslow moved toward him. He wished his heart would stop pounding so hard. The fear burning his eyes threatened to humiliate him even more. At least he wasn't losing his grip as Isaiah was.

"I have my share," he admitted. There was no point pretending. Robert recognized that it was highly unlikely either of them would survive this day. "You know the police will have the house surrounded by now. They'll come in after you. You won't get away unless you—"

He patted his chest. "Not to worry, Senator, I have a backup plan. I may not get out of here, but neither will the two of you."

"You don't have to do this, Bernie."

"Do you have any idea what you and the others did to him?" He removed a small device from his pocket.

Robert couldn't quite make out what he held in his hand. A small, black rectangular object about the size of a cell phone. "We were wrong." Robert met his furious gaze. "We were selfish and indifferent. There is no excuse."

"I promised him each of you would get a taste of what he endured before you take your final breaths." He pressed the black object to Robert's neck. "I won't let him down the way you and the others did."

"What about the shameful actions we took against you?" Robert searched the other man's face. "We let you go to prison for a crime you didn't commit to ensure you were properly discredited as a potential witness. We should pay for that, too." Robert prayed his delay tactic would work. He worried a little now that Isaiah had abruptly fallen silent. Had Kinslow already administered a lethal dose to Isaiah as he had done to Harmon and Joe?

Kinslow's jaw tightened. "I was beaten every day for the first four months in that place. Eventually I learned how to avoid attention. I kept my head down and I did whatever I had to do to survive. And I learned all I could from those who actually were criminals. There was just one thing that kept me going." He leaned his face close to Robert's. "The knowledge that when I got out I was going to make you all suffer for what you'd done."

"Wilson is very fortunate to have you as his friend," Robert said quietly. "Few have the chance to share such a friendship."

"I'm the one who's lucky," Kinslow sneered. "Now, close your eyes and remember all that you have enjoyed because he chose you. You would be nothing if not for him."

"That's not true."

Kinslow glared at him, his lips curled back with fury. "What do you mean it's not true? Mr. Hilliard made you just as he made the others!"

"He supported my efforts, nudged the right contacts," Robert argued, "but he didn't make me who I am. I supported his efforts as well, until he asked for something I couldn't give."

"And then you sent him away to be tortured with shock treatments and all manner of unethical treatments! You left him to rot." Kinslow jabbed what Robert now recognized as a Taser into his throat. "Just like you did me!"

Robert wanted to deny the charge but there was no denying the truth. Both he and Isaiah had looked the other way too many times…they had agreed that steps had to be taken to keep Kinslow quiet. "Will this change what we've done? Don't you want us to face years in prison as you did?"

"Ha! Your hotshot lawyers would find a way out for you." Kinslow shook his head. "You were the worst of all, senator. You represent the people. They trust you. Mr. Hilliard trusted you and you failed."

"I have no excuse," Robert confessed. "Do what you will, but I still believe you could make a much stronger statement by forcing our foul deeds into the open. Simply ending our lives rather than making us suffer for years as Mr. Hilliard did is clearly the easy way out."

Kinslow grinned a malevolent expression. "Do you really think I'd allow *you* an easy way out? You just don't know, senator. But you will. Any minute now."

Robert felt sick to his stomach. "What do you mean?"

"He made me do it," Isaiah wailed.

Fear roared through Robert. "What have you done?"

The sound of the doorbell echoed through the house.

Kinslow's grin widened. "That will be your daughter and that lady cop friend of hers."

Robert opened his mouth to shout a warning but a jolt of electricity rendered him mute.

CHAPTER
TWENTY-SEVEN

Jess's instincts were on high alert. "Where's Taylor's car?" She surveyed the cobblestone parking area as they crossed to the front door.

Sylvia shook her head. "Maybe he didn't want to get out of the car out here in the open with all those reporters on the street."

"Guess so." Jess gazed toward the street. The driveway was a long one but a telescopic camera lens wouldn't have any trouble. Anytime there was police activity involving the city's elite, the media followed. Jess scanned the property. She didn't like that it was so damned quiet. Lori had already rung the doorbell but no one had answered. "Lori, have a look around before you come inside."

"Sure thing." Lori palmed her weapon and headed down the steps.

218

Since Sylvia was busy digging in her purse, Jess pressed the doorbell again.

"Found it!" Sylvia held up a single key. "I always let myself in."

While Sylvia unlocked the door, Jess unearthed her weapon from the bottom of her bag. She stretched her back and wished the pain would go away. It was worse today than last night. She wasn't about to complain and hear more warnings that she should be taking it easy.

Three men were dead. The killer was still out there. Who had time to take it easy?

"Hello!" Sylvia called out as they moved along the entry hall. She peeked into the great room as they passed but it was empty. "They must be in Daddy's study."

The house was too damned quiet.

Jess put a hand on Sylvia's arm, then pressed a finger to her lips. Sylvia's eyes rounded. Jess pointed to the front door about a dozen yards behind them. Sylvia nodded and they started back in that direction.

"Leaving already, ladies?"

Jess halted.

"You just got here," the male voice said. "We've been waiting for you. Now, lower your weapon and come along before I have to do something we'll all regret."

Jess lowered her weapon and slowly turned to face the threat. Dammit. She should've listened to her instincts. This meeting hadn't felt right.

The tall thin man staring at her smiled. "Looks like that baby's coming any time now. We don't want to do anything rash. Put the gun down on the table and follow me."

Jess hesitated long enough to look him up and down once more. If he had a weapon, it wasn't visible.

"It would be better if you came with us, Mr. Kinslow," she countered.

He chuckled. "I see. You think I'm unarmed." He held up his right hand. "This is a detonator." With his left hand, he opened the lapel of his jacket. "I'm certain you know what this is. If I release this trigger—" he waved his right hand "—we'll all go boom."

A belt of what appeared to be explosives looped his waist. Evidently, drugs weren't the only things he'd been ordering on the Internet.

Jess placed her weapon on the table. "Can we see the senator and Mr. Taylor now?"

"That's why we're all here." He motioned for Jess and Sylvia to precede him.

Jess hoped Lori had gotten a peek in one of the windows or had simply decided something was off and called for backup. All the times Dan had told her she needed to be especially careful echoed through Jess. Fear trickled through her veins. Whatever happened next, she had to protect their baby.

At the door to the senator's study, Jess got a glimpse of the senator as well as Taylor secured to chairs before Sylvia hurried around her to get into the room.

"Daddy!" Sylvia rushed to her father. His head hung forward.

Taylor looked up and immediately started apologizing. Both men were restrained in the same manner as Kinslow's other victims. The newspaper clippings and photos had already been arranged on the wall.

Kinslow ushered Jess inside and then took a position next to his intended victims.

Sylvia glared at him. "What did you do to my father?"

"We were just getting started," Kinslow said with a smirk. "Step away," he ordered. When Sylvia held her ground, he repeated, "Move over next to your pregnant friend or else."

Sylvia looked to Jess, her lips quivering. Jess nodded, and the terrified ME did as Kinslow instructed.

"Before I finish this," Kinslow said, "I want you to hear from their own mouths what these two did. I realized after I ended Baker's sorry existence that I'd only made those men martyrs. What I should have done was made them admit what they'd done on a video before I killed them." He shrugged. "Maybe we'll just tell their stories as well to the two of you. Since Congressman Moore ran like the coward he is, I mailed a letter to that reporter Gina Coleman about him. She'll get it in tomorrow's mail. He won't escape his fate."

"I think that's a very good idea," Jess offered. "Would you like me to take notes?"

Kinslow thought about her question for a moment. "No." He looked at Sylvia. "I'm pretty sure she won't forget." He nodded to Jess's bag. "Put your purses on the floor and push them away with your foot."

They both did as he asked. Another pain stabbed Jess in the lower back and she almost flinched. She didn't need this man seeing any sign of weakness. What she needed was a plan.

When he would have spoken again, she cut him off, "We interviewed Mr. Hilliard."

Kinslow schooled his face but not before Jess saw a glimpse of emotion. "Mr. Hilliard was a great man."

Jess smiled. "That's exactly what he said about you, Bernie." She touched a hand to her mouth. "Is it all right if I call you Bernie? Mr. Hilliard spoke so fondly of you I feel as if I know you already. He said you were a fine, loyal assistant."

Confusion cluttered his face. "When did you speak with him?"

"Just before we came here," Jess explained. "We were at his house looking for you." She sighed. "Bless his heart. We called an ambulance for him. The paramedics took him to the hospital. He's doing well considering what he's been through."

Kinslow's head started to shake before Jess stopped talking. "Mr. Hilliard is dead."

"Oh no," Jess assured him, "he's going to be fine."

"They've already pumped the oxy out of his stomach," Sylvia put in, seeming to understand where Jess was going.

"An oncologist will be taking him to surgery soon. They're going to cut out the cancer. The doctor called me on the way here. He says the prognosis is surprisingly good."

"You're lying!" Kinslow shouted. "He's dead!"

Think, Jess! "If you don't believe me, you could speak to him yourself." Jess hoped Sylvia wasn't staring at her as if she'd lost her mind.

Kinslow seemed to stall on the suggestion.

Thankfully the senator, who had regained consciousness, and Taylor were keeping quiet. All Jess needed was to buy enough time for Lori to get help in here.

"If you're lying to me," Kinslow said in a quiet roar, "I will—"

"I'm not," Jess lied. "All I have to do is call my detective and have a Skype call set up. That way you can not only speak to Mr. Hilliard, you can see him." Jess had learned all about Skyping last summer.

Anticipation replaced the confusion on his face. "Do it. Quickly."

"Should I use the house phone?" Jess gestured to the senator's desk.

Kinslow nodded. "And tell your cop friends if they come near this house we all die."

"I understand." Jess went to the desk. The shutters on the massive windows behind it were closed tight. Lori wouldn't be able to see them at all. Since she had no idea where Lori was, Jess couldn't call her. She could be inside the house at this point.

Her hand shaking just a little, Jess picked up the phone and called Sergeant Harper. He answered immediately. "Sergeant, I need you to prepare a Skype call for me."

"Put it on speaker," Kinslow shouted.

Jess pushed the speaker button and placed the receiver back in its cradle. "Can you hear me, Sergeant?"

"Yes, ma'am."

Jess moistened her lips and said a silent prayer as she instructed Harper. "Sergeant, I explained to Mr. Kinslow how the paramedics took Mr. Hilliard to the hospital for surgery. But Mr. Kinslow would like to speak to his friend personally. Would you call the oncologist, his name is Dr. Martin Leeds, and tell him that we need to set up a Skype call so that Mr. Kinslow can see Mr. Hilliard. He doesn't believe that his friend is still alive."

"Absolutely, ma'am. I'll make that call right now."

What else? What else? "I know this is a big request since they're preparing Mr. Hilliard for surgery, so if Dr. Leeds gives you any trouble you call Chief of Police Burnett and tell him that we have a volatile situation here. If the doctor won't cooperate this situation will blow up in all our faces."

"Yes, ma'am. I'm on it."

"Thank you, Sergeant."

The call ended and Jess took a deep breath before facing Kinslow once more.

A grin split his face. "I like the way you let him know about the explosives." The grin disappeared. "I hope that's the only coded message you attempted to pass along. I'd hate to have to kill the senator's daughter."

"Do what you came here to do, Kinslow," the senator demanded. "No one else needs to be hurt. Send these women out of here. They're innocent in this."

"Shut up!" Kinslow growled. "How long will this take?" he asked Jess.

"It depends on whether or not they've already taken Mr. Hilliard into surgery." She shrugged. "Fifteen or twenty minutes if he's not in surgery."

"You'd better hope he's not," Kinslow threatened. "Until then, let's play truth or dare." He turned to Taylor. "You can go first, Your Honor."

Taylor screamed in agony as Kinslow alternately tasered him and demanded answers. The senator pleaded with Kinslow to leave Taylor be and to let him speak. Kinslow ignored him.

Jess put a hand on Sylvia's arm and gave it a reassuring squeeze. Cops would be everywhere outside. SWAT was no doubt getting into place. This would be over in no time. Meanwhile, Jess scanned the room looking for any sort of weapon. All she needed was the right opportunity...

Please let my baby stay safe.

By the time the telephone rang, Sylvia was trembling. Jess gave her arm another squeeze before turning her attention to Kinslow. "Would you like me to answer that?"

He nodded.

Jess moved around behind the desk again and answered the call, putting it on speaker. "Is that you, Sergeant?"

"Yes, ma'am. Everything has been arranged. All you need to do is place the call from any handy computer." He rattled off the contact information. Jess grabbed the nearest pen and wrote it down on the desk blotter.

"Thank you, Sergeant. We'll set it up now."

The call ended and Jess looked to Sylvia. "Can you get me into your father's computer?"

What Jess wanted was Sylvia behind the desk with her. She didn't trust her not to make any sudden moves.

Sylvia turned on the computer and then stepped back while Jess brought up a screen and entered the necessary information. Within moments, Dr. Martin Leeds, Jefferson County's Coroner, appeared on the screen. Behind him, Jess could see Wilson Hilliard in what appeared to be a hospital bed. An IV was in place, along with a heart monitor, clearly monitoring someone else's heart. An oxygen mask had been placed over Hilliard's mouth and his chest moved up and down as if he were breathing. Jess didn't know how they'd managed considering the old goat was as dead as a doornail, but it looked real enough to her.

"Dr. Leeds," Jess said, "can you hear me okay?"

"I hear you perfectly, Chief."

"Good. Good. Mr. Kinslow is here and he'd like to speak to Mr. Hilliard."

"I'm afraid Mr. Hilliard is sedated right now. We're about to take him into surgery."

"Let me see him," Kinslow shouted as he stormed around the desk. "I want to see him breathing."

"Let me get out of your way." Jess eased back just a little.

She couldn't help staring at his hand and the detonator he held. It was right there in front of her. Her heart skipped a beat. If he released the pressure on that button it was over. If she could just take it away from him without the loss of pressure on the button…

Even as the thought formed in her mind, movement in the corner of her eye warned that Sylvia was about to make a move. Whatever she had in her hands she swung it hard against Kinslow's head. Jess grabbed his hand in both hers and squeezed a thumb over his.

He struggled.

Jess held on.

Sylvia hit him again.

This time he went down, dragging Jess to her knees.

"What part of *we'll all go boom* did you not understand?" Jess demanded, her heart pounding.

Sylvia dropped the statue she'd used to clobber Kinslow. "What can I do?"

"I need the bomb squad in here now!" Jess shouted. "Call Lori." Jess held as still as possible even as her arms started to tremble. She reminded herself to breathe, deep breaths.

Sylvia rushed to her purse and dug out her cell to make the call.

Jess held on tight and prayed the son of a bitch didn't wake up and start struggling again. He was breathing. At the moment that wasn't necessarily a good thing.

Sylvia rushed back over to her. "What now?"

"Release your father and Mr. Taylor and get out of here." Shit. Shit. Shit. This was a bad, bad situation. Sweat dampened her body and her back was hurting like hell. *Calm down, Jess. Deep breaths.*

"Are you insane?" Sylvia straddled Kinslow and sat down on him, pinning his free arm beneath one knee just in case he moved, Jess supposed. "Let me have that." She reached for the detonator.

"Get out of here!" Jess ordered. "Now! There's no way I'm letting go!"

The senator and Taylor were shouting for someone to release them as they struggled to get free.

"Very carefully I'll put my hands where yours are," Sylvia insisted, "and then you take that baby out of here."

Jess couldn't do that. "I have to—"

"Listen to me, Jess," Sylvia said, tears spilling past her lashes. "You do not get to be the hero this time. Now go. The only thing that matters is that baby you're carrying."

Her heart thundering, tears blurring her vision, Jess inched her fingers away from Kinslow's as Sylvia inched hers over his. Sylvia pressed her thumb on top of Jess's and she slowly, slowly tugged hers free.

"Now, untie Daddy and Mr. Taylor and get out of here."

Jess scrambled to her feet. She grabbed a pair of scissors from the desk and rushed to the hostages.

"Get out of here," the senator roared.

The sound of boots pounding in the entry hall warned that SWAT was in the house before Jess could get the senator free of his bindings. Dan rushed into the room, Buddy right behind him. *What the hell?*

"What're you—?"

Dan pulled Jess into his arms before she could finish the question and hugged her. "Thank God," he murmured.

"We'll take it from here, Chief," the SWAT commander declared.

Two techs were already on the floor next to Sylvia. Jess didn't want to leave her but she knew she had to. Sylvia gave her a nod and Jess allowed Dan to pull her toward the door.

"I want everyone out who doesn't need to be here," the SWAT commander ordered.

Bodies started filing out—all but one. Buddy Corlew stood his ground. Jess could still hear him shouting at the SWAT commander when she and Dan exited the front door. He was not leaving Sylvia.

"You okay?" Dan asked as he ushered Jess farther from the house.

"I'm good. Sylvia scared the hell out of me but otherwise all went well." She glanced over her shoulder. *She hoped.*

By the time they reached the end of the driveway, Sylvia, the senator, Buddy, and Taylor were coming out of the house. Paramedics rushed forward to assist.

Jess looked around. Half the department appeared to have descended on the scene.

She didn't breathe easy until she heard the announcement that all was clear. Then she wilted against Dan. She tried to breathe but couldn't seem to catch her breath.

Sylvia hurried over and hugged her. "You all right?"

Jess opened her mouth to answer but a strange shift in her pelvis region had her gasping. Water gushed down her thighs.

"Oh my God." She turned to Dan. "I think my water just broke."

CHAPTER TWENTY-EIGHT

Sylvia had long ago removed her shoes. Her feet were killing her. "This is taking forever." She turned and paced the length of the waiting room for the two hundredth time.

"Now, now, Sylvia," Katherine Burnett scolded, "these things take time. Why I was in labor for eighteen hours when I had Dan."

Sylvia clamped her mouth shut. Part of her wanted to tell Katherine she, too, knew a little something about having babies but this was not the time. This was Jess's time. Sylvia blinked back the tears that gathered in her eyes. Jess had saved her father's life today while she had almost gotten them all killed. What had she been thinking when she'd hit that fool over the head?

231

Buddy touched Sylvia's elbow. "Why don't I get us all some coffee?"

Sylvia took a breath. "Coffee would be nice."

Dan Senior stood. "Why don't I give you a hand, Buddy?"

"I could help," Chet Harper rushed to say.

Before Sylvia could blink Buddy, Dan Senior, Harper, Hayes and Chad had exited the waiting room. Sylvia turned to Lori. "Do you think they planned that?"

Lori laughed. "I'm thinking that's exactly what they did."

Katherine waved them off. "Men are not very good at this part. Come on over here and sit with me, sweetie." Katherine urged Andrea Denton, Dan's former stepdaughter with whom he remained close, into a chair. "You look exhausted."

"I had a huge exam," Andrea explained. "And then I drove straight here from Tuscaloosa."

Andrea was a student at the University of Alabama. Dan was very proud of her. The young woman had grown close to Jess as well.

"Any news?" Lily, Jess's sister, her husband Blake and their little girl, Maddie, along with Jess and Lily's Aunt Wanda, piled into the room. They had taken Maddie for ice cream in the cafeteria.

"Not yet," Lori said before Sylvia could.

Blake took a seat and Maddie curled up in his arms. She looked ready for bed. Wanda sat down next to Katherine. Katherine had decided to take

Wanda under her wing by inviting her into several of her ladies' clubs and civic organizations.

Lily checked her watch. "We should be hearing something soon."

"I was just telling the girls," Katherine said, "that I was in labor for eighteen hours with Dan."

"I had my kids fast," Lily said. "Blake Junior came in less than four hours. We barely reached the hospital before Alice made her appearance."

Sylvia surrendered and dropped into a chair. "I'm exhausted." She should check on her mother. Her flight back to Birmingham was supposed to have landed at seven. The paramedics had taken her father to UAB just to be sure he was okay. Once he was settled at Sylvia's house, she'd come here. Her parents would stay with her for a few days since their house was a crime scene for now. Dan had assured her that nothing her father had done would incur criminal charges. For that she was immensely grateful. No matter, her father clearly felt a tremendous amount of guilt.

At some point, she had to tell them about Addison. It wasn't fair to keep her parents in the dark about their granddaughter. However things turned out with Addison, Sylvia intended to do all within her power to make this right.

Plus, she had to tell her family about Buddy. Her father had shaken Buddy's hand for staying at Sylvia's side while the detonator and explosives were deactivated. There'd been no time for real introductions then. Sylvia's heart fluttered with excitement. She wanted her family to know Buddy.

The men returned with coffee all the way around. Sylvia was glad Buddy remembered that she liked hers with two creams.

"Thank you." She sipped the fragrant brew.

He sat down beside her. "You doing okay?"

She nodded. "I'm okay." She turned to him, knowing full well his question was more about her daughter than today's events. "I guess standing in Daddy's study knowing that we could all die any second put things into perspective. I want to know her, Buddy. I do. But if she doesn't want me in her life, I'll understand."

Buddy gave here one of his classic lopsided grins and her heart did a little flip-flop. "She's going to see exactly what I see."

"And just what is that, Mr. Corlew?" she asked quietly. With all the conversations going on in the room no one was paying attention to theirs.

"A smart, gorgeous, and courageous lady."

Sylvia smiled. "I did take out the bad guy today."

"You sure did." He smiled, pride shining in his eyes.

The door opened again and, dressed in scrubs, Dan appeared. The room fell quiet. He grinned from ear to ear. "It's a girl."

Much cheering and hugging and plenty of happy tears took place before Dan made another announcement, "Five people at a time can come in to see Jess and the baby." He beamed a smile at his parents. "Starting with the grandparents and the aunts and uncle." He winked at Andrea as he ruffled Maddie's hair. "I think we can sneak in a couple more."

Maddie squealed with happiness.

Sylvia felt so warm inside. She couldn't wait for her turn to see the baby. She couldn't wait for whatever came next.

She was so glad to be alive. She glanced at Buddy. From this moment forward, she wanted more in her life. Starting with this man.

CHAPTER
TWENTY-NINE

Jess stared at her sweet baby girl. She couldn't believe it. All those years she'd been certain she didn't have time for children. Her career had been top priority. She touched her baby's nose and then opened the blanket swaddled around her to count those precious fingers and toes. Tears filled her eyes yet again.

"You are so beautiful, little one." The baby had a tuft of golden hair. She weighed seven pounds and was twenty inches long. She was perfect. Absolutely perfect. The baby squirmed and stretched. Jess wrapped the blanket around her once more. "Mommy loves you so very much."

Her heart full, she reached up and fingered the precious necklace Dan had given her. The blue agate mother-child cameo hanging from a delicate white gold chain was a gift she would treasure for the rest of her life. She smiled down at the precious bundle in her arms. How was it possible to love anyone else as much as she loved Dan? Yet, she did. The bond had started to form months ago.

A light rap on the door sounded before it opened. Dan stepped in, still grinning broadly and leading his parents as well as Lil and her family and Wanda. And Andrea! Jess's tears started anew. She had never been so happy in her life—except for her wedding day—and she couldn't stop crying.

"Hi, everyone." Jess wished her lips would stop their foolish trembling.

Lil moved to her side. For a moment she couldn't speak. She stood there, fingers pressed to her lips, staring down at the angel in Jess's arms. "She's beautiful."

Her sister kissed Jess on the forehead and then lightly brushed her lips across the baby's sweet little head. "You did good, sis."

Jess tried to blink back the blasted tears but they refused to slow down.

"Oh my heavens," Katherine leaned down and pressed a kiss to the baby's forehead, "she's perfect." She turned a watery gaze to Jess. "Perfect and absolutely beautiful, Jess. I am so proud."

Dan Senior stole a kiss next. "Too precious for words."

Wanda and Andrea took their turns.

"Your mother would be so proud," Wanda assured her.

"Thank you," Jess managed to say.

Dan handed Jess another handful of tissues for the tears that just wouldn't stop flowing. "Thank you. She is perfect, isn't she?"

"What do you think of your little cousin, Maddie?" Blake hoisted the little girl up to have a look.

"I want to play with her," Maddie said without hesitation.

"Soon, sweetie," Jess promised.

Dan cleared his throat to get everyone's attention. "I'd like all of you to meet Beatrice Irene Burnett."

"Oh." Katherine clutched her chest. "She's named after my mother and yours, Jess. How thoughtful of you."

Jess looked up at Dan, and he nodded for her to go ahead. "Dan told me your mother," she said to Katherine, "was called Bea."

"That's right," Katherine said, dabbing at her own new wave of tears.

"We're going to call her Bea."

Dan leaned down and kissed Jess on the cheek. "We're very lucky to be able to share this wondrous event with all of you."

Jess watched as her family exchanged hugs and cried more tears of joy. In her heart, she wished her parents were here as well. She smiled as she watched Dan's father hug him and then shake his hand. But she was okay. She and Dan had their own family now.

Bea was a very lucky little girl.

When the first wave of visitors were out the door, she and Dan had a minute or two alone before the next group would arrive. Everyone wanted to see the baby. Jess was more than happy to show her off, but she would be very glad to have some quiet time alone with her husband and baby girl.

Dan sat down on the edge of the bed. "If you're too tired, we can take a break from visitors for a bit."

Jess shook her head. She didn't want to make anyone wait. For now, she was enjoying watching Dan stare at his little girl. Jess lifted the baby toward him. "You want to hold her again?"

Dan had helped cut her cord, he'd washed and diapered her, but since they were settled in this room he hadn't gotten to just sit down and hold the baby.

"If you don't mind."

Jess passed the soft bundle over to him. Seeing the way he looked at her took Jess's breath. A year ago she wouldn't have believed this moment would ever come. She was so grateful and so very happy that she and Dan had found each other again.

She looked around the room at the dozens of flower arrangements. There was one from Ralph Gant, her old boss at the Bureau. One from Wesley Duvall, her ex. He truly was happy for her. He'd just gotten engaged and would be married later this year. Jess was happy for him, too. Everyone deserved to find their true love. She hoped this one would be Wesley's.

The sound of laughter in the corridor brought Dan's head up. "Here we go." He passed little Bea back to Jess. "I love you."

Jess looked into those gorgeous blue eyes of his and smiled. "I love you."

CHAPTER THIRTY

Lori was on cloud nine as she, Chet, Sylvia and Buddy were allowed their turn to see Jess and the baby. The moment they stepped into the room, Lori clamped her hand over her mouth. Tears spilled down her cheeks.

Jess smiled and motioned her on over.

"You look so beautiful." Lori's voice trembled.

"Thank you."

Jess literally glowed. And the baby...

"She's beautiful." The child looked like an angel. All that pink skin made Lori want to scoop her up and hug her tight.

"Wow." Chet shook his head. "She's so tiny. Chester was eight and a half pounds."

Corlew gave Jess a nod. "You did good, kid."

Sylvia hugged Jess. "She really is beautiful, Jess, and so are you."

"Thank you."

Corlew shook Burnett's hand. "Danny boy, you two sure did it up right. That's one gorgeous little girl."

DEBRA WEBB

The time they could visit passed far too quickly. Lori wished they had more time but Hayes, Cook, and Gina Coleman were still waiting.

Lori gave Jess a hug. Chet gave her a pat on the arm and then shook Burnett's hand. Lori could hardly contain herself as they said their goodbyes.

In the corridor, she tugged Chet toward the nursery. "I want to see the babies before they turn out the lights."

Corlew and Sylvia headed back to the waiting room. Lori was pretty sure those two were an item. "Did you see the way Corlew was holding Sylvia's hand?" she asked in a whisper meant only for Chet.

He nodded. "Hey, I heard how he refused to leave her in there with that bomb. He's got it bad."

Lori moved up to the nursery window and gazed across that sea of babies. She felt giddy. She couldn't wait to have this baby. She wrapped her arms around Chet's. "Can you believe it? We're going to have one of these this year?"

He kissed her on the temple. "It's a dream come true." He leaned down to whisper in her ear. "I think we should go home and celebrate."

Lori tiptoed and kissed him. "I'm ready."

They had plenty to celebrate. They'd solved their case and no one on the team had been injured in the process.

Life was good.

CHAPTER THIRTY-ONE

Sylvia sat in her car for a few minutes before going inside. She and Buddy had talked long into the night last night. Thankfully, her parents had been fast asleep by the time they made it home from the hospital.

She hadn't asked her father about his dealings with Wilson Hilliard and he hadn't volunteered any answers. The truth was, it didn't matter. Whatever happened between her father and that man was in the past. Robert Baron was a good man. Whatever he had done it was for the greater good, of that Sylvia was completely certain.

He would be a fine grandfather as well.

Sylvia gazed across the leather seat and smiled. Buddy parked his Charger and shut off the engine. She had officially introduced him to her parents this morning. Her mother had looked a little uncertain at first but then she'd smiled and given Buddy a hug. Her father, on the other hand, had shaken his hand again and then hugged him as well. Somehow, over breakfast, Buddy had charmed her parents completely.

"Let's do it," Buddy suggested. He got out and came around to her side of the car.

Sylvia willed her body not to shake as Buddy opened the door and she climbed out. He had made *the* call this morning. Addison had agreed to meet with Sylvia. According to Buddy, she had been pleased that Sylvia wanted to know her.

"Deep breath." Sylvia drew in two or three for good measure, and they entered the café Buddy had chosen.

He ordered a couple of beers and escorted her to a table. The waitress left the order at their table.

Sylvia made a face. "I'm not a big fan of beer."

Buddy grinned and pushed the Corona toward her. "You'll learn to like it."

"The way I learned to like you?"

He winked. "Exactly."

Sylvia fingered the label. "Is she here?"

He scanned the small crowd. "Not yet. But she'll be here."

When Sylvia looked up, he added, "I don't mind a little alone time with you."

Warmth spread through her. They'd almost made love last night. He'd had her so hot and bothered she'd nearly ignored the fact that her parents were right down the hall. He'd been the one to hold back. The way he'd kissed her goodnight still made her lips tingle whenever she thought of those few seconds. Buddy Corlew was a master kisser. As well as an inordinately skilled lover.

"I've grown attached to you, Sylvia."

There was something about the way he said the words or perhaps it was the words he chose that made her giggle. She hadn't meant to…couldn't remember the last time she'd made such a silly sound.

"You find that amusing, do you?"

He gave her a stern look but all Sylvia could think about was removing that leather tie from his hair and running her fingers through that silky length. "No." She cleared her throat. "Really. I guess I'm just giddy."

"As I was saying," he began again, "I have feelings for you. Feelings I don't quite know how to handle."

Sylvia bit her lips together. She would not make another sound. Her heart was racing and she could hardly sit still.

"If you don't feel the same way, I totally get it. I just wanted you to know how I feel and that I would like to take our relationship to the next level. Especially since you introduced me to your parents."

Sylvia couldn't bear it any longer. She stared directly into his eyes. "I have feelings for you, too, Buddy. I'm not sure how to handle mine either, but I do know that I want to explore them. I want to spend more time with you…if that's what you want."

He grinned. "That's all I think about night and day."

He kissed her and the weight of the world lifted from her shoulders. Somehow being with Buddy made her completely happy.

When the round of applause started, they pulled apart.

Buddy waved off the cheers. "Most folks who know me have been waiting a long time for this to happen."

"I know I have," Sylvia confessed.

The bell over the entrance door jingled and her attention swung in that direction. Addison wandered in, her gaze sweeping the crowd. Sylvia's breath caught. She turned to Buddy. "I don't know what to say."

He squeezed her hand. "Say what's in your heart."

Sylvia scooted from the booth, smoothed her sweater, and took a deep breath. She walked up to the gorgeous young woman who was her daughter and thrust out her hand. "Hello, Addison, I'm..." And then her jaw locked.

Addison accepted her hand. "You're my mother."

Sylvia nodded. "I'm sure you have a lot of questions."

Addison drew her hand away and shrugged. "A few. Mr. Corlew answered most of them."

Sweet Jesus, Sylvia owed Buddy big for this. She gestured to their table. "Join us. Have you had lunch?"

Addison shook her head. "I hear they have great burgers."

"I'm sure they do."

Sylvia and her daughter spent the next two hours getting acquainted. They both cried and laughed... and cried some more. Eventually, they would discuss other painful topics like the truth about her biological father, and they would talk about Chad. For now, getting to know each other was enough.

Buddy was next to Sylvia, squeezing her hand under the table whenever she needed a little backup.

Right there in that eclectic pub her feelings for Buddy deepened just a little more and they were only getting started.

Look for my next standalone suspense novel, SEE HIM DIE, coming June 25, 2015! Meanwhile, did you miss Jess and Dan's wedding? Did you have a chance to read the story about Jess's first encounter with serial killer Eric Spears? Read on for my gift to you – both Faces of Evil short stories are included with this novel!

THE WEDDING

A FACES OF EVIL SHORT STORY

DEBRA WEBB

CHAPTER ONE

Lost in thought, Deputy Chief Jess Harris removed the crime scene photos from her case board. Her team had caught a double homicide early in the week. The case had appeared cut-and-dried at first. An intruder had entered the home and murdered the homeowner and his best friend. The house had been ransacked and any items of cash ready value such as jewelry had been taken. Sadly, the wife and two teenage daughters had arrived home later to find the awful scene.

Jess studied the photo of the wife and daughters before taking it down. The case had turned out to be anything but a random break-in. The father had been leading a double life that included drug dealing for extra income. The slow economy had driven him to make bad decisions. He and his friend had paid the ultimate price for his mistake.

Within forty-eight hours Jess and her major crimes team had uncovered the truth. None of it was pretty and finding justice for the murdered father and his friend hadn't made any of them feel one iota better. The wife was still a widow and the two daughters were still without a father.

"You know," Lori Wells moved up beside Jess and took the photos from her hands, "this was an unfortunate case to catch this week."

Jess smiled at the detective who was her good friend as well as her maid of honor. "Everyone has secrets, some are just worse than others." Jess removed the final photo. "Tomorrow I'm marrying the man I've been in love with for most of my life. I know him better than most women know the men they marry. More importantly, I trust him completely. That said, it's impossible to know everything."

"She knows all my secrets." Sergeant Chet Harper grabbed the eraser and started removing the written timeline from the board.

Lori narrowed her gaze and issued a warning, "I'd better."

From his desk, Lieutenant Clint Hayes tossed in his two cents worth. "That's why I'm never getting married."

Jess laughed as she turned to the lieutenant. "Because you won't trust anyone with your secrets?" She'd long suspected he had a few.

"I'll never tell." He grinned. "Some secrets should stay that way."

Chad Cook, newly promoted to detective, joined them at the case board. He still walked with a bit of a limp, but he was doing great. His up-close encounter with a follower of the depraved serial killer Eric Spears hadn't kept him down. *Thank God.* Chad had been back to work for a month now. Jess imagined those eight weeks of recovery and physical therapy had been the longest of his life.

"By this time next year," Chad said, "I plan on having a wife of my own with a baby on the way—if I'm lucky."

Jess grinned at him. Chad and Dr. Sylvia Baron, who was Jefferson County's associate coroner and closer to Jess's age than Chad's, had decided they were better at being friends than lovers. Jess was immensely grateful the break-up had been an amicable one. Chad was wise beyond his years. Having just turned twenty-four he had plenty of time. His recent brush with death had obviously made him decide not to waste a moment of it.

"That'll make you the only bachelor, Hayes," Harper challenged as he set the eraser aside. "You might want to rethink your strategy."

Chet Harper and Lori Wells were engaged. The two were getting married next June. Jess still counted her blessings they had been able to pull off their personal relationship without it interfering with their work on the team. Jess didn't want to lose anyone on her very specialized major crimes team. The Special Problems Unit had proved its worth in Birmingham as well as all of Jefferson County. So much so that the Sheriff's Department and the BPD had decided to make the SPU permanent. Jess and her team would be fighting crime throughout Jefferson County for a long time to come.

"Not a chance," Hayes declined. "I like my status and my strategy."

"As interesting as this conversation is," Lori announced, "the Chief and I are calling it a day. We're having a mani-pedi party." She rubbed her hands together in glee. "Twenty-four hours until the wedding!"

Jess checked the time and groaned. "I have so much to do." She headed for her desk. "I don't know why this wedding has to be so complicated."

"Last night's rehearsal went well," Lori reminded her as she gathered her purse and keys. "The dinner was amazing."

Jess hummed an agreeable note. Katherine, Dan's mother, had insisted on a lavish rehearsal dinner for the wedding party since Jess and Dan had opted not to have a sit-down meal after the wedding. Neither she nor Dan wanted to delay their honeymoon flight until the day after the wedding so the dinner option had been taken off the agenda.

As pleasant and fun as last night had been the whole evening had been exhausting. Her soon-to-be mother-in-law and her sister, Lily, had organized a genuinely lovely but hectic wedding week down to the last detail. Jess had sworn she wouldn't complain. She wanted to be happy and to enjoy all the festivities. The truth was, she was simply tired. At forty-two years old and five months pregnant, she wasn't your typical blushing, energetic bride. Right now she'd trade her mani-pedi for a nap.

"We don't get a mani-pedi?" Harper teased.

Lori waved him off. "Please. Tonight is ladies night."

"I guess that means we get a guys' night," Hayes suggested.

Harper shrugged. "I have my son tonight, but you and Cook are welcome to come over for pizza."

"Before you go," Cook said, interrupting the male bonding moment, "we have a little something for you, Chief."

Bag slung over her shoulder, Jess hesitated as she rounded her desk. "What? You guys have done too much already. You shouldn't have bothered with a gift." She'd lost count of the gifts she and Dan had received. In the past two weeks there had been a shower hosted by the bridesmaids, another one hosted by Dan's mother, and yet another one from the BPD. There were also endless gifts from long distance friends—like Wesley Duvall, her ex-husband, and Ralph Gant, her former boss at the Bureau. She didn't need more presents.

From beneath his desk Cook removed a gift wrapped in the traditional snow white paper and tied with an elegant silk ribbon in the same white.

What was she going to do with this wonderful group of people? "You better not make me cry."

"No promises." Lori placed the package on Jess's desk. "It's from all of us."

Jess shrugged off her bag, letting it slip to the floor. She opened the gift with shaking hands. Foolishly, she had hoped to make it through this day with no tears. At this point she wasn't sure she could keep blaming her emotions on the pregnancy. Beneath the glossy wrapping was a white box stuffed with tissue paper. Wrapped carefully in the paper was an eight-by-ten photograph of the entire team framed in Waterford crystal.

"When was this taken?" She didn't remember anyone snapping a photo like this. Judging by the outfit she wore it had been taken in the past couple of months. Lately, she'd had to go with fabrics that had a little stretch to them. The crime scene looked vaguely familiar.

"I had one of my buddies from the Crime Scene Unit take it when we worked that case with the missing cousins," Chad explained.

"Read the inscription on the frame," Lori suggested.

Before she'd even read the engraved words Jess was already swiping at her eyes. "Your family away from home."

"While you're on your honeymoon and then staying home with the baby," Harper said, "we didn't want you to forget about us."

"You don't ever have to worry about that," Jess assured them.

After hugs were exchanged and Jess had totally ruined her mascara, Lori insisted they had to go.

It was Friday after all. The case was closed and Jess had less than a day before her wedding to the man she'd loved for twenty-five years.

CHAPTER TWO

3309 DELL ROAD
MOUNTAIN BROOK, ALABAMA
SATURDAY, DECEMBER 19, 1:30 A.M.

Empty boxes were scattered all over the floor. The distinct evergreen scent of the Fraser Fir mingled with the lingering smell of sugar cookies. Jess stood back and surveyed the enormous tree. Dan had borrowed his father's truck and driven out to the Christmas tree farm first thing Thursday morning. He'd brought the tree into the house and set it up so they could hang the first ornament together before leaving for the office. The beautiful angel sitting on the very top of the tree made Jess smile. They'd hoped to get home early enough after the rehearsal dinner to finish decorating but that hadn't happened.

This morning—yesterday morning, technically—she and Dan had left for work and, according to his mother and Jess's sister, it was bad luck for the groom to see the bride again until the wedding. It was a ridiculous superstition in Jess's opinion, but she wasn't about to test fate. Particularly after the summer she and Dan had survived.

Though she'd missed Dan, Jess and Lily and the bridesmaids had spent the evening doing fun, girlie things. The mani-pedis had been first, and then dinner and going over the preparation list for the big day. Everything was set. Except Jess didn't feel fully prepared.

She wrapped her arms around herself and ran down her mental checklist. Bear, their sweet but huge yellow Lab, was staying with Detective Cook for the next week. Cook had picked him up after work yesterday. Hayes would be keeping tabs on the house for Jess and Dan while they were in Barbados. Harper was in charge of the team in Jess's absence.

Everything had been arranged. She and Dan were packed. Although Katherine and Lily had taken care of all the wedding planning, Jess had selected her gown, the veil and shoes as well as all the flowers and most of the music. The rest she had gladly left in their capable hands. She had never been more grateful for that decision than she was this week. Despite the careful planning and meticulous execution of every little thing, Jess felt oddly out of sorts as the final hours before the wedding ticked away.

Somehow there seemed to be too many things undone. She stared at the tree, inhaling the rich scent. It was almost Christmas and she hadn't hung the rest of the ornaments. She supposed it didn't really matter since they wouldn't even be here for Christmas. Yet, not having a decorated tree in their new home for their very first Christmas as a married couple felt wrong. She wanted to return from their honeymoon and smell the scents of the season all through the house. She wanted them to take down the decorations together the way they had in that tiny apartment near Boston College all those years ago.

Maybe this unsettled feeling was just nerves. Jess pressed her hand to her belly. Her sister had been right about most everything so far. She had hit the twenty-week mark in her pregnancy and only gained a few pounds. The worries about her gown fitting had been unnecessary. It fit like a glove. Finding one she loved hadn't been nearly as problematic as she'd feared. She'd known the moment she saw it that it was the one.

Jess smiled. Tomorrow—today, she reminded herself—she would become Mrs. Daniel Thomas Burnett. She blinked at the emotion that immediately filled her eyes. She had been in love with him since she was seventeen years old. As their college days had come to a close, so had their relationship. They'd spent almost two decades apart and both of them had been married before. Somehow none of that had been able to keep them apart.

"Jess?"

Lily Colburn, Jess's older sister by two years, shuffled into the room, rubbing the sleep from her eyes. The huge hair rollers and well-worn chenille robe reminded Jess of their mom. She vividly recalled watching their mother, dressed in a similar robe and slippers, at the stove making breakfast. On Sunday mornings her hair had always been up in rollers.

"I hope I didn't wake you." Jess had tried to be quiet.

Lily draped an arm around Jess's shoulders and surveyed the tree. "Sweetie, you do realize it's almost two o'clock in the morning and that you're getting married in just over twelve hours? You should be sleeping."

Jess reached up and touched the matching rollers in her own hair. "How can you sleep with these things boring into your skull? Wouldn't it have been easier to go to a salon?"

Lil rolled her eyes. "No salon. I want to do this. Now, all you have to do is climb into that big comfy bed, close your eyes, and focus on something else." She stared at Jess's hands and frowned. "You didn't mess up your manicure, did you?"

"No," Jess grumbled. "I was stringing lights not scrubbing floors." She sighed. "I wanted to decorate the tree before we left." If she'd taken Friday off from work, as everyone had wanted her to, she might have had time. Maybe this child would give her the ability to walk away from work at a decent hour even if all the i's weren't dotted and all the t's crossed.

"All right." Lil walked over to the waist high stack of ornament boxes Jess had accumulated since the middle of October when they started showing up in stores. "We'll decorate your tree, and then you are going to bed."

Jess smiled. "You're sure you don't mind?"

Lil made a sound that was more a grunt than anything else. "As long as we can see to walk down the aisle tomorrow, I don't mind at all."

Jess picked up the box of red crystal bells. "I spent a lot of time selecting these ornaments."

"Money, too," Lil teased.

After hanging an ornament on the tree, Jess shrugged. "It means a lot to Dan and to me that we start traditions that we'll keep year after year. The ornaments are part of it."

Lil hung a shiny silver star. "I know what you mean. Blake and I have ornaments from our first Christmas, too. Those and the ones the kids made when they were little are my favorites."

"You're a good sister, Lil."

"I know." Lil smiled. "You, too."

Jess's cell chimed with an incoming text. She picked up her phone and smiled. "Dan can't sleep either. He and his father are playing cards."

Lil laughed. "We're all going to need naps before the wedding."

I love you, Jess.

Jess smiled as she replied with *love you, too.*

As she reached for another ornament, she decided that maybe she didn't want to sleep at all.

This day was too important to miss a single minute.

7:30 A.M.

A second cup of coffee cleared the haze sufficiently to have Jess tugging the rollers from her hair. Long spirals of blond hair fell around her shoulders. She groaned. Between her puffy eyes and the not so happy feeling in her stomach, she wasn't sure how she would get through the day.

A tap on the door and Lil appeared in the bathroom mirror behind Jess. "Dan's at the door and he insists on speaking to you."

Jess's heart leapt. "He's here?"

"He can't see you, Jess," Lil cautioned. "It's bad luck. Don't you dare poke your head outside that door."

Jess considered her reflection. "Don't worry. If he saw me looking like this he might get cold feet."

"Not a chance, but keep in mind that I'm the one who would have to answer to Katherine if she found out I let Dan see you."

"I won't let him see me," Jess promised. She didn't want anyone seeing her like this!

"All right. Go."

Lil stepped aside, and Jess hurried through the bedroom and down the hall. Sitting on the floor near the Christmas tree, four-year-old Maddie looked up and smiled.

"We gots the same hair, Aunt Jess." She tugged at a long lock of her blond tresses.

Jess smiled down at her little niece. "We sure do. Your mommy swears she can make it beautiful."

Maddie looked about as convinced as Jess felt.

In the entry hall, Jess hesitated to catch her breath. She couldn't actually see Dan through the front door's stained glass, but she could make out his form. Tall, broad shoulders. Her mind easily filled in the rest. With every fiber of her being she wanted to go to him. She wanted to feel his arms around her and to rest her cheek against his chest.

Just a few more hours.

She went to the door and opened it just a crack so they could hear each other without shouting. She pressed her hand to the glass, wishing she could somehow touch him through it. "Good morning."

"Hey. I know I'm not supposed to be here."

Jess heard the smile in his voice and her heart melted a little more. "The rules don't say we can't talk."

His soft laugh had her trembling with the renewed urge to throw open the door and fall into his arms.

"I have something for you." His hand appeared inside the door, a small black velvet box clutched in his fingers.

"Dan." She reached for the box, her fingers lingering on his. The delicious tingles that shivered through her body were almost her undoing. "You didn't have to bring me a gift."

"I know you don't wear a lot of jewelry, but I wanted you to have these."

Her heart pounding, Jess opened the box. Diamond earrings sparkled up at her. "They're beautiful." They must have cost a small fortune.

"I've waited for this day my whole life, Jess. It means the world to me that you want to spend the rest of yours with me."

God, she was going to cry. She pressed her hand to the glass again. "Love you."

On the other side, his hand closed over hers. "Love you."

Jess dabbed at her eyes with the back of her hand. "I'll see you at the altar."

"I'll be there."

CHAPTER THREE

Before Jess could turn away she heard her maid of honor and the bridesmaids coming up the sidewalk. Greetings were exchanged with Dan as he walked away, and then the doorbell rang.

Hoping no one would run when they got a good look at her, Jess opened the door wide and beamed a smile. "Good morning."

"Good morning!" her friends shouted in unison.

"I brought donuts," Gina Coleman, Birmingham's award winning television journalist announced as she waltzed in carrying a Dunkin Donuts box.

"Coffee!" Lori said, strolling in right behind her with a tray of cups from the same donut shop. "And a milk for Maddie."

Dr. Sylvia Baron cruised in next. She lowered her sunglasses enough for a closer inspection of Jess's face. "You look like hell, Harris. We have to do something about that ASAP."

266

Jess wanted to hug the snarky medical examiner. This was exactly what she needed this morning. *Normalcy.* "To the kitchen, ladies."

Halfway down the entry hall, the group stopped at the door to the living room to admire the Christmas tree.

"It's very elegant, Jess," Gina raved.

Jess was quite proud of how the tree had turned out. She and Dan had selected genuinely beautiful ornaments that evoked the Christmas spirit. Nothing too frilly or showy, just—as Gina said—elegant.

"Wow. You have to show me how to do this." Lori turned to Jess. "It's really gorgeous. So's the mantel."

"Lily is the one with the real talent," Jess admitted. "Save your compliments for her. All I did was follow her directions."

"You have to stop this," Sylvia scolded. "You and your sister are making the rest of us look bad."

Laughing, they moved onward to the kitchen. Lil and Maddie were already munching on bacon and eggs.

After greetings and hugs were exchanged, the ladies gathered around the kitchen island to indulge in the scrumptious breakfast Lil had prepared. She'd even baked homemade biscuits. Her sister was really going the extra mile to make this day special.

Jess sipped her coffee. "Did you sleep at all after we finished the decorating?"

Lil grinned. "I'll never tell."

"Okay. We're supposed to be at St. Paul's by two, right?" Sylvia surveyed the faces around the island.

Lil nodded. "Katherine has a limo picking us up at one-thirty."

"The groom and his party have a suite at the Tutwiler. They're getting a limo, too," Jess said. "They won't be arriving at the cathedral until after three."

The Tutwiler, Birmingham's historic hotel, was only a few blocks from St. Paul's, but Katherine had insisted on taking care of all transportation needs for the entire wedding party. The reception would be held in the Tutwiler's grand ballroom. From there, Jess and Dan would be whisked away to the airport for the flight to their weeklong honeymoon.

"You're all packed for the honeymoon?" Gina asked as she selected another slice of crunchy bacon.

"We are." Jess reached for another slice as well. "Everything's at the Tutwiler. We'll be able to change there before we leave." She looked around the kitchen. "We won't be back home for a whole week." She had never stayed away from work for seven days. Her vacations had always been working ones or short visits with Lil and her family.

Strangely enough the idea that she wouldn't be *home* for all that time and wouldn't see Bear bothered her the most. For the first time since she was ten years old, she felt a connection to a place.

This was home.

"Did you get the nursery decorated?" Lori asked.

Jess sighed. "We decided to wait until we get back. There's just been too much to do with settling into the new house and pulling together a wedding in barely three months."

"Don't worry," Sylvia said with a mischievous glance at Jess, "Katherine will probably have it done by the time you get back."

Jess waved a finger. "No sarcastic remarks or thoughts about my soon-to-be mother-in-law. I live by that rule now."

The laughter that followed her announcement warmed Jess. She genuinely cherished these women.

Maddie licked the milk from her upper lip. "I want make-up now."

"Princesses always go first," Gina said, tapping the little girl's nose.

"Before the make-up," Sylvia announced, "we have massages, facials, and the removal of any unsightly hair."

This was the first Jess had heard about a mini-spa—not that she was opposed, mind you. "I hope I wasn't supposed to schedule those."

The doorbell chimed. Sylvia smiled. "That will be Antonio."

Uncertain what to expect, Jess and the other ladies, including Maddie, followed Sylvia to the front door.

"Antonio." Sylvia opened the door wider. "You're timing is perfect as always."

"It's a pleasure to be at your service, Dr. Baron."
Antonio gifted Sylvia with an air kiss.

"Come in, gentlemen." Sylvia waved her arm and
Jess along with the rest of the bridal party backed
out of the way.

Antonio, followed by four other muscular, good-
looking men of Latino descent, swaggered into the
entry hall.

Sylvia hung an arm around Jess's shoulders.
"This is the bride, gentlemen. She needs a nice,
deep massage before her facial."

"I want Sylvia to be my wedding planner," Lori
murmured.

Jess smiled. Leave it to Sylvia to keep things
interesting.

NOON

The sound of the doorbell echoed through the
house.

"That's probably the delivery guy!" Lori shouted
from the kitchen. "I'll get it."

Jess was absolutely certain she could not eat—
unless it was chocolate. Thankfully breakfast had
stayed down, but if she dared consume a bite now
she was doomed. Her nerves were frayed. She stared
at her reflection and heaved a big sigh.

"This is the happiest day of your life so far."
And it was. It really was. She wanted it to be perfect. She wanted it to be all that Katherine Burnett
had dreamed it would be, and more importantly,

she wanted it be filled with memories she and Dan would cherish forever. The facial and massage had been wonderfully relaxing. All would be exactly as it should be if her hair would only cooperate.

"We'll get it," Gina assured Jess as she gazed over her shoulder and into the mirror. "I know what you're going for."

"That's what Lily said an hour ago." Jess was going to be the first bride to stroll down the aisle at St. Paul's who looked a mess.

For some reason Lily and Maddie's hair had fallen into soft, lush waves. Maddie wore the sweetest sparkly tiara. Lily's hair was up in a French twist. Lily swore that sleeping in those massive rollers had given her hair just the right amount of fullness and body.

Jess was reasonably confident her sister had made up that part.

"I don't know. Maybe I'll have to go with an up-do like Lil's." Jess had really wanted her hair down since her gown was an off-the-shoulder one.

She still remembered the one and only photo she'd ever seen of her parents' wedding day. The small, framed photograph had sat on the bedside table in their bedroom. Her mother had worn an off-the-shoulder gown, and her long blond hair had draped her shoulders like a curtain of wavy silk. Jess supposed she'd been thinking of her mother when she chose her own gown.

"Try not to worry." Gina dug her cell phone from her purse. "I'll call my stylist and see if I can get her over here ASAP."

Jess felt ill. Her nerves were twisted into a thousand knots.

"Jess."

She turned as Lori entered the master bathroom. "Tell me you have a hair genie who can transform this…" Jess stared at her reflection again. "Oh, for heaven's sake."

"Your aunt is in the living room," Lori said gently. "She said she has something for you."

Jess frowned. Wanda Newsom had been invited to the wedding. She'd received her invitation. No question. Jess had gotten the RSVP. Had something come up? Was she here to give her regrets in person?

Whatever mistakes Wanda had made in the past, Jess's new motto was never to take family and friends for granted—or to hold their past transgressions against them.

"I'll be back," she promised Gina.

How was it that women like Gina and Sylvia could look so beautiful so effortlessly?

Jess sighed as she tightened the sash of her robe and headed for the living room. Her hair didn't have to be perfect. The gown, the flowers, and the cathedral would be perfect. No one was going to care what her hair looked like.

"Besides you," she muttered.

Wanda stood in the living room admiring the Christmas tree. Jess paused at the door a moment and considered how nice her aunt looked. She wore a well-fitting skirt and jacket, both in a soft powder pink. Her gray hair was styled in an attractive fashion.

Sensing Jess's presence, Wanda turned around and smiled. The apprehension on her face warned that she worried she'd intruded or overstepped somehow by coming to the house.

"Your home is just beautiful, Jessie Lee."

"Thank you." Jess moved into the room, noting that Wanda carried a small white gift bag. "You didn't need to bring a gift."

Wanda held the bag out. "I came across this as I was digging through a couple of old boxes I found in the attic. I thought you might want it for today."

Jess accepted the bag. "That's very thoughtful of you." She gestured to the sofa. "Won't you sit down?" Jess wanted to shake Lil for not joining them. Lori had no doubt told her Wanda was here.

"I know you're busy. I don't want to be in the way."

As much as Jess resented that Wanda had not been there for her and Lil when they had needed her so very badly, she simply didn't have the heart to hold it against her any longer. "You're not in the way." Jess sat down with a plop. "Right now I'm so frustrated with my hair, I need a break anyway."

Wanda settled on the sofa, her back stiff as if she feared she'd chosen the wrong place to sit. "I'm certain you'll be beautiful no matter how you wear it. You look so much like your mother."

The compliment caused a decided bump in the rhythm of Jess's heart. "Thank you." She opened the bag and reached inside. The delicate silver chain bracelet was adorned with small blue gemstones. "It's lovely."

"It was my mother's," she explained. "Your grandmother's. I wore it at my wedding and your mother wore it when she married your father. I don't know how I managed not to lose it or…anyway, I thought you might want to wear it. It's so delicate it's hardly visible so it won't clash with your colors, and it gives you something blue."

Her hands trembling, there was no way Jess would even attempt to fasten the bracelet around her wrist. "I'm so glad you found it. Thank you."

"You know," Wanda knotted her hands together in her lap, "I fixed your mother's hair for her wedding. Would you like me to try doing something similar with yours?"

Jess thought of her mother's wedding photo. "You know, that's a wonderful idea. The half up, half down do my mother wore is what I wanted."

"I'll give it a try, if you'd like."

Jess stood, the delicate bracelet clutched in her right hand. "I would really appreciate your help."

While she showed Wanda through her home, the doorbell rang again. This time it was the pizza. Surprisingly, Jess's appetite had awakened. She might have a slice after all.

CHAPTER FOUR

Dan reached for his tux jacket. He slipped it on and adjusted the lapels.

His father clapped him on the back. "It's almost time, son."

Dan smiled. He was so grateful to have his father as his best man for this amazing moment. A few months ago he'd thought he had lost him, but Daniel Thomas Burnett, Senior, had survived his second heart attack as well as the brutal assault of a serial killer.

"I'm ready." Dan couldn't wait to begin this journey with Jess. "You have the ring."

His father patted his chest. "Interior jacket pocket."

"You're not getting cold feet on us, are you, Danny boy?"

Dan glanced at the most recent addition to his lineup of groomsmen. "Not a chance, Corlew."

Buddy Corlew was Jess's oldest friend. Dan's cousin had ended up in the hospital earlier this week with acute appendicitis. Corlew was standing in for him. Fortunately, his cousin's tux had been a perfect fit since it had been too late to order and tailor another one. Dan doubted Corlew had ever or would ever again be caught in a tuxedo. A former BPD detective and a little rough around the edges, Corlew made his living as a private investigator. He was a damned good one, Dan had to admit, even if some of his methods skirted the law.

Frank Teller slid his cell into his pocket and held his hands up in surrender before Dan could remind him yet again to turn the damned thing off.

"It's off. I swear." The man was one of Dan's oldest friends and a highly respected Birmingham attorney. "You know how it is, there are some calls you just have to take."

"I guess I missed the bachelor party," Corlew said, drawing Dan's attention back to him. He leaned against the conference table. "What'd you guys do, discuss your financial portfolios?"

"Funny, Corlew." Dan adjusted his black bow tie. "My bachelor days have been over for a while."

"I figured as much." Corlew grinned. "Don't worry, last night I celebrated the demise of your bachelorhood for you. Umm-hmm. Not one but two strippers—twins—helped me celebrate. It doesn't get better than that."

"Did you take pictures?" Frank wanted to know.

"Don't encourage him," Dan advised. "Corlew, you're the only person I know who would talk about strippers in the boardroom of St. Paul's."

"Come on now. I'm just pulling your leg. I was on surveillance last night. I'm working a big case. It does, however, involve twins. They share an apartment and apparently don't ever close the blinds. They did this little—"

A rap on the door preceded Mary Green's entrance. "Gentlemen, we'll be proceeding to the sanctuary in five minutes."

Anxious to get started, Dan smiled. "Thank you, Mary."

"I'll just have a quick look to make sure all is in order." She surveyed each of them from their red rosebud boutonnieres to their well-polished black leather oxfords. "Very good, gentlemen. I believe we're ready."

She flashed Dan a smile of approval and closed the door once more. Mary, the cathedral's wedding coordinator, had kept his mother in line. Katherine Burnett had a tendency to go overboard. Dan had to give her credit though, she had done a wonderful job with the wedding. More importantly, she'd been respectful of Jess's wishes. He'd worried about that in the beginning.

"Have you and Jess decided if you're running for mayor next year?" Frank asked.

Dan had wondered how long it would be before his old friend would inquire about those rumors. Dan had been offered the position when Joseph Pratt had stepped down, but he'd decided to hold off. He liked being chief of police. He and Jess had been busy with their personal lives the past few months. Buying a home, getting settled, and preparing for the baby's arrival next spring had been their primary focus. The timing simply hadn't been right. The deputy mayor who had actually planned to retire stepped in until the next election. The powers that be were still leaning on Dan for an answer on the upcoming election. Jess insisted the decision was his. He wasn't saying no just yet, but he was far from a yes.

"We'll consider the proposal in the spring." The position of mayor required a tremendous commitment, personally as well as professionally. With the baby coming he wasn't sure he wanted to spend more of his time away from home. They had a great deal to consider before he made a decision.

"I spoke to Sylvia at the rehearsal dinner," Frank said, "she mentioned that Nina is doing extraordinarily well at the new clinic."

Nina was Dan's second wife and Sylvia's younger sister. She'd suffered with mental illness her entire adult life. The outlook had been quite dire the past few years. Now, however, a new medication recently approved by the FDA was helping her to make great strides at an innovative facility in New York.

"If she continues on her current path, she may be home in a few months. She's made an incredible turnaround."

"It's a miracle," his father agreed. "Your mother and I are very happy for her family."

"Speaking of miracles and Barons," Corlew said, "what kind of miracle would it take to get you to swap bridesmaids with me, Teller?"

Frank raised a skeptical eyebrow. "I think Mrs. Burnett and Mrs. Green would have something to say about that, Corlew."

Dan grinned. It shouldn't but the idea that Corlew was uncomfortable escorting Sylvia gave him just a little glee. "What's the matter, Corlew? You afraid Sylvia might bite?"

"I don't think she likes me too much." He shifted his attention back to Frank. "I'll even throw in a bonus and teach that investigative team of yours some of my secrets."

"No way," Frank said. "I'm not getting in trouble with Dan's mom. I've been down that road, Corlew. Believe me, you do not want to go there."

Dan laughed. "You'd better listen to him, Corlew."

"I know I would," Dan Senior agreed.

Corlew shook his head. "Maybe you have a point. She's been on my back all week about cutting my hair." He shook his head. "I was afraid to go to sleep at night. The lady is persistent."

Dan hadn't missed the wedding coordinator's raised eyebrows at Corlew's ponytail. Corlew was about as far from a good Catholic boy as one could be, but he was Jess's friend. Back in high school, Dan and Corlew had been serious enemies, but those days were over. Dan owed the man. He was proud to have Corlew as one of his groomsmen.

The door opened and Mary waved her arm. "This way, gentlemen."

His father placed a hand on Dan's arm. "Just a minute, son."

"We need a moment," Dan said to Mary.

"We'll be waiting for you." Mary ushered Corlew and Frank into the corridor and closed the door.

His father took him by the arms and smiled. Dan didn't miss the sheen of tears in his eyes.

"You're a good man, Dan. Your mother and I are immensely proud of you, not only for the way you've served this city but also for the outstanding human being you've always been. From the time you were old enough to have a paper route you were kind and helpful to others. It makes our hearts glad to know that we had a little something to do with making you the man you are today."

Dan blinked back some tears of his own. "Thank you, Dad. I wish I could take the credit, but I have an excellent role model to follow."

His father smiled. "We've always respected your decisions, and never once have we doubted the plans you've made." His father squeezed his arms. "I just want you to know that we are especially thankful you're marrying Jess."

Dan couldn't speak for a moment.

"You and I both know your mother wasn't so keen on Jess back when the two of you were kids, but she realizes now how wrong she was. Jess is a wonderful woman. We're very pleased to be welcoming her to the family not only as your wife but as our daughter."

"That means more than you can know, to both of us."

"We're going to spoil your children every single day." His father laughed. "I can't tell you how grateful I am to be here for this day. Your mother and I are looking forward to many, many more wondrous events with you and your new family."

Dan hugged his father hard. "I love you, Dad."

"I love you, son." His father drew back. "Today you'll watch your bride walk down the aisle toward you the way I watched your mother walk toward me all those decades ago."

"I can't wait."

"Right now," his father laughed, "if we keep Mary waiting any longer, she'll be calling your mother to come and light a fire under us."

Dan laughed. "We should go then."

He'd been waiting for this moment a very long time.

CHAPTER FIVE

While Lily helped Maddie pick up the rose petals she'd decided to spread around a little early, Jess took a moment alone before the call to take their positions. She stood in the room that had been designated as the dressing room for the bride. When Katherine had first suggested having the wedding at St. Paul's, Jess hadn't been very happy. She hadn't wanted a big formal wedding. She'd wanted a private ceremony with only close family and friends. Sometime during the past couple of months, Jess had changed her mind.

This cathedral had graced downtown Birmingham for more than one hundred twenty years. It's neo-gothic architecture and incredible stained glass windows made it awe inspiring. Jess had never been inside until the wedding planning began. If she'd thought the exterior was beautiful, the interior was breathtaking. The granite columns, vaulted ceiling, and arches soared high overhead to the ornate domed ceiling. Rich hand hewn wood floors filled the space with warmth. Something about the sacred beauty and history had changed her feelings about a big wedding. Knowing that Katherine and Dan Senior had taken their vows here had sealed the deal for Jess. This was another of the traditions she and Dan wanted to have in their lives.

She pressed her hand to her belly. A few months from now, they would be baptizing their child here. Perhaps their son or daughter would one day take his or her vows in this cathedral.

Jess moved to the full-length mirror and checked her reflection one last time. The gorgeous earrings Dan had given her twinkled from her earlobes. Her wedding gown was only the third one she'd tried on and both Lily and Lori had urged her to look at others, but this had been the one. The gown was made of soft, elegant tulle overlaid with lace and accented with a grosgrain belt and a crystal gemstone bow. The three-quarter-sleeved wrap-over bodice was fashioned from the most exquisite lace. Jess loved the way it hugged her body. The floor length A-line skirt of the gown was embellished with lace appliques and a scalloped hem. The matching sheer veil fastened at the back of her head allowing the gauzy fabric to drape down her back and along the length of her gown. Jess adored the way it featured the same lovely lace and crystal appliques. The soft ivory color of the gown and veil made her skin appear more radiant.

Wanda had done a marvelous job with her hair. The half up do was exactly the look she'd wanted. Wanda was right about Jess looking like her mother. Blinking back the tears that would ruin her make-up, she fingered the delicate silver bracelet. "Wish you were here."

A knock on the door sounded about two seconds before Lily, Maddie, and the others poured into the room with the soft rasps of tulle, satin, and taffeta.

"Oh my God, Jess," Gina cried. "You look…" She pressed her fingers to her lips.

Sylvia smiled, her lips trembled just a little. "What she's trying to say," she finished for Gina, "is that you look stunning."

Lori nodded. "You were right, Jess. This gown was the one."

Maddie touched one of the lace appliques. "Looks like my dress."

"It sure does," Jess agreed. As the flower girl, Maddie's little dress had been made to complement Jess's.

"Dan is simply going to melt when he sees you," Lily promised.

"Thank you." Jess surveyed her sister and dear friends. "And look at all of you." Lily and Lori wore dresses of silver satin and taffeta. The formfitting bodices and long sleeves flowed into cinched waists and floor-length A-line skirts. Gina and Sylvia's were a deep Christmas red in that same striking fabric. The dresses glittered as if they'd all been dusted with diamonds. Jess sighed. "Just wow."

Lily hugged her, careful of their make-up and dresses. "I'm so happy for you and Dan."

"Okay, okay, ladies," Sylvia scolded, "no tears. We have a few last minute details to cover."

Lori stepped forward. "You have something new."

Jess touched one of the diamond earrings Dan had given her and smiled. "Yes."

"The chief also gave you something a long time ago that you asked me to be sure you didn't forget to bring." Lori held out the locket Dan had given Jess when they were seniors in high school.

Jess's breath caught. "Thank you for remembering, Lori."

Gina held Jess's hair and veil aside while Lori fastened the tiny catch. The cool white gold of the locket rested against Jess's throat. Inside was a photo of her and of Dan. God, they had been so young. Jess had kept this locket safely tucked away for more than two decades.

She touched the cherished locket, relished the feel of it against her skin. "This was the first important gift Dan gave me."

"Stop," Lily protested, "you're going to make me tear up again!"

"Moving on," Sylvia announced. "You have something blue, that leaves the something borrowed. I brought the something borrowed." She handed Jess a lady's handkerchief. Tiny pink flowers were embroidered on the soft ivory linen. "My great grandmother brought that handkerchief with her from Ireland. You may borrow it for this auspicious occasion."

Gina produced Jess's bouquet. "We thought you could tuck it into the bouquet in case you need it."

"Good idea." Jess bit her lips together to stop their trembling. Tears brimmed on her lashes as she clutched her bouquet. She had selected every flower being used today and simply looking at them made her heart glad. They were so very lovely. Roses of red and varying blush shades, cream colored tulips, and orchids, with baby's breath and delicate silver sprigs as accents. In the cathedral were more roses, tulips, and orchids, along with hydrangeas. The ends of all the pews were festooned with silk ribbons and hanging drifts of the gorgeous flowers. It was so lovely.

"Since I'm walking you down the aisle for Dad," Lily spoke up, "I brought the six pence for your shoe."

More emotional laughter had Jess battling tears. Lori helped Lily to place the small silver coin in Jess's shoe.

Jess took her sister's hand in hers. "Thank you, Lil, for being an amazing big sister."

Lil squeezed her hand. "Any time."

A fluttering deep inside made Jess gasp.

"Are you all right?" Lori searched her face, worry in hers.

Jess smiled, more of those confounding tears burning her eyes. "I think I just felt the baby move."

"Oh!" Lil placed a hand on Jess's belly. "Isn't it incredible?"

Another of those little butterfly flutters made Jess gasp again. "It's incredible."

"Tissues!" Sylvia rushed across the room and grabbed the box.

Jess couldn't help smiling as her friends dabbed their eyes. Lori handed Jess a tissue and she did the same. A rap on the door made them all jump.

"That's probably the wedding coordinator," Lil warned. "It's almost time."

Lori went to the door and opened it. She looked surprised. "Just a moment," she said to whoever was on the other side of the door before turning to Jess. "There's someone here to see you."

"As long as it's not Dan," Lil cautioned.

Lori shook her head and opened the door. Wesley Duvall walked in.

Jess's breath caught again and this time it had nothing to do with the baby. "Wesley!" He'd said he was coming. She was glad to see he'd made it.

"Jess." He nodded to the others. "Ladies."

Before Jess could make any introductions, Wesley kissed her on the cheek. "You are simply glowing, Jess."

Wesley Duvall was her ex-husband. They'd realized soon after the marriage that they were better at being friends. "Thank you, Wesley." Jess glanced at her friends. "Does everyone know Wesley? He's—"

"The fool who let her get away," Wesley announced.

Sylvia thrust out her hand. "Sylvia Baron."

Wesley shook Sylvia's hand. "Wesley Duvall."

"Gina Coleman." Gina shook his hand next.

"We've met," Lori said with a nod and a brush of palms.

"Yes, Detective Wells, we certainly have."

Lil took her turn but opted to give him a hug rather than shake his hand. "Did you see Blake and the kids out there?"

"I did. In fact, I'm sitting with your family. The usher said that's where I was to sit. I hope that's right."

"You are family," Jess assured him. She and Dan had discussed the issue of exes. Annette Denton and her daughter Andrea were seated with Dan's mother. Technically, now that all the required paperwork was done, neither she nor Dan had an ex. This would be their first and only marriage in the eyes of the Church.

Wesley smiled. "I have to leave right after the ceremony and I was afraid I wouldn't be able to say hello so I convinced the wedding coordinator to give me a moment." He took Jess's hand in his and gave it a squeeze. "I wanted to tell you that I'm so happy for you and Dan. I look forward to an invitation to the christening."

"Absolutely," Jess promised.

After a careful hug, Wesley hurried away to take his seat. Mary returned with the three-minute warning.

After more careful hugs and air kisses, the bridal party filed out of the dressing room and moved to the vestibule. Jess could hardly hold herself together as the heartrending notes of Canon in D Major filled the cathedral. Buddy sneaked over and gave her a hug.

"Love you, kid," he murmured, almost starting a flood of fresh tears. Thank God for Sylvia's great-grandmother's hankie.

A moment later Buddy wrapped Sylvia's arm around his and started their walk down the center aisle.

Next Frank Teller escorted Gina along that same path.

Dan's father left a kiss on Jess's cheek before taking Lori's arm and heading down the aisle.

"Ready, sis?" Lil asked, her face beaming with the same happiness filling Jess so completely.

Jess nodded.

The wedding coordinator gave the signal.

With Maddie leading the way, Jess and Lil moved into the main aisle. The guests rose and turned to watch as Jess and Lil started forward. Sweet little Maddie wandered along just as she'd been instructed, leaving a trail of red and cream colored rose petals.

Jess's gaze settled on Dan who looked so very handsome in his black tuxedo. Despite how much time had passed, they had never stopped loving each other. No force on earth had been able to keep them apart.

When it came time to take their vows, Dan and Jess stood facing each other. It was as if they were the only two people in the cathedral. All other thought vanished and there was only the man Jess loved with all her heart standing before her.

"I Daniel Thomas take thee Jessie Lee…"

The sweet words he spoke wrapped her heart with such love and tenderness, filling her with a sense of being honored and treasured.

"I Jessie Lee take thee Daniel Thomas…"

She pledged her endless love and devotion to him, her voice catching ever so slightly at the incredible happiness shining in his blue eyes.

"You may kiss your bride…"

Dan smiled down at her for a moment before taking her into his arms and kissing her breath away.

"Ladies and gentlemen, I give you Mr. and Mrs. Daniel Thomas Burnett."

CHAPTER SIX

The photographer didn't need to tell Jess to smile. She couldn't stop. The formal photos had been taken. The toasts had been made and the gorgeous cake had been cut. Jess wasn't sure she'd ever seen a cake so beautiful or so enormous. Five luscious layers of decadent red velvet cake covered in sweet cream cheese frosting generously embellished with sweet fondant jewels. The middle layer was monogrammed with the letter B and crowned with silver and crystal columns that supported the top two layers. It looked as extravagant as it tasted.

"Are you enjoying yourself, Mrs. Burnett?"

Jess peered up into Dan's eyes and her smile widened. "I am, Mr. Burnett. The wedding was everything I'd dreamed it would be." Jess laughed. "Once I got used to the idea of a *big* wedding anyway." She gave her head a little shake. "Really, Dan, it was perfect. Absolutely perfect."

"The Tutwiler was a good choice for the reception." He surveyed the hundred fifty or so guests still celebrating, some swaying to the soft notes of the music drifting from the band, others simply mingling.

Dan's mother had personally overseen the decorating of the ballroom. The lights, the classic holiday ornaments, and the flowers, all of it was simply magnificent.

"All right, ladies and gentleman," the bandleader announced, "let's clear the dance floor for the bride and groom's first dance."

Dan leaned close. "You finally get to hear the song I selected for our first dance as husband and wife."

"I can't wait to hear it." He smiled and Jess's heart skipped a beat. His smile had always had that effect on her.

Dan led her to the middle of the dance floor accompanied by a round of applause. She wished she'd held onto Sylvia's great-grandmother's handkerchief now. She'd been afraid it would be lost so she'd given it back to Sylvia once all the formal photos had been taken.

The slow easy notes of the song began as Dan took her into his arms. The female member of the band stepped to the microphone and started to sing.

At last...

My love has come along...

Jess's eyes filled with emotion as Dan guided her smoothly to the easy, gentle rhythm of the music. She looked up at him and whispered, "Good choice."

Their life together was finally exactly where it should be.

At last...

"I love you, Jess."

She smiled. "Love you, too."

"Earlier you said you had something to tell me."

After the ceremony there hadn't been a moment of time alone. Though they weren't alone now, the dance allowed a hint of privacy. "I felt the baby move."

"You did?" His face lit up. "Did it feel like a butterfly's wings?"

The books they'd read had described the first movements a mother could feel as a fluttery sensation. "It really did."

"I can't wait to feel him move."

"Her," Jess reminded her new husband.

Dan laughed. "I guess we'll know when the time comes."

They had opted not to be told the baby's sex. Why spoil the fun? They were planning to decorate the nursery in shades of soft yellow and green with a little blue and pink here and there.

"When I saw you coming toward me, Jess, I couldn't breathe for a minute. You are so very beautiful. I wouldn't have thought it possible for you to look even more stunning than you do everyday and somehow you did."

"I felt the same about you, Mr. Burnett."

"We're very lucky."

Jess nodded. "We surely are."

The final notes of the song faded and the applause began. Dan leaned down and kissed Jess until she was dizzy.

"Excuse me, son."

Jess turned to Dan Senior and smiled. "Are you cutting in?"

He gave Jess a nod as Dan stepped aside. "No one can take the place of your father, Jess, but, if you'll have me as a stand-in, I'd love to share the father-daughter dance with you."

Battling another wave of tears, Jess hugged him. "I would be honored."

What a Wonderful World floated through the air and Jess felt as if she were bursting with happiness. Across the dance floor, Dan danced with his mother. Soon, more couples joined them. Blake and Lil made a lovely couple. Blake Junior twirled Maddie around the floor. His sister Alice carried three-year-old Chester, Chet's son, around the dance floor.

Jess almost laughed out loud when she saw Buddy with Sylvia cuddled in an intimate embrace. She was reasonably sure Sylvia had indulged in a little extra champagne to allow Buddy Corlew to put his arms around her so tightly. Chet and Lori whispered to each other as they swayed with the music. Chad Cook danced with Gina Coleman and Clint Hayes maintained his wallflower status. Jess was very happy that every member of her team was here, alive and well.

As the official parts of the evening were concluded, Jess lost all track of time. There were so many congratulations and hugs exchanged her head was spinning. Lori was still beaming after having caught Jess's bouquet.

Ralph Gant, Jess's former boss at the Bureau, had even traveled all the way from Virginia for the wedding. Jess had spent a few weeks trying to be angry with him, but she'd failed miserably. Gant would always be a sort of father figure in her life. As much as she might deny it, she'd worked with him for two decades and she couldn't pretend she didn't care about him.

Deputy Chief Harold Black caught up with her at the bar when she went for another glass of water. No matter that he'd lost his wife last month, he found a way to be here and that meant a great deal to Jess.

"Harris, I have to tell you, with the exception of my wife, I have never seen a more radiant bride."

Jess smiled. "Thank you, Chief. I'm glad you came." She wouldn't have blamed him if he'd wanted to pass on the invitation. The loss of his wife was so recent.

"I wouldn't have missed it." He gave her a hug. "You and Dan have a wonderful honeymoon. I'll check in with your team from time to time to see if they need anything."

"Thank you, Chief. That's very thoughtful of you."

"I suppose it's time we dropped all the formality. If you'll call me Harold, I'll call you Jess."

"I can do that."

He gave her another hug. "I'll have a word with Dan and then be on my way."

Jess watched as Dan chatted so easily with the power players of the city and the elite of Birmingham society. They were all here, too. Senator Baron, Sylvia's father, was among them. They all wanted Dan to agree to run for mayor. If he agreed, they would make it happen. Jess intended to stay out of that one. She was fine either way.

"Jess."

She smiled as Katherine Burnett joined her. "I don't think I've had the opportunity to tell you how lovely you look, Katherine."

Dan's mother had chosen a striking beaded suit in a gorgeous deep rose. The fit of the jacket as well as the pencil skirt showed off her trim figure. Her dark hair was fashioned in a lovely bun that accentuated her high cheekbones. Katherine really was a beautiful woman.

"Thank you, Jess." She gazed across the crowd. "Everything turned out beautifully. Sharon Pace from the *Birmingham News* was quite impressed. I expect a full page in the Lifestyle section as well as a front-page headline. This was the event of the year, hands down."

Jess hugged her. "Thank you, Katherine, for making this day more special than I could have ever imagined."

Katherine blinked rapidly, holding back tears. "Why, you're welcome, Jessie Lee." She dabbed at her eyes with a handkerchief. "I wouldn't have wanted anything less for you and Dan. The two of you are my world."

Jess tried to hold back the tears but it wasn't happening. "I know that." She nodded. "And…I love you for it."

"Oh, sweetie." Katherine hugged her tight. "I love you, too."

When they had their emotions under control once more, they both laughed and shared Katherine's handkerchief. Jess would never forget that moment. Something had changed in Katherine…or maybe Jess was the one who'd changed. Either way, it felt good.

Before the crowd could thin too much, Jess and Dan changed into their traveling clothes and said their goodbyes. More photographs were snapped as they rushed from the entrance of the historic hotel beneath a shower of bubbles.

A gleaming white limousine waited. Jess settled into the elegant leather seat and Dan slid in next to her. Their luggage was already in the trunk. With final waves, the limo rolled forward, leaving the crowd of well-wishers behind.

Jess leaned against Dan and sighed. "I'm exhausted. I'm certain I'll sleep the entire flight."

Dan hugged his arm around her. "Rest while you can, Mrs. Burnett. Once we arrive in paradise, there won't be a minute of rest for either of us."

Jess looked up at him. "Is that a promise, Mr. Burnett?"

"Definitely."

He kissed her. The taste of champagne and cake icing made her want to devour him right here and now. But she could wait. The future was theirs.

At last...

THE FACE OF EVIL

(A FACES OF EVIL SHORT STORY)

DEBRA WEBB

CHAPTER ONE

BIRMINGHAM POLICE DEPARTMENT
BIRMINGHAM, ALABAMA
SUNDAY, AUGUST 29, 11:30 A.M.

Deputy Chief Jess Harris closed her notepad and placed her pencil on the shiny conference table. Her heart thudded so hard it made her chest hurt.

Another young woman was missing, Monica Atmore, a legal secretary in Montgomery. This time there were no games. No question as to who the victim was. The twenty-five year old hadn't come home on Friday night. Her husband reported her missing first thing Saturday morning.

No need to look any farther. Monica Atmore was with Eric Spears aka the Player—one of the most prolific serial killers on the planet. The one obsessed with Jess. The one who wanted to destroy all that she loved. He sent photos of his victims to her just to taunt her. Fury combined with the fear paralyzing her, making her want to scream.

"You'll get an update the moment I have one."

The sound of Supervisory Special Agent Ralph Gant's voice jarred Jess back to attention. Gant was lead in the Joint Task Force attempting to find and stop Eric Spears. He was also Jess's former superior, what felt like a lifetime ago, when she'd worked as a profiler for the Bureau.

Gant's image on the screen faded as the video conference call ended. Chairs squeaked and suits rustled as the rest of the attendees around the table prepared to leave the room. No one said a word to Jess.

There was nothing else to talk about. God only knew where Spears was. He had at least two hostages at this point and there wasn't a solitary lead on his whereabouts or theirs. They had nothing except the reality that every move he made was about *her*.

Jess didn't bother standing nor did she miss the glances from the rest of the members of the Joint Task Force. The two local Bureau agents were the first out of the room. Deputy Chief Harold Black, head of the Crimes Against Persons Division, walked out with Mayor Pratt at his side. Jess didn't care that Black and the others blamed her for this—fact was she blamed herself. What tore her apart was the damage being done to the man she loved.

When the silence had thickened in the room once more, there was only the two of them. She could hardly bear to look at Chief of Police Dan Burnett.

Dear God, she had crashed her career with the Bureau and now she had all but destroyed his. To torment her, Eric Spears had targeted Dan, pitching his career into turmoil and his life into jeopardy.

How in the world would she stop this insanity?

"At least we're not chasing down dead ends trying to identify his latest victim," Dan said, voicing her earlier thoughts. The hint of hope in his tone fell just shy of optimism.

Dan was no fool. He understood the situation was grave for all concerned.

Jess tucked away her pad and pencil and pushed out of her chair. "That's something, I guess." She shouldered her bag and tried her level best not to let him see her hands shaking. "I should get to my office."

As deputy chief of the department's Special Problems Unit, she had work of her own to do. Even as the thought formed, her head spun. Spears would not stop until he had what he wanted. Even if it meant everyone around her was destroyed.

Dan caught her at the door. He cupped her face so gently with his strong hands that she wanted to weep. "This will be over soon. You have my word on that."

The sincerity in his blue eyes was almost her undoing. How could he hope to fulfill that promise? He knew what they were up against—what *he* was facing. And the baby—her heart lurched—protecting the child she carried was her constant worry just now.

"We're doing all we can," she agreed, for his benefit. She tiptoed and brushed a kiss across his jaw.

The warmth and certainty in his eyes chased away some of the cold that seemed her constant companion. "I'll see you tonight."

She left before her emotions got the better of her. That was the thing about being pregnant—keeping her emotions in check was a serious challenge. Good grief, who would have thought when she returned to her hometown, just a few short weeks ago, that she would end up staying for good and back in the arms of the only man she'd ever loved? *And pregnant.*

No wonder her head was spinning.

Sergeant Chet Harper waited in the corridor outside Dan's office. *Her escort.* She wasn't allowed to go anywhere, not even the ladies' room at this point, without an escort.

Harper gave her a nod. "Ma'am, you have a visitor waiting in your office."

Jess frowned. "Should I avoid my office, Sergeant?" She was in no mood to see anyone not part of her team. The media frenzy that hit the news last night was enough attention for the next couple of decades. In the last week, she had gone from being the favored new cop in Birmingham to being the pariah of the city.

"Maybe," Harper allowed. "It's Gina Coleman. We told her you were tied up but she insisted on waiting."

Gina Coleman was the Magic City's award winning investigative journalist. If she was determined to get the scoop on Spears' latest move, she could forget it. Then again, she had done some favors for

Jess recently, and she was undeniably the voice of integrity and substance in the local media. Maybe she could give Gina something. Since returning to her hometown, Jess had learned just how important it was to have an "in" with the local media—even if they made her nuts most of the time.

"All right then, I might as well see what I can do for Ms. Coleman this morning."

By the time they had gone down a flight of stairs and made it to her office, Jess had pushed aside the mountain of worries and prepared a kernel of information she hoped would satisfy Gina.

The other members of the SPU team present this morning looked up as Jess and Harper entered the office. Their working space was nothing more than one big room filled with desks and an empty case board, but it worked. They'd solved their latest case less than forty-eight hours ago.

Gina Coleman stood at the window behind Jess's desk. She looked amazing as always. Sleek, form-fitting white jacket and skirt. A killer pair of white stilettos. Also as usual, not a strand of her lush brunette hair was out of place. Jess resisted the urge to sigh. How was it that some women made looking that good appear so effortless?

"Chief Harris," Gina smiled, "I hoped you might be available for lunch."

As if on cue, Jess's stomach rumbled. Everything tasted better these days. By the time she was ready to have this kid she would surely be enormous. A groan rose in her throat but she kept it to herself.

She and Dan were the only ones who knew about the baby. As if she'd telegraphed the thought, Lieutenant Clint Hayes, the newest member of their team, opened one of his desk drawers. Hayes had learned her secret but he'd sworn to keep it to himself. Jess hated secrets but she just couldn't share this news right now. Not and risk Spears finding out. He would love another pawn to use against her. She couldn't afford to give him any more ammunition.

"Today is not a good day for lunch," Jess admitted. She glanced at Lori Wells, the only female detective on her team. "We usually have a working lunch."

"I called in an order for pizza from Gino's," Lori said, taking Jess's cue.

The uncertainty in her voice almost made Jess cringe. How she wished she could make Lori see that she hadn't done anything wrong. The events that played out in that restaurant on Friday couldn't have been anticipated by anyone.

Coleman gave a nod. "I see." The gleam in her eyes warned she wouldn't be so easily deterred. "I guess you're not interested in what I can do to help."

The hint of something beyond the usual self-confidence in her expression nudged Jess's curiosity. She turned to Lori. "Miss Coleman and I will need some time."

Without meeting Jess's gaze this time, Lori grabbed her purse. "I wasn't in the mood for pizza anyway."

So far, nothing Jess had said had penetrated the layers of guilt overwhelming Lori. She needed time. Unfortunately, time was something they had little of to spare.

"I love pizza," Hayes spoke up.

Jess would have liked nothing better than to tell the newest member of her team to go with the others. Why waste the energy? She understood that wouldn't be happening, and, for the most part, had come to terms with that inevitability since her safety wasn't only about her anymore.

"Good," Jess told him. "You can make sure we're not disturbed, Lieutenant."

That was her one complaint about their shared space. Though the open concept worked well when the team was brainstorming on a case, there was no privacy for meetings like the one she was about to have with Gina.

"Happy to oblige, ma'am," Hayes said, in his best southern drawl.

When she and Gina had the office to themselves, Jess opted to set the ground rules. "You're aware there are certain things I can't talk about yet."

Gina moved to the front of Jess's desk and made herself comfortable in a chair. "I doubt you know anything the media doesn't have already."

There was that.

Jess settled behind her desk. So much for the tidbit she'd decided to give the reporter. "Then why bother coming? I can tell you right now the pizza isn't that good."

"I have a proposition for you, Jess."

Jess leaned back in her chair. "I'm listening."

"Tell me your story," Gina began. "The real story of how Spears came to be in your life and how he ruined your career with the FBI. The citizens of Birmingham will eat it up. They love you."

Jess laughed. "I think you'd better check your sources on that one. This city has quickly fallen out of love with me."

"All these murders have them running scared," Gina argued. "*Spears* has them running scared. Let me tell them how he's taken over your life—what he's done to you and the people you care about. The world loves a martyr, Jess. And you're a martyr if I've ever seen one."

Jess was reasonably sure that was not a compliment. "The story starts back in February, more than six months ago," she warned. The truth was it started even before that. Like five years before that, but the real trouble had begun this year. "What makes you think people want to hear old news?"

Gina smiled. "You'll have to trust my instincts."

No arguing that point. The woman hadn't gotten where she was by going after the wrong stories.

"What do I get in return for spilling my guts to you?"

Gina shrugged. "Tell me what I can do for you. I'm confident there's something. Name it."

As if the answer had suddenly been scrawled across her bare case board, Jess knew exactly what Gina Coleman could do for her.

"I'll give you the story," Jess granted.

Victory, or maybe euphoria at getting the interview every reporter in the state would no doubt wish they'd landed, sparkled in Gina's eyes.

"If," Jess qualified, "you help me find a discreet way to warn the citizens that their beloved chief of police is being framed."

Now Jess had the reporter's attention.

"I can definitely help with that," Gina agreed.

Jess ignored the tinge of jealousy that came automatically at the idea the other woman had once shared Dan's bed. Didn't matter. All that mattered was making sure Dan didn't suffer more than he already had. His home had been burned to the ground. He was being investigated in the case of a missing BPD division chief, Captain Ted Allen. She had to do something to stop this downward spiral.

"Eric Spears," Gina said, drawing Jess's attention from the painful thoughts and to the small recorder now sitting on her desk, "start at the beginning."

Jess shuddered at the idea that she'd once owned a recorder very much like that. Funny, how something so seemingly harmless could change one's life.

Jess took a breath and began. "It was Valentine's Day." She closed her eyes for a moment. "Feels like a lifetime ago."

CHAPTER TWO

Special Agent Jess Harris stared at the massive bouquet of red roses on the corner of her desk. She shook her head. The divorce papers were signed and though the marriage had ended months ago, the legal dissolution wouldn't be final until the end of this month. Still, it was over. Why in the world did Wesley waste his money sending her flowers? She lifted the card from the lush arrangement.

Thinking of you. Wesley.

Jess tossed the card into a desk drawer. "That must be why you accepted a position on the opposite coast."

She stared at the open folder in front of her but her mind just didn't want to stay focused. The idea of holding the divorce against Wesley was ridiculous. Their failed marriage was more her fault than his. He was a very nice man and an excellent agent. Wesley Duvall's only mistake had been being in the

310

wrong place at the wrong time. Jess had turned forty and getting married promptly went from nowhere near her priority list to practically the top. Forty had felt so old and she'd never been married. Everyone around her was or had been at least once in their lives. The idea that her old flame, Dan Burnett, had been married twice already hadn't played a part in her reasoning. At least, not one she would acknowledge. That was a secret she fully intended to take with her to the grave.

A rap on her office door drew her errant attention from those foolish musings. She really didn't have time for a pity party. All work and no play was her choice. If she ended up old and alone she had no one to blame but herself. Her sister Lily reminded her of that fact regularly.

"Come in." Jess had nothing to prove to anyone except to those who needed her assistance with finding criminals.

The door opened and Supervisory Special Agent Ralph Gant walked in. Judging by the bulging case file he carried he had a new assignment for her. Or maybe he wanted to remind her that an all hands staff meeting included her.

"I was on a conference call," Jess said before he could chastise her. "It took me three days to get that time with the coroner on my current case. The detectives are waiting for this profile." She tapped the folder on her desk. "I knew you'd bring me up to speed and here you are." She topped off her excuse with a broad smile.

Gant grunted a disagreeable sound, closed the door and then deposited himself into the chair next to her desk. "I'll send you an email."

So this was about a case. She'd anticipated a reminder that as a career agent and seasoned profiler she was expected to set the proper example.

"We need to talk about the Player case."

Anticipation coursed through her. She forced herself to relax. No need for him to see the immediate interest and hope, frankly, his words elicited. "I gave everything I had to Taylor five months ago like you asked."

Gant shrugged. "Unfortunately, we don't have anything new to add to that."

Why wasn't she surprised? The Bureau had been on the Player's trail for the past five years and still he remained an unknown subject. Jess had consulted on the case for most of that time. She had studied his victims. His MO. She knew all there was to know about the phantom and his games. Truth be told, she had done almost as much searching for this unsub as any agent in the field.

No matter, she, like everyone else involved, had no idea who he was beyond the probability that he was a white male in his late thirties to early forties. Intelligent. Resourceful. And ruthless. If Jess's profile was correct, he was a sociopath in the purest form.

"He's like a ghost," Gant grumbled.

Jess didn't believe in ghosts. "It's difficult to identify a suspect when he leaves no evidence and never strikes in the same place twice."

Gant nodded. "That doesn't help me sleep at night."

Insomnia went with the job. How was she or any agent supposed to sleep when every imaginable evil roamed their heads all hours of the day and the night? Only when a case was closed successfully, and the criminals involved were either dead or on their way to justice, did she feel she had done enough. Unfortunately, there were far too many, like the Player case, which remained unsolved. Those were the cases that robbed her of sleep. The average civilian couldn't understand how a serial killer, like the Player, who had raped and murdered at least six women every year for the past five, that they knew of, hadn't been caught by now. It was simple. No witnesses and no evidence. Until the Player made a mistake, there was no identifying him much less catching him.

"Taylor and Bedford have done all they can and they've gotten nowhere."

Jess bit back *I told you so* and reminded her boss of what he knew all too well. "It's time for him to start again." Goose bumps rose on her flesh. About this time every year the Player's cycle started. As the date on the calendar had neared, she'd pretended it wasn't her problem. Had done all she could to ignore the inevitable. But he was there, night and day, on the fringe of her mind.

It was time for a new game.

Jess steeled against a shudder.

"I shouldn't have taken you off the case." Gant shook his head.

Jess wasn't sure whether to jump for joy or to scream at the man. She had studied the Player since the Bureau first became aware of his existence. But five months ago her boss, likely prompted by the lack of movement on the investigation, had assigned the case to Agents Taylor and Bedford.

Burnout happened. A profiler worked closely with the agents and local law enforcement personnel involved with a case. As angry as she had been about Gant's decision, deep down she had understood that new insights might make a difference. Taylor had been a profiler a year longer than her and Bedford had moved to BAU only two years ago, but they were both good. She'd pretended to understand.

Like local law enforcement, the Bureau was taking a beating in the news. Any time that happened something had to change—whether it did any good or not.

Jess reached for the file that would contain an overview of any updates on the case as well as the lengthy reports she had provided. The actual case file would be much larger. Not that she needed to see any of it. The details were etched into her brain. The only case she'd ever been assigned that she hadn't helped solve. *Yet.*

She placed the file on her desk. "I have maybe another two hours work on my current case and then I'll start on this one again. If Taylor's available, maybe we can talk tomorrow morning."

"I know you two are a little on the competitive side," Gant said, "but you should know, he admitted you're the one who should be working this case."

She appreciated Gant saying so, but she had her doubts as to whether Taylor would ever admit any such thing unless it was because he saw failure coming and decided to bail. No one wanted to be the profiler or the field agent assigned to a case when the death toll was about to rise. "Thank him for the vote of confidence."

Gant pushed to his feet. "You might want to keep that part to yourself. I'm reasonably sure he didn't mean for me to pass along the comment."

"I won't say a word."

When Gant was gone, Jess took a deep breath and opened the file. She shook her head as she considered that it was time for his cycle to begin again and they had nothing.

He was too good at protecting his identity. Too careful in his every step.

"Not your garden variety sociopath, that's for sure," she muttered as she closed the folder.

Just another monster that had gotten away with his evil deeds for far too long.

PRESENT DAY...
BIRMINGHAM

Gina shut off the recorder. "You look like you need a break."

With effort, Jess dismissed the memories. She cleared her throat. "I could use a Pepsi."

What time was it? She glanced at her cell. Just past noon. Had it only been half an hour since she and Gina started the interview? Felt like a lot longer.

Where was that pizza? Maybe a few M&Ms would get her through. She reached for the drawer where she kept her backup chocolate stash.

Gina stood. "I'll check with Lieutenant Hayes and get an ETA on that pizza."

Jess decided she must look like hell if Gina was worried about her. Pretty soon folks would recognize that something was off.

How much longer could she keep the pregnancy a secret?

CHAPTER THREE

"She was a good girl," Mona Clark said of her twenty-year-old daughter. "She made the Dean's list every semester at the college."

Jess kept her smile in place. She wished there were comforting words she could say to the woman, but there were none. As usual, the Player had chosen his victims, one every seven to twelve days until he had taken a total of six, and as with the other victims in each of the games over the past five years, none had survived.

Frieda Clark had been the final victim in this latest game. She was also the youngest ever taken by the Player.

Following his typical pattern, he left no evidence. Nothing.

Now, the Bureau and all other law enforcement agencies involved had about ten and a half months to find him before the next game started.

The Player called his annual ritual a game. Each victim was abducted, tortured for approximately seven days before being given a chance to escape that was doomed to failure, and then she was murdered. How twisted was that? Just when the victim was almost defeated, he gave her hope, and then extinguished it as well as her life. Tracing the last hours of their lives was as simple as reading a map—the map of cruelty drawn on their bodies.

There was little deviation in his MO and the only thing the victims had in common was physical appearance. The Player preferred tall, brunette and beautiful women. Intelligence appeared to be a factor as well.

"According to your statement, Mrs. Clark," Jess said, hoping to draw the poor woman from her painful thoughts, "Frieda hadn't mentioned any new friends. You said she wasn't dating anyone special."

Mona shook her head. "She always told me about her friends." Her shoulders sagged. "She wanted a boyfriend but she hadn't met anyone who lived up to her high standards." A smile trembled across her lips. "My daughter was a little picky. I raised her that way. I wanted her to have a good husband. The kind of husband she deserved."

Jess understood. "When it comes to men, picky is good." Then again, being too picky carried a cost of its own. Funny, she had never considered herself lonely until the last couple of years. *What was it about turning forty that changed so much?* She found herself questioning every decision she'd ever made. Even her career had come under scrutiny lately, and her career was the one part of her life where she'd always felt completely confident. Work defined her. No one had worked harder than Jess. She had a near perfect record. If she worked a case, the bad guy always got his.

Except one.

The Player. The single blemish on her record.

Mona gazed at Jess hopefully. "Do you think you'll be able to stop him this time?" She batted back the tears shining in her eyes. "If you do, at least my sweet Frieda won't have died in vain."

Jess forced away the doubt nagging at her. "We're doing all we can, Mrs. Clark. You have my word on that. We are going to stop him." She refused to admit defeat on this case. She would identify the Player and he would be stopped.

If it was the last thing she did, she would find him.

The older woman's lips trembled as she visibly struggled with her emotions. "I hope so."

By the time Jess was in her car, she was mad as hell. Six more dead women. She closed her eyes and braced her forehead against the steering wheel. And not one speck of evidence that would lead them to the serial killer who was probably laughing at them right now. She straightened and stared at her reflection in the rearview mirror. Let him laugh. She was not done yet.

Her cell clanged with that old-fashioned ring tone. She hated the sound but it made recognizing hers from everyone else's in a crowd easy. She dug the phone from her bag and checked the screen. *Richmond telephone number.*

One of the local cops working the case, maybe. "Harris."

"Agent Harris, this," the female caller cleared her throat, "this is Naomi Proctor."

Jess's heart thumped. "Naomi, hi. Did you think of something else that might help with our investigation?"

Naomi Proctor was the best friend of Sierra Timmons, victim four in the latest Player murders. Naomi had spoken to Sierra just minutes before her abduction. Her statements so far had provided nothing to advance the investigation. Par for the course. Not once in five years had a friend or family member been able to provide useful information. The Player was too smart for that.

Jess hoped his luck was about to change.

"There was this older guy," Naomi said. Her voice quavered. "Like forty or forty-one. His name was Eric Spears. He came to the restaurant a couple of times. Sierra said he gave her the creeps but he was a really big tipper. Like a hundred dollars each time."

Jess's hopes drooped. It wasn't unusual for older men to hit on younger women. A college student, Sierra had worked as a waitress on weekends. Tips had helped keep a roof over her head. Being attractive had ensured good tips. "Was there something in particular about this man that bothered Sierra?"

"He told her she was the kind of woman he liked, and that he was going to play a game with her."

Jess sat up a little straighter. "You're certain those were his exact words?" That thumping in her chest grew harder.

"That's what she told me."

Laughter in the background—the canned kind from a television program—punctuated her statement. A frown furrowed Jess's brow. She found it more than a little strange that Naomi would be watching some sort of comedy program while mulling over her friend's murder. Even stranger was the fact that nothing about this older man was in her previous statement. "Is there a reason you didn't mention this man before?"

"I...I just remembered. I guess I was in shock until...now."

That vacant sound in the woman's voice grew more distant with each word she uttered. "Why don't we talk about this in person?" Jess suggested. "Are you home, Naomi?"

"Yeah." A big, shaky breath vibrated over the line. "Okay. Sure."

The words were hesitant, chock full of trepidation. "Stay right there, Naomi." Jess started her car. "I'm on my way now."

Jess tossed her phone onto the passenger seat and drove like a bat out of hell. Still it took her half an hour to get to Naomi's home. Whatever was going on, the young woman sounded under duress.

Emptiness and anxiety had resonated in her every word.

After skidding into the first available parking slot, Jess jumped out of her Audi and raced toward the row of two-story townhouses. Maybe she was over reacting, but her instincts warned that something was very, very wrong.

With a deep breath to slow her pounding heart, Jess rapped on the door of Naomi's townhome. The silence inside ratcheted up Jess's tension. When they'd spoken on the phone, she had heard the television playing in the background.

Had Naomi changed her mind and left to prevent talking to Jess? A quick survey of the parking lot answered that question. Naomi's blue Fiat with its Life is Good plate on the front sat in a spot a few doors down. Had she decided in the last half hour that she didn't want to talk after all?

Why had she sounded so upset? Did she know more than she was telling? It wasn't impossible that she'd only just remembered the information, but it was highly unlikely. Either way, Jess needed to speak to her in person. Body language told far more than the words alone.

Jess rapped again, harder this time. The door opened a few inches as if the latch hadn't been engaged.

"Naomi?" Jess reached for her Glock as she took a position next to the door. "Naomi, I'm here if you still want to talk?" She gave the door a push with her free hand. It swung inward.

It was so quiet Jess could hear the blood surging through her veins.

She leaned around the doorframe and had a look. Her breath jammed in her lungs.

Naomi hung from the banister on the second floor landing.

Jess moved across the threshold, weapon ready and braced for anyone who might be inside. She hesitated, couldn't see a way to get the young woman down without a ladder and something to cut the rope. Didn't matter at this point, she realized. Naomi Proctor was dead. After calling for backup, Jess moved cautiously through the rest of the home.

Back downstairs, the sirens wailed. Jess started for the door, but something on the floor in the corner next to the staircase stopped her. A piece of paper lay on the white carpet. Jess tugged out a glove and snapped it into place. Picking the paper up by one corner, she read the words scrawled across the page.

I wasn't supposed to tell.

Jess shivered with the abrupt sensation that someone was watching. She wheeled around. Two uniformed officers were barreling up the sidewalk.

He'd won again.

But this time the Player had taken a victim who wasn't a part of his usual game. This one he'd taken just to show everyone who was boss. The move was a deviation from his usual MO. Jess hoped the unexpected departure from his usual pattern would lead them to something besides another woman's body.

"That's when you knew it was him?" Gina asked, her eyes wide with the excitement. "You knew Eric Spears was the Player?"

Jess reached for the bottle of water on her desk. The pizza wasn't sitting well. Or maybe it was the topic of conversation. Spears had ruled her life for so long the very thought of his name made her ill.

Would she never be rid of him?

Not until he's dead.

That was the one thing she now understood with complete certainty.

"No," she said in answer to Gina's question. "I didn't know Eric Spears was the Player then. But I know now that was the day..." A moment was required before Jess could finish her statement. "That was the day it began."

Gina frowned. "It?"

"His obsession with me."

CHAPTER FOUR

JUNE 25, TWO MONTHS EARLIER...
QUANTICO

"You don't have enough evidence."

Jess wanted to tear out her hair! Gant wasn't listening! "Naomi Proctor is dead," she reminded her boss. "I believe she's dead because she gave me his name."

Gant wagged his head from side to side in the most infuriating manner. "The autopsy showed no conclusive evidence that she'd been forced to hang herself, Harris. She put that rope around her neck and climbed over the banister. Those are the only two facts we can prove."

He just wouldn't see it. Jess pointed to the case board she had created on the wall in her office. "Not one of her friends or family members saw this coming. Not a single one. No history of depression or any other mental illness. Proctor was at work the day before and no one noticed anything out of the norm."

"It happens," Gant argued.

Jess shook her head. She was not letting this go. "No, it doesn't." She propped her hands on her hips and stood her ground. "There are always warnings when something like this happens. Always. People see what they want to see, or maybe they're afraid or feel guilty and won't admit what they noticed, but there are warnings. *Always*," she repeated just in case he didn't get it the two other times.

He shrugged. "So no one noticed or no one wants to admit what they saw. Either way, Naomi Proctor committed suicide and we have no evidence Eric Spears was at the restaurant where victim four worked."

"Sierra Timmons," Jess corrected.

Gant frowned. He was annoyed at her insistence on following this lead. "What?"

"Victim four's name was Sierra Timmons."

Gant glanced at her case board then heaved a big breath. "No one wants to solve this case more than me, Harris. But what you have on Spears is nothing. You don't have a witness who can place him at the restaurant during one of Proctor's shifts even if that would prove anything. Your job is to help identify and anticipate the movements of the unsub in the Player case, not track down potential suspects. We have agents in the field for that. You've already stepped on too many toes with the locals in Richmond. The lead detective is more than a little pissed at you."

Jess didn't care. No one was listening! She had two employees at the restaurant who kind of, sort of remembered Spears. But, unfortunately, Gant was correct. No one could corroborate Naomi's story. And Jess was way outside her jurisdiction on this case. Still she argued. "Spears owns businesses in all five of the cities where the previous murders occurred."

"SpearNet is global, Harris. What city doesn't he have assets in?" Gant challenged.

Eric Spears was one of those "garage entrepreneurs" who'd created a Fortune 500 company from nothing that had propelled him to the top of the top one percent.

"He fits the profile." There were a number of traits that identified a sociopathic serial killer. More than enough of those applied to Spears. Jess collapsed into her chair. She refused to give up on this lead. She was onto something. Dammit.

"But he has no record. Nothing about his past screams serial killer."

Jess was the one heaving a big sigh now. "Just because no one ever caught him killing a puppy when he was a kid doesn't mean he didn't."

She had never met the man but she'd read the one interview he'd granted to GQ. Spears was a recluse for the most part. He'd created his international corporation, and now he gave his instructions from wherever in the world he decided to land for the day. He owned his own jet, among other things. Most who'd met him personally called him an arrogant genius. Spears had never been married and had no friends that Jess could find. Not that she could mention that particular fact since certain things she'd been doing weren't technically in her job description.

Not that being friendless outside of work made him a serial killer. If that were the case, most in the Behavioral Analysis Unit would fit the profile. Who had time for friends?

"I warned you about this before, Harris." Gant leaned across her desk and tapped the photos of Spears. "Your obsession with this case makes your assessments unreliable. This is why I took you off the case last year."

When she would have contended otherwise, he held up a hand to stop her. "You're the best." He glanced at the closed door. "Not that you have permission to tell that around, but it's true. Be that as it may, this case has gotten under your skin and you're operating on emotion. We all hit a brick wall on a case eventually, Harris. No one can find the killer every time. Not even you."

If that was supposed to make her feel better, it did not.

"I need your total objectivity on this case," he went on. "Get past this Spears thing and help all those other agents and cops who want to find the Player. You're operating as if you're the only person on the team. That has to stop for the job to get done. I know it and you know it."

Jess stared at the photos of Spears for a moment. Somehow, in her heart, she knew this man was the Player. But Gant was correct in his conclusion. She couldn't prove it. Worse, she had no right to leave everyone else out of the loop. Guilty as charged. Her job was to provide information, not to take off on some maverick investigation.

"You're right." She gathered the photos and placed them back into the case file. "I'll set up a meeting ASAP to brief Richmond PD on my latest assessments."

As Gant left, satisfied he had ushered Jess back into line, she considered whether SpearNet would still be open when she arrived in Richmond if she left now.

Only one way to find out.

RICHMOND

The corporate offices as well as one of the largest labs belonging to SpearNet were nestled amid the city center of downtown Richmond. Twelve stories of sleek tinted glass, SpearNet specialized in electronic security, but the mega corporation dabbled in everything from drones to medical technology. The founder was so proud of his accomplishments he offered tours of certain areas of its research and technology laboratories.

Jess strolled along with the crowd of folks who listened intently to the tour guide's every word. Her senses, on the other hand, were honed in on the facility. Giant monitors and floor to ceiling windows provided firsthand views of the newest technology. Staff members in crisp white coats hurried around the corridors.

The perfect place to hide if one was a killer. Eric Spears was surrounded by dazzling displays of his financial portfolio as well as his brilliance. This was a man with immense, possibly endless, resources. He could do anything, go anywhere…and no one would be better at hiding than someone who specialized in security.

Briefly Gant's words echoed a warning, but Jess ignored them. She needed to soak in the atmosphere of Eric Spears' life's work.

His blond haired, blue-eyed likeness stared out at her from a two-story poster proclaiming him the gifted CEO of SpearNet. Sophisticated. Charming. Determined. Ruthless in all things business.

She had driven by his home as well. Like this building, his home was austere. Sleek, modern, and so very cold. A fortress complete with a guard booth and most likely a state of the art security system.

No one was getting close to Spears without an invitation.

Yet, all she needed was a few minutes in a room with him and she could confirm if he was the monster she thought him to be. So far, her attempts to get an interview had proven futile. Eric Spears was always on one continent or another but rarely on this one, it seemed.

Jess followed the crowd, reminded herself she had an appointment with Richmond's lead homicide detective in just one hour. The hair on the back of her neck stood on end and she froze. Instinctively, her hand went to her bag but she'd had to lock her

Glock in the car for this tour. She turned around, surveyed the long, broad corridor before lifting her gaze to the walkways above. A man standing on the walkway to her right appeared to stare directly at her. He didn't wear a white coat and he didn't appear to be a part of one of the tour groups.

Unable to stop herself, Jess reached into her bag for her glasses. He surely knew she was staring at him since she made no attempt to hide it and still he didn't look away. She pushed her glasses into place and zeroed in on his face.

The man smiled.

Her heart skipped a beat.

Eric Spears.

PRESENT DAY...
BIRMINGHAM

"He was watching you," Gina Coleman suggested, breathless.

Jess rubbed at her temples. "He was."

"Did you talk to him that day?"

Jess shook her head. "No. He just wanted me to know he was watching. Then he walked away. What I didn't know at the time is that he'd been watching me too."

Gina pressed a hand to her throat. "With what I've learned about Spears, it must have been terrifying just being in the same room—no matter how large—with him. When did you actually speak to him?"

Memories of those minutes in the Richmond PD interrogation room filled Jess's mind, causing her chest to constrict. "It would be twelve days before I interviewed him." She remembered every hour of every one of those days and nights. Her life had grown consumed with Eric Spears.

Had it only been two months ago? Seemed like a lifetime. Jess closed her eyes. That had been the beginning all right.

The beginning of the end of her life as she knew it.

CHAPTER FIVE

Jess pressed the brew button on her coffeemaker and waited for the cup to fill. She had a little more work on the new case she'd been assigned yesterday, and then she intended to get some sleep.

Between the homicide detective in Richmond having moved on and her inability to connect Eric Spears to Sierra Timmons, Jess had decided to try and find some distance from the Player case.

Gant was grateful, that was for sure. He didn't want his ace profiler, as he called her when his mood was right, getting bogged down with a dead end.

"Moving on." She snagged her coffee and headed to her home office. She'd bought this house almost ten years ago, and still she hadn't hung a single picture on the walls. Only two of the four bedrooms were furnished and one of those served as her office. During her brief marriage to Wesley, he had used one of the vacant bedrooms as his office. He'd also used that room as a place to sleep near the end.

333

Jess hesitated at the door of the room Wesley had used. The indentations in the carpet from his desk and bookcase were still visible. She stared at the wedding band on her left hand. She probably should take it off and put it away. But then she'd just have to explain that her marriage was over due to irreconcilable differences.

As long as she wore the ring, no one asked questions. Except Gant. He and Wesley had been friends. Wesley had told him the relationship was over. Gant hadn't admitted as much, but he'd asked Jess on several occasions if she was okay. To anyone who overheard, he could have been asking about her health or a case. She knew the real motive behind the question. His not so covert glances at the wedding band she wore when he asked was all the explanation she needed.

She moved on to her office. Before taking a seat behind her desk, she stared at the case board she'd made on the wall. Graphic photos from the crime scene, including those of the victims, along with dozens of handwritten notes she used in creating her profile dotted the wall. She'd poked hundreds of tiny holes in the drywall of this room with all those pushpins. Her sister's kids had managed to get a peek on their last visit. They had immediately proclaimed that their Aunt Jess had the creepiest office in the world. Her sister Lil had been appalled.

The chair creaked as Jess got comfortable and set her coffee next to the keyboard. She nudged the mouse and opened her inbox. She smiled as she read an email from the detective in charge of a case she'd recently profiled. Her suggested method of questioning had garnered a confession from the suspect.

A quick reply and she was on to the next email. The subject line surprised her.

The evidence you need...

She tapped the necessary keys and the email opened.

I know you're watching him. I can help. I know where he keeps his mementoes. Your Attic Mini Storage. Raines Tavern Road. Unit 12.

Jess hit print, her fingers cold. What the hell kind of joke was this? She stared at the address of the sender. Watcher01. The Internet Service Provider was one used by millions. Anyone could create an ID and begin sending messages.

But this sender knew she was watching someone. With a few more keystrokes, she plotted the address, which was just outside Richmond. It was late. Almost ten. She could be there before midnight.

Jess chewed her lower lip.

Or she could be smart and wait until morning and turn the email over to Gant.

This wouldn't be the first time she'd made a not so smart decision.

Hopefully it wouldn't be the last decision she made.

FARMVILLE, VIRGINIA

Twenty minutes before midnight Jess parked in the lot of the Your Attic Mini Storage. She'd circled the property. Three long rows of storage units. No other vehicles were in the lot. Thankfully there was plenty of lighting. The road was pretty much deserted but visibility in either direction was good. No sign of another house or vehicle for miles.

Unit 12 was only a few feet from where she'd parked, and she'd positioned her car in such a way that it couldn't be blocked in by anyone who might have decided to set her up. As a profiler she worked behind the scenes most of the time. The media rarely heard her name. Credit for support to local law enforcement was always attributed to the Federal Bureau of Investigation not to any one person.

Since her name wasn't bandied about in the media, the most troubling aspect of the communication she'd received was how the sender had obtained her name much less her personal email address. She gave it only to those with whom she worked closely on a case and even that was rare. Of course, if someone with the right resources wanted her personal information it could be procured.

"Damned hackers." One day the Bureau would be able to police Internet crime a little better.

Any way she looked at this, chances were it was a set up or a game someone wanted to play. There was a remote possibility that someone who knew the Player had decided he or she couldn't live with the guilt any longer.

"Right," she groused. Few sociopaths, much less serial killers, trusted anyone with their darkest secrets.

Still in her car, Jess scanned the lot once more. "You going to just sit here, Jess, or are you going to do this?"

Since she hadn't completely lost her mind, she decided to send Gant a text just in case this was the kind of set up you didn't walk away from. She gave him her location and reason for coming. He was likely in bed and wouldn't see it before morning. At least if she ended up dead, someone would know where to start looking and why she'd been way out here in the middle of the night.

"Enough stalling."

She donned a pair of latex gloves, opened the car door and climbed out. In the distance she could hear faint traffic noise from the interstate. Otherwise it was eerily quiet. The gravel crunched beneath her sneakers. She'd thrown on her favorite pair of jeans and a t-shirt but now she wished she had grabbed a sweatshirt. The air felt cool against her bare arms.

Though it had been a while since she'd worked as a field agent, she'd done this plenty of times before. As confident as she felt, the weight of the holstered Glock nestled against her torso was reassuring. The flashlight in her right hand was the Mag type easily used as a weapon. She was prepared.

"Or stupid," she muttered, with another long, slow look around.

There was no lock on unit 12. Not a good sign. If there really was any evidence inside, why wouldn't there be a lock?

She'd been had. "Dammit."

Her cell phone vibrated with an incoming text and she dug it out of her back pocket. If Gant had gotten her message, he was going to blow a gasket and she would have some major explaining to do. All for nothing. She stared at the screen.

Open it.

Her pulse jumped. Jess surveyed her surroundings again. There were no cameras on the buildings. No other cars in sight.

How the hell did he or she know Jess was here? Or get her cell phone number?

She turned to head back to her car. Whatever was going on here, she intended to call the locals for backup.

A sound whispered across her senses.

Jess stilled.

It was low, scarcely audible...but it was there. Soft weeping or whimpers.

The next sound to fill the air was the steel of her Glock sliding from its leather holster. Jess eased closer to the door of unit 12. The soft sound was coming from inside. Keeping her attention on her surroundings, she shoved the Mag light in her waistband and bent down to tug up the door with her free hand.

The grate of metal on metal drowned out the whimpering. She raised the door and reclaimed her flashlight. Definitely a woman crying. The sound was louder now. Heart thundering, she clicked on the light and surveyed the space beyond the door. A single cardboard box sat in the middle of what appeared to be an otherwise empty unit of about ten by twelve feet. She leaned in, tried to get a better look at anything that might be hanging overhead.

Nothing.

"Well hell." She wished whoever had set this up were here and she could just shoot the bastard.

Her cell vibrated again. Shaking her head, she dragged it out.

Evidence is in the box.

She had to be out of her mind. Gant would go ballistic. There were rules and she'd already broken several.

Still, she had to look.

Checking behind her once more, she approached the box. Inside were articles of clothing. Bras and panties. The weeping was louder this close to the box.

"Where the hell is that coming from?" She surveyed the interior of the unit, top to bottom, once more. *Clear.* The sound had to be coming from something in the box. A recording or cell phone set to speaker. Cautiously, she picked through the garments, and then stalled. *Blood.* Some of the garments were bloodstained.

The weeping suddenly stopped with an audible click.

She moved aside the rest of the bloodied under garments and at the bottom of the box was a handheld recorder. The same kind Jess had in her desk drawer at home.

"Shit," she hissed.

"What the hell are you doing in here?"

Jess whirled around, her weapon and the beam of her flashlight leveled on the man who held a shotgun aimed right at her. "FBI." She steadied herself. "Let's just stay calm, sir. I'm Special Agent Harris."

"I don't care who you are," he growled without lowering his weapon. "You're trespassing. I already called the sheriff."

Jess exhaled a chest full of tension. "Good. Can you call him back and tell him we need a forensic unit, too."

PRESENT DAY...
BIRMINGHAM

"It's a miracle he didn't shoot you!" Gina proclaimed. She shuddered. "Harris, you really are lucky to be here."

More so than anyone knew. "He wasn't looking to shoot anyone. He was only protecting his property."

Confusion lined the reporter's smooth brow. "I thought you said there were no houses along that stretch of road."

"There wasn't. He received a call that someone was prowling around his storage facility."

"The call was from an untraceable cell phone, I take it."

Jess nodded. "A burner. Same as the text messages I received. The email, I learned later, was sent via the Wi-Fi from my own house. His goal was to prompt a reaction from me and he got one. I made

340

the first and last mistake of my career with the Bureau."

"But the stuff in the box belonged to the victims from the Player's most recent murders, right?" the reporter guessed.

"That's right. The box even had Spears' prints on it."

Gina put up her hands. "I don't understand."

"You will," Jess assured her, "when you hear the rest."

CHAPTER SIX

Jess stared at the man beyond the glass. She hugged her pad and pencil to her chest and tried unsuccessfully to chase away the cold that had settled there.

Eric Spears. The Player. The man who had brutally tortured and murdered thirty or more women.

Lieutenant Randolph, the lead homicide detective on the Richmond case, had already interviewed Spears. Jess would have preferred that he wait for her but it hadn't worked out that way.

The local authorities were in a frenzy. The articles of clothing found in the box belonged to the six victims from the Richmond area. Blood matching that of two of those victims had been found on the undergarments.

Eric Spears' prints were on the box.

That was where the good news ended.

The box was from his company, SpearNet. Anyone who worked there, or who had access to the

342

trash taken from the facility, could have picked up the box and used it for nefarious purposes. Once the box left the SpearNet facility, it couldn't be connected to Spears. Other prints were on the box but no matches so far.

They couldn't connect Spears, or anyone with whom he was associated, to the storage unit, to the box or to the items in the box, much less the burner phone used to lure Jess there.

The text messages she had received and the call to the storage unit manager were from the same burner phone that was conveniently untraceable. A cyber expert was attempting to track down where the email she'd received had come from.

Gant and the locals were in an uproar because she'd gone into the storage unit without a warrant. Jess wasn't a fool. She'd had exigent circumstances, in her opinion. How was she to know the weeping was coming from a recording device? It could have been coming from a victim via a cell phone set to speaker inside the box.

She'd had no choice but to go in. At least that was the story she was sticking to. Maybe she could have decided to stand down once she saw there was only a box inside—not one large enough to hold a person, by the way. But she'd needed to know what was inside and the scenario about the cell phone wasn't totally outside the realm of possibility. At least not unless a judge said so anyway.

As if her worrisome thoughts had summoned him, Gant appeared at her side. "They've agreed to allow you to interview him."

Jess resisted the impulse to roll her eyes. She hated, hated, hated when local law enforcement treated the support from the Bureau as if it were more in the way than anything else. "I'd be grateful except they wouldn't have a suspect in custody if not for me."

Gant shot her a look. "We don't need to talk about this right now."

He was not happy that she'd gone rogue, as he called it, last night. In hindsight, it wasn't one of her better choices but then she'd known that at the time.

"Fine." She turned her attention back to the man waiting alone in the interview room. "Whatever you say."

"Tread carefully in there," Gant cautioned.

As if she didn't know how to interview a suspect. "You're well aware this isn't my first dance with a sociopath."

"He has three attorneys, Jess." Gant stared at her until she met his gaze. "Three legal eagles who are right now looking for cause to toss out your evidence. Spears is so sure he has nothing to worry about he's agreed to talk to you alone—against the counsel of those three attorneys."

"Got it." She should have known Spears would have the best lawyers money could buy. If she'd taken a minute to think about it, she would have been telling Gant that instead of the other way around.

Maybe he was right. Maybe her head wasn't on straight with this case.

"I'll be watching," Gant reminded her as she prepared to enter the room where Spears waited.

Before she could open the door, the chief of police as well as the lead detective on the case and the Richmond Bureau field agents working the task force had gathered behind the one-way mirror to watch.

She stepped into the interview room and closed the door. She could almost feel the camera in the upper left corner of the room zooming in on her. The scent of extravagant cologne, subtle and undeniably appealing, filled her nostrils.

Jess cleared her head and took a seat across the table from him. Her pulse jolted before settling at the realization that only about two feet separated her from the man she was absolutely certain was the Player. "Good afternoon, Mr. Spears." She placed her pad on the table and readied her pencil for taking notes. She liked doing certain things the old-fashioned way. Recorders and electronic notepads were fine for some, she'd given both a shot, but she preferred her pencil and paper.

Spears watched her for a long moment before he spoke. Assessing her no doubt. He deliberately inventoried every part of her visible to him before he was through.

"Special Agent Jess Harris," he said. His voice was deep, smooth, elegant—like the obscenely

expensive silk suit he wore. "I finally have the pleasure of meeting you face-to-face. I'm a lucky man,
indeed."

Jess ignored his attempt at humor. "I have a few
questions for you, sir."

"You've been watching me," he said. "Driving
past my home. Touring my SpearNet facility."

How nice of him to tell the world. She felt certain
Gant was shaking his head this very second. Spears
was trying to rattle her. She wasn't going to let him.

"I'm a profiler, Mr. Spears. Part of determining all
that I can about a subject involves learning about his
life. His work. As a successful business strategist, I'm
certain you grasp the concept of understanding your
target. Once a goal is set or a choice is made, it's important to gather as many facts as possible. Routines.
Strengths. Weaknesses. It's the only way for any hunter
to win the game and ultimately catch the prey."

He smiled. If it was not for the fact that she knew
he was a vicious murderer, the expression would
have been pleasant. Eric Spears was a handsome
man. A charming man. A brilliant one.

A cunning and deadly animal.

"The only hunting I do, Agent Harris, is in the
world of technology."

The situation became perfectly clear at that
precise moment. This was not going to go down the
way she wanted. Spears was far too smart to make
a mistake. Unless he could be connected to that
damned box, he would walk. She would never have
this opportunity again.

She returned his smile with an amiable one of her own. "You choose six women each year to hold hostage and murder, one at a time. Why six?" she asked. "Why not five or seven? Is there some relevance in the number six? Is that how many women rejected you as a young man—before you were rich enough to buy attention and affections."

Those watching in the viewing room would be demanding that Gant get her under control. She hoped like hell he didn't end the interview before she said what she had to say to this bastard.

"Six is the devil's number, Agent Harris. Did you know that?" Spears inclined his head and studied her. "Perhaps your monster chooses six victims for that reason."

Fury started to simmer deep inside her. *Don't let him get to you.* "I'd say you're right, Mr. Spears. He is a monster and a devil. Both of those terms are in my profile."

"Are you analyzing me now?" He angled his head the other way as if needing a different perspective of her. "Have you labeled me a psychopath or a sociopath?"

"I think you know the answer to that."

He laughed. "Oh yes. A sociopath. I fit most of the criteria, don't I?" He shrugged casually. "What successful businessman doesn't?"

"You may be right about that." Might as well go along. Maybe he'd trip up in spite of his brilliance. All that arrogance had to be hard to carry around.

347

"Your reasons for bringing me here still elude me, Agent Harris." He turned his hands up. "You have no evidence. I can't fathom your point." He leaned forward, his face so very close to hers. Jess stood her ground without as much as a flinch. "If you wanted to meet me that badly, you should have left a message with my assistant. Blondes are not usually my type, but I've been known to make the occasional compromise."

That fury that had been simmering boiled over. "It isn't the murder that turns you on, is it?"

He stared so deeply into her eyes she couldn't breathe, could hardly hold his gaze. "I don't know what you mean, Agent Harris."

"It's the torture." This time she inclined her head, studied him openly. "That's the part you enjoy." His eyes turned ice cold. Jess barely staved off a shudder. "You see, Mr. Spears—"

"Call me Eric," he said softly, something menacing in the gentleness.

"Eric," she amended, her throat so damned dry at this point she could hardly swallow. "I've spent a lot of years studying the levels of evil and you, sir, are at the very top. The only way you get any pleasure in this life is to inflict pain. You feel nothing without the pain of others."

He inhaled deeply as if trying to catch her scent. "Since you have me all figured out, Agent, what else is there to talk about?"

Jess forced a smile. Oh he was good. So very nonchalant. "April North. Sierra Timmons. Wendy

Commers. Lola Wayans. Allison Fleming. Frieda Clark. And, of course, Naomi Proctor. That's what I want to talk about, Eric. Where would you like to begin?"

He leaned back in his chair. "As entertaining as this lovely visit has been, I've grown quite bored, Agent Harris. I think I'd like to speak with my attorneys now."

"First," Jess reached into her pocket for her cell phone, "do you mind if I snap a photo of you?" She shrugged. "You're the first sociopath at the top of the evil scale I've ever interviewed."

"This is your party, Agent Harris. Be my guest."

"Thank you, Eric." Jess took his picture and gathered her pad and pencil. "I'll see that your attorneys are called for you."

Before she could rise from her chair, he reached across the table and touched her. Just the briefest caress of his fingertips across her hand. She shuddered before she could block the reaction.

"The pleasure was all mine, *Jess.*"

CHAPTER SEVEN

"He touched you…"

The words were hardly more than a breath. Jess nodded in response to Gina's stunned comment. "He hasn't stopped touching my life since." Jess rubbed her hand as if she could erase that moment in her past. Eric Spears had marked her.

"What about the anonymous contact? Did it continue? Do you still get emails or text messages from him or whoever sent them?"

Jess suddenly felt more tired than she had in her entire life. "The emails continued for a few days. Then they stopped. I didn't hear from him again until the text messages started after I came here." She remembered the first text message she'd received from Spears after his release. Jess sucked in a sharp breath. "As it turned out, the emails were sent through my home computer. The handheld recorder in the box at the storage unit was the one I'd bought years before and tucked into a desk drawer after carrying it around for months. It was just something else cluttering my bag. Who knew it would become the linchpin in the demise of my career."

"Spears' prints were only on the box?"

That was the most frustrating part of all. "Only on the box that came from his place of business. A place where any number of folks could have picked it up. The recorder, however, only had my prints."

"So the evidence was thrown out."

Jess nodded. "Between the evidence being a step below circumstantial and my method of obtaining it, yes. The evidence was thrown out and Spears was released from holding."

"That was just a few days after you returned to Birmingham," Gina said.

"Right before Detective Wells was abducted." Jess realized now that Eric Spears had chosen her for some reason. Maybe he'd known she'd been searching for him, for five long years. Whatever it was, his perverse murder games had evolved into something else...something that involved her.

"He picked you," Gina offered, reading her mind.

"He wanted me to know the monster I'd been tracking with no success was him. He couldn't help himself. It was an ego thing."

"He took a significant risk reaching out to you."

"He knew what he was doing," Jess countered. "He planned every move too carefully to be trapped.

I was the one who ended up caught between a rock and a hard place. I was so involved in my own game of trying to figure him out I made mistakes I'd never made before."

"He destroyed your career with the FBI."

"He did." There was a time when Jess had regretted that so very deeply, but coming home was the right thing. Spears had done her a favor on that one. "Although, my name was eventually cleared and Gant offered me my job back, there are some who will always see what happened as a failure on my part."

Gina contemplated her for a moment. "You could have gone back to Quantico and yet you decided to stay here."

"I did." Jess thought of the child she carried and the man she had loved since she was seventeen years old, even when she'd refused to admit it. "It was the right choice."

"Do I hear wedding bells in the future for you and our chief of police?"

Jess reached across her desk and shut off the recorder. "That's not part of this story, Miss Coleman."

Gina ducked her head in acknowledgement. "Off the record, then. You said Dan's in trouble."

Jess hesitated for only a moment. "Someone inside the Birmingham Police Department is setting him up for the disappearance of Captain Ted Allen."

"That's ludicrous." Gina shook her head. "Allen was head of the Gang Task Force. More likely some drug lord he pissed off took him out."

Jess feared it wasn't that straight forward. "Whatever happened to Allen, we both know Dan couldn't have been involved with anything like that." *Impossible.*

"Do you think this has anything to do with Spears?"

"I can't rule it out, but it may be about jealousy. There are those who would like to be where Dan is."

"Are you suggesting Deputy Chief Harold Black is out to get the promotion he thought he should have had four years ago?"

Now they were getting somewhere. "Black wasn't happy when Dan was selected as chief of police?" Jess had suspected as much, but she hadn't returned to Birmingham until the middle of last month. She had no idea what happened four years ago. Dan would never speak ill of Black. He was far too classy to stoop that level.

"Not at all," Gina confirmed. "There was tension for a while."

"Check with your sources," Jess urged. "See what you can find out."

"Here you are with a deranged serial killer after you and you're worried about taking care of Dan. Who's going to take care of you?"

Jess forced a smile. "I know what I'm up against. Better the devil you know, as they say." Dan spent most every waking hour trying to take care of her. She intended to do the same for him. She needed Gina's support on this. "What I need from you," she pressed, "is help pinpointing the source of this threat to Dan."

"Count on it," Gina promised.

"This stays strictly between us." Jess couldn't allow any member of her team to pursue her theory. Though any one of them would gladly do just that if they knew about her suspicions, she would not permit them to risk their careers.

"You have my word," Gina promised.

The door opened and Dan walked in.

"I hope I'm not interrupting," he announced with a smile that didn't reach his eyes.

Jess had done that to him. She had brought this evil to his door.

Gina pushed to her feet. "Jess was just giving me an exclusive on Spears." She looked from Dan to Jess. "It's quite a story."

"That it is." Dan's gaze rested on Jess.

His concern wrapped around her, but rather than comfort her it tightened so that she could hardly breathe. It was his love for her and their child—his determination to keep them both safe— that was going to cost him far too much. That terrified her more than anything. She wanted to protect him as much as he wanted to protect her.

"I'll call you," Gina said as she gathered her recorder and bag.

"Thank you." Jess hoped her eyes conveyed how much the other woman's help meant to her.

Gina hesitated at the door and gave Jess a nod. Jess wasn't going to second guess her decision to ask for Gina's help. Certainly, the reporter hadn't climbed to the top in Birmingham without walking over a few bodies. But it was a risk Jess had to take.

"You had lunch?" Dan glanced at the pizza box.

Jess pushed away the worrisome thoughts and produced a smile. "I did. You?"

Dan shook his head. "It's Sunday. With the briefing over there's nothing else we can do here. What do you say we go someplace where we can relax for a little while?"

Part of her resisted. How could she relax when Spears was out there, planning his next move...his next murder? She stilled. No. Dan had the right idea. They wouldn't even be in the office on Sunday if not for the special briefing Gant had called. There was nothing else she could do today. She and Dan had no promise of tomorrow but this moment was theirs. She didn't intend to take a single minute of her time with the man she loved for granted.

"That sounds like a plan," she agreed.

Dan came around to her side of the desk and drew her into his arms. "I love you, Jess. If it's the last thing I do, I will protect you and our child."

That was the very thing that terrified Jess the most.

Don't forget to look for my next standalone suspense novel, SEE HIM DIE, coming June 25, 2015!

ABOUT THE AUTHOR

DEBRA WEBB, born in Alabama, wrote her first story at age nine and her first romance at thirteen. It wasn't until she spent three years working for the military behind the Iron Curtain—and a five-year stint with NASA—that she realized her true calling. A collision course between suspense and romance was set. Since then she has penned more than 100 novels including her internationally bestselling Colby Agency series. OBSESSION, her debut novel in her romantic thriller series, the Faces of Evil, propelled Debra to the top of the bestselling charts for an unparalleled twenty-four weeks and garnered critical acclaim from reviewers and readers alike. Don't miss a single installment of this fascinating and chilling series!

READ ALL THE FACES OF EVIL BOOKS!

Visit Debra at www.thefacesofevil.com or at www.debrawebb.com. You can write to Debra at PO Box 10047, Huntsville, AL, 35801.

94871148R00219

Made in the USA
Columbia, SC
01 May 2018